bush and pointed his thumb over his shoulder. "I spent the morning planting around the edge of my lanai. I was working on the other side when I heard something that sounded like digging. It was your dog. Are you aware there's a leash law in Calusa?"

Rachel directed his attention toward the torn screen, bit her lower lip and counted ten. No use getting off on the wrong foot. She had enough on her plate without getting into an argument. Did he think had the market cornered on having a bad morning?

"I'll keep Daisy in the house until I get the screen repaired. I'll get to it right after I call the plumber to fix the bathroom sink. That is third on the list after I get a new belt for the vacuum cleaner," she said, trying to sound calm and dismiss the salty burning in her eyes. She shook her head. "Sorry, I apologize. I shouldn't take out my frustration on you."

"Why don't you get your husband to give you a hand? I'm sure once he gets home he'll have everything taken care in no time."

Rachel stared at the man's blue eyes and wanted to make both of them black. What gave him the right to interfere in her private life? It was none of his damn business if her husband was working or didn't take care of things. She was amazed he hadn't said one of the neighbors told him Dave had split.

Aglow Again

by

Virginia Crane

The Calusa Series

Aglow Again

Cover Art by *Tina Lynn Stout*

The Wild Rose Press, Inc.
PO Box 708
Adams Basin, NY 14410-0708
Visit us at www.thewildrosepress.com

Publishing History
First Mainstream Women's Fiction Edition, 2014
Print ISBN 978-1-62830-448-0
Digital ISBN 978-1-62830-449-7

The Calusa Series
Published in the United States of America

Dedication

To my husband, Richard

Virginia Crane

Chapter 1

Eyes narrowed and menacing, Dave Benton pounded the kitchen table so hard his startled wife, Rachel, almost fell off her chair. The bowl of soup in front of her danced, then splashed, splattering vegetables in a kaleidoscope of colors over the white tablecloth. Peas rolled onto the floor like balls breaking in a game of billiards.

Dave pushed away from the table. "I can't believe you're so damn thick headed. How many times do I have to tell you I want my vegetables cooked until they're soft? Not crunchy; not medium firm. And don't think of serving me soup for dinner again, ever. Your diet buddies at the hospital may like this garbage," he bellowed, "but I don't. Fry up some bratwurst or frozen hamburgers. And do it quick."

Enough was enough. Rachel had held her tongue over the past few weeks, but no longer would she be cowed by another one of her husband's outbursts. Lately his explosions had come closer together. Either she had to take a stand or she would end up being his floor mat for the rest of her life. No way would she let that happen. Not in this lifetime.

Trying not to match him in the nasty department, she started counting to ten—but only made it to five. "Be patient, Dave. The soup is only the first course. It's healthy and good for you."

"This isn't a friggin' restaurant. I don't want *courses*, I want my damn supper. I want meat and potatoes. Some hot biscuits and gravy. Not this shit."

Rachel closed her eyes, mentally counted to ten again. This time she made it to nine. She'd spent a lot of time preparing this meal and wanted to enjoy it. "Taste it. I made it with a seven bone pot roast, there's plenty of meat for you, as well as potatoes. As for the vegetables, I like mine crunchy. They retain more vitamins. Good heavens, Dave, you chew the gristle on chicken bones; I don't see why you can't chew a few crunchy vegetables."

He shot out of his chair, rested his fisted hands on the table and leaned close, nostrils flared. She quickly closed her eyes as spittle spewed from his lips and touched her cheeks when he inched closer. "This is *my* house and *I* want *my* food cooked the way *I* like it. Do you understand?"

She rose to her feet, bent forward, almost touching her nose to his nose and stared straight into his angry brown eyes. "This is also *my* house, and sometimes *I* like to have *my* way. If you don't like the way I cook, do it yourself—and if life here isn't to your liking, don't let the door hit you in the ass on the way out."

"You'd like for me to leave, wouldn't you? You're probably counting on getting a big alimony check. Then you could get it on with the new neighbor next door. He's probably one of those health nuts who like lots of salad and crunchy vegetables. I bet he even eats bean sprouts or some other damn sissy ass kinds of food."

Wondering, not for the first time, about the directions the man's mind sometimes took, Rachel's brow furrowed. "What are you talking about?"

She hadn't smelled alcohol on his breath tonight, like in the past when he'd come home acting strange. Could it be he'd switched to drugs?

Dave stepped back, crossed both arms across his chest and growled. "Don't try to deny it. I happened to be looking out the side window yesterday and saw you getting all chummy and making goo-goo eyes at him when he sauntered over to introduce himself."

After all these years, had he stooped to spying on her? Unless he planned to live to be a hundred, he was past the usual time for a midlife crisis. Maybe he was having a *late* life crisis?

"You've got to be kidding." Pointing a thumb over her shoulder toward the house next door, she hooted a wry laugh. "Are you referring to Jeremy Dunn, the guy who moved in a couple of days ago?" No sooner had the words left her mouth when she knew she'd made a mistake. Reason didn't always work with Dave. In fact it rarely did.

"See? I knew it," he said, face beet red, spittle spewing from his lips. "You know his full name. For all I know you've already had him over for coffee and a quickie in the morning after I leave. Maybe you meet him for a drink after work."

With a shake of her head, she plopped into her chair. "Honestly, Dave, I think you're losing your mind. You know I always leave the house before you each morning and I've had to work late the past six days. I *always* come straight home unless I stop at the grocery store. When I do have to make a stop, I call. Right?"

He nodded, but didn't sit.

She went on. "Since you can't be bothered to take out the trash, I do it. Mr. Dunn happened to see me, introduced himself, and asked which day the garbage is picked up. Believe me; I am not the least bit interested in having another man in my life. One is more than I can handle, and you're the one."

Dave glared at her for a nanosecond, pushed the soup bowl aside, scrunched the tablecloth toward the middle of the table, then stomped out of the kitchen, cursing a blue streak.

In the wink of an eye she heard the door to the den slam shut. Then the television went on, volume cranked. Tempted to tell him to turn it down, she decided to back off. His hearing had markedly diminished recently, but she'd refrained from saying anything. The one time she did make reference to it, he accused her of mumbling, telling her if she spoke plainer, there'd be no problem.

Rachel sat quietly for a few minutes, trying to process what had just happened. She glanced around her bright kitchen with its soft butter yellow walls and wine country accents. While none of the amenities had changed, the atmosphere was heavy with anger and resentment. In spite of promising herself not to cry anymore, tears leaked out of the corners of her eyes. She was not going to allow this kind of scene to be repeated.

Appetite gone, the smell of the cooked pork nauseated her. She cleared the dishes from the table, dumped the food down the garbage disposal and set the bowls in the sink. Going back to the table, she folded the brightly colored cloth and took it outside to shake before putting it in the laundry. Maybe the birds or the bunnies would enjoy the vegetables. If not, the raccoons certainly would. Returning to the kitchen she swept up the peas and put them in the trash.

So much for sharing a nice quiet dinner at the table. Until recently, most nights Dave wanted to eat in front of the TV…alone. Tonight, she'd decided to make things a little more elegant. Table set fancy, a couple different courses. Thank goodness she resisted using candlelight. There was enough fire in Dave's eyes as it was. Besides, he would've thought for sure she had something going on with the neighbor. The whole idea of doing anything with Jeremy Dunn was comical, but she wasn't laughing.

What ticked her off the most was she had made the soup with beef, like she'd told him, but after the way he carried on she wasn't about to inform him she had made his favorite main dish: baked pork chops with dressing. She had been keeping it warm in the oven to serve after the soup course. Was his sense of smell diminishing like his hearing?

The more she thought about the scene, the angrier she became. Two could play this game. She'd be damned before she gave Dave a bite. Hell, the dog would have a feast. What happened to the quiet, loving man she fell in love with thirty-five years ago? She knew people changed with time, but his behavior had taken a total one-eighty turn. She had often heard in order to know your husband in his later years, observe his father. Not a chance there; his father was killed during the Vietnam War when Dave was a little one.

Tonight he'd gone *too* far. In the morning she would talk to him, provided he had calmed down. At this point, she could only pray he would be easier to talk to by then. Recent experience had revealed that any attempts at conversation were useless when he was in the throes of a major snit. Deep in her heart she knew they were headed for a separation, probably a divorce, unless he agreed to counseling. She knew he wouldn't. With Dave, it was always the other person who had to change. She had gone along with his juvenile behavior for too many years. Giving in to keep the peace was no longer an option.

Maybe she shouldn't have lost her temper, but tonight she'd been unable to keep it in check. She looked down at her slightly crooked right index finger, a reminder of the one and only time she'd lost control. Her oldest son, Davy, had taken a bottle of dish washing soap and squirted it all over the kitchen floor. She grabbed him by the arm to swat his bottom, but when he tucked it under, her hand jammed straight into the wall. The pain of overriding joints quickly brought her to her senses.

Even though she had been up to her elbows in soap suds trying to clean the floor, she had promised herself she would never allow herself to become that angry again. She recalled her mother saying it was Davy's guardian angel who pushed her hand into the wall. Be that as it may, she managed to last all these years without raising her voice at her husband or her kids.

Now she could only wonder if holding back her feelings was good thing. One thing she was sure of...there wouldn't be a valentine for Dave sitting by the coffee pot tomorrow morning. It would go into the trash tonight—or maybe her desk drawer for next year. No way could she do the customary love and kisses without feeling like a total hypocrite.

****

Dave stuffed his hands in the pockets of his jeans

and stared out the window as hot tears of guilt, frustration and anger stung his eyes. He knew damn well he was the problem, not Rachel. Feeling stuck, he acted like a first-class bastard. He had lived in Calusa all his life, rarely traveled out of Florida. In fact, the only time he went out of state was when Rachel's brother-in-law Pat was buried in Arlington Cemetery— and that was more years ago than he cared to count. It was August and so damn hot in Washington, DC, he'd refused to go sightseeing and insisted they get in the car immediately after the service. He drove straight home even though Rachel had pleaded with him to stop and spend the night in Charleston or Savannah. He had refused to listen to reason, but complained the rest of the way home.

It was painful to admit it was his fault they didn't go more places. In spite of his behavior in Washington, Rachel often begged him to go on vacations. He always turned her down before she mentioned where she would like to go. Bottom line, the boys drove him crazy when they were little and more so when they were teens. He could never keep up with them energy-wise, making excuses not to be around when they had friends over. The boys were always dashing somewhere to do some damn thing—or playing music loud enough to wake the dead. He'd left the job of raising them to Rachel.

Before he knew it, they were grown and married and made him a grandfather. Where in the hell had the years gone?

During the past month he'd gotten closer to his oldest son, Davy. Had even sort of talked his feelings over with him rather than his other son, Mike. Davy had three kids, Mike didn't have any. Davy would understand. What had caused him to talk about his restlessness with his son was hearing Davy tell his wife he didn't want to go to Disney World with her and the kids. It was like having a flash back and for the first time told his son to live a little or else he was going to end up like his old man.

Dave had to make a change soon, before he exploded and did something he might regret. The past six months had been tough. Outrageous ideas, like lashing out and hitting Rachel, which he came close to doing tonight. A prime example was when he accused Rachel of having an affair with the new neighbor. A ridiculous statement if he ever heard one, because Rachel was not a flirt. In fact, she was the exact opposite. Keeping a good home was important to her. He knew exactly what went on during her conversation with this Dunn guy. Hadn't he stood by the open window and heard every word?

Man, he was beginning to scare himself.

Oddly enough, he'd always wanted to travel—but on his own. It had been his dream to get up one morning, get in the truck and drive, no fixed destination in mind. He wanted to do this while he was still in good health. Who knew how much longer he had?

His dad died in 'Nam. Taken prisoner, he died in a POW camp at a young age. He hadn't even been a career military man… enlisted for a hitch and ended up being sent overseas.

A heart murmur kept Dave from serving in the military which didn't bother him a bit. No way did he want to follow in his father's footsteps. When Dave left this world he wanted it to be while he was having a great adventure. That was never going to happen if he stayed in this one-horse town.

He had smelled the pork chops in the oven, but instead of eating the soup and waiting for the main meal, he'd gone off half-cocked and made an ass out of himself. Rachel must be feeling the tension, too. Tonight, for the first time, she took a stand. He could never recall her saying she fixed something she liked *for a change*. She had always bent over backwards to please him.

Had he deliberately been trying to goad her into making a decision to end the marriage? Have her take the first step so he'd be off the hook...could say it wasn't his fault. Wasn't that his pattern over the years? There was this deep seated burning—the need to get away. Away from everything. He was starting to feel claustrophobic living in Calusa. Always around the same people, going to the same places. Same every damn thing.

When was the right time to put his plan into place? It had better be soon because his naturally short fuse was getting shorter every day. He had no painting contracts pending. As a matter of fact, he had purposely put customers off this past month. Dropped a hint here and there, mentioning he was giving early retirement some serious thought.

The bigger question was would he have the guts to pack his bags, get in his truck and leave? He felt the west coast calling to him. Not California, but he would like to see Oregon or Washington State.

After all, Rachel told him not to let the door hit him the ass on the way out.

****

Rachel opened the trunk of her car and took out the

groceries, looping the cloth totes over each arm. After pausing for a few moments, she let out a deep breath, closed the trunk, and reluctantly made her way through the garage and into the kitchen.

The first thing she noticed was the absence of 'forgive me' flowers on the table. There wasn't even the usual valentine card propped up by the coffee pot.

A curtain of sadness shrouded her spirit. Dave's comments of last night rang loud and clear; she'd made the right decision by not to putting out the card she had bought him. Granted it was a gesture of thoughtfulness, but it was also too flowery with I love you written all over it.

She'd tossed and turned all night, rehearsing a conversation, then stayed preoccupied all day, tweaking here, adding there while she went about her work duties. Several co-workers had asked if there was something wrong because she seemed preoccupied. Of course she had blamed work, and that was partially true because it had been crazy busy.

She wished she'd had time to talk with her friend, Anita, before she got home tonight, but when she drove by The Hair Lair she saw several customers through the front window so she cruised on by and went directly to the grocery store.

This emotional roller coaster ride had to stop. She and Dave had to come to an agreement…and soon because she couldn't go on like this. Either they called it quits or they sought professional counseling. If not, she was going to end up getting counseling on her own, and the end result would likely be the same: He would do as he pleased and she would be out the money.

He didn't come to bed last night, and she figured

he had slept in Davy's old room next to the den. He'd been sleeping in there a lot lately. He'd even taken to keeping most of his clothes in there. Not that it mattered. He was not an easy person to sleep with. Many times she had gotten up and gone into another room in order to get a decent night's sleep because of his restlessness and snoring. Even though he took time to make the coffee, like he always did every morning, he was gone before she got up.

She would most likely abandon all the rehearsed scripts, get straight to the point and tell him what was on her mind. That was probably the best way to handle the situation. She would do it as soon as he got home.

When she was a young girl and going through stressful times, her mother had always told her to relax, not to get upset before the fact because there were no accidents in life. Events happened and were usually part of a greater plan. Then again, her mother was a good Presbyterian and also big into predestination. Rachel remembered her mother crying when they got the news about Rachel's father dying from a sudden massive heart attack. Mrs. Fehrenbacher had gathered her two daughters together, held them close and reassured them this was all part of God's plan and they would survive.

If her mother was right about 'what would be would be', what in the world was the plan in this particular case? It had better manifest itself pretty damn soon because she couldn't take living under this stress much longer.

"I'm home," she called out as she turned and closed the door with her back. No answer. It figured.

Dave was always among the missing when it came to giving her a helping hand. She shook her head to clear it. Of course, he couldn't help her. His truck wasn't in the driveway when she drove up. He wasn't home from work yet.

She was in a hurry to get supper started. After all his carrying on last night she had given serious thought to telling him to fix his own dinner. She couldn't do that to a man who had worked hard all day. He at least deserved some supper.

She had put too much in one of the bags to save a trip. As fate would have it, before she could get to the table, the side seam on the cloth bag split, sending grocery items rolling all over the floor. To make matters worse, when the jar of olives hit the tile floor, the bottom broke and brine leaked all over the floor. She picked up the glass, dumped it in the trash can, and ran to the sink to grab paper towels to sop up the liquid.

If having things end up on the floor continued, folks would be able to eat off her floor because she spent so much time cleaning it. Was this a premonition of another clean-up based on the previous evening?

No, she had to stop and look on the bright side. The jar didn't shatter. She got down on her hands and knees and crawled under the table to retrieve the rest of the cans and a couple of baking potatoes. She even found some dried up peas she had missed the night before.

Then she found the note.

She backed out from under the table, rolled over on her behind and sat with her back against the cabinet door, ignoring the knob poking her in the back. It was a brief message. It must've blown off the table when she opened the door. In his simple scrawl, he wrote he was unhappy and had to leave. To go off and find himself. It was signed with only his first initial.

He left no clue as to where the journey to 'find himself' might end. Had he found someone to help with the search? Did he intend to call and tell her what he found when he finally arrived at this place of discovery?

She stared up at the sky light in the kitchen ceiling. Dark clouds rolled overhead, creating an eerie light in the room as she listened to the rain hammer against the glass. There had to be a way of getting answers.

She would call him on his cell phone and find out where he was. She got up and grabbed the phone from the dock on the counter and dialed—then heard the sound of the ring coming from the junk drawer.

The lousy bastard.

She crumpled the note and threw it across the floor. Of all the gutless cowards. She got up, walked across the room and picked up the note. Sitting on a kitchen chair she smoothed it out and read it again. Like the storm raging outside, emotions churned in her stomach. She didn't know which emotion to address first.

She truly didn't care if the marriage was over. As far as she was concerned, that was a given. But she was angry he wasn't man enough to discuss what legal steps should be taken. She'd lived with this man all these years, thought she knew him inside out—yet deep down, she didn't know him at all.

She rested her elbows on the table and propped her chin in her hands. Refusing to shed a tear, she bit her lower lip so hard it hurt. It had taken him thirty-five years, two children and three grandchildren to find out he was unhappy? Most guys found out much earlier before they took off for greener pastures.

She had been lucky in that respect. At least he had

stuck around until the boys were raised. Maybe he couldn't deal with being a grandfather. Come to think of it, he had always insisted the grandkids refer to him uncle rather than grandpa.

Taking everything into consideration, she'd thought he was satisfied with the status quo. That place where you become the old married couple. Each one doing their thing, staying together for security.

Apparently Dave wasn't at all comfortable with the security scenario. Was that the reason for his recent outbursts? Granted life was not peachy keen and lovey-dovey, especially for the past year, but, overall, life wasn't awful. Maybe she was too easily satisfied—or too close to the situation to see a problem.

Well, *maybe* it was okay if you took into account they never went anywhere together, had absolutely no interests in common, and couldn't even agree on what television programs to watch. Consequently, he went out and got his own flat screen set and took over the den. She converted the spare bedroom into a sitting room with a daybed and a small TV, which she rarely watched. She preferred to read a book.

Unless it was a holiday and she insisted holding a family gathering he would make plans to be somewhere else, or he would show up an hour late. Was there another woman? Possibly, but she didn't think so. Not in Calusa anyway, especially with the Fearsome Foursome living down the block, keeping an eye on everybody and everything that happened in the neighborhood.

Bottom line, Dave was very selfish when it came to how he spent his time—and especially his money. One of the reasons she went to work after the boys were grown and gone was so she didn't have to account for every penny. As for being social, Dave did what Dave wanted to do.

It could be he took her seriously last night when she told him if he was not happy with the way their life was going right now, he was free to leave. Though she had made the comment in the heat of the moment, there was no way she could be a hypocrite and rescind it now. She had meant it, from the bottom of her heart.

All she could hope for now was when he did find himself he would not entertain any thoughts about coming back home. As far as she was concerned once he walked out the door that was it. This front door did not revolve.

She looked around the kitchen. It was quiet...much too quiet. She folded her hands in prayer. The only thing that would make her life perfect would be if he'd taken Miss Daisy, the dog-from-hell with him.

No such luck. She heard the familiar sound and turned to look down the hallway leading to the bedrooms. There was Miss Daisy, busily gnawing on the footboard of the antique sleigh bed. The dog looked up at her with innocent brown eyes, then turned back to the task at hand.

Rachel hurried to the pantry and grabbed the spray bottle of Bitter Yuck and doused the footboard with the stuff. Daisy gave her a brief glance, then licked the spray off the wood and began chewing all over again.

Tears running down her cheeks, she shouted, "Damn you, dog, stop."

The dog blithely carried on with the chewing as if nothing had happened.

"Don't you know you're supposed to hate this

stuff?" she shrieked. "Let me tell you, young miss, your days of not listening and doing as you please are over. There is new order about to be instituted in this household. You *will* go to obedience school and you *will* graduate *cum laude* this time."

The dog obviously picked up on the shrill tone of her voice because she laid her golden head on the carpet, crossed her paws over her ears, heaved a sigh and looked up with liquid brown eyes. Miss Daisy's sad expression made Rachel feel guilty.

"Sorry I yelled at you. Come on, pup, time to go outside. Things are going to change around here. Trust me; it will be for the best, for both of us. You and I will hang tough and get started on a new set of rules. It might be hard at first, but we *will* have fun."

Rachel walked to the back door, Miss Daisy trotted along at her heels. Should she call her sons and let them know what was up? Not tonight. She had to get her thoughts in order before she could face them. How long should she wait before contacting an attorney? Should she do nothing until she heard from Dave? She didn't want to flounder in limbo. This whole situation was starting to aggravate her. How dare he leave her hanging like this?

This was the time a girl needed to talk to her sister. She walked to the phone and picked it up so she could call Trina at her home in Wyoming. Then something clicked inside her muddled brain. No, she couldn't. When she spoke to Trina last week her sister mentioned she was driving west to Spokane to visit an old friend and would call when she got back home.

There were certain things her sister refused to do in this day and age. One was to own a cell phone, or a computer, so email was out of the question. She'd have to put that conversation on hold.

Since Trina wasn't available, as soon as she cleaned up the olive juice on the kitchen floor, Rachel promised herself she'd call her neighbor, Anita. She glanced at the clock on the stove. Anita should be home from her beauty shop by now. Rachel went to the fridge and took out a bottle of white wine. After pouring a glass, she took a sip and let it swirl around on her tongue. The oaky taste of the chardonnay felt good on her tongue. She swallowed, went to the phone and punched in Anita's number.

A good confab about the present state of affairs was exactly what she needed.

Chapter 2

Anita Scott rapped a knuckle on the sliding glass door before pushing it open with one foot. A clear plastic rain poncho draped over her head protected the tray of sandwiches she carried. A small bowl of Kalamata olives was centered in the middle of the tray. The Publix Market tote she'd looped over her left arm swung against her thigh. When Rachel went to lend a hand she saw the neck of a wine bottle peeking out of the top of the tote, along with a large bulge next to it.

"Take this; I don't want to drip water all over your kitchen floor."

Anita slipped the tray through the side opening of the poncho and handed it to Rachel before going out to the lanai to shed the poncho and kick off her flip-flops. She hurried back inside and closed the slider. "Man, the rain is starting to blow. Storm or no storm, I figured from the panic in your voice we'd need something to absorb the alcohol we're about to consume, so I brought food."

"Oh, come on. I didn't sound that bad." Rachel grimaced. "Did I?"

She placed the tray on the kitchen counter. It rattled when she set it down to remove the plastic wrap, so had to make a quick grab for the olive bowl when it tilted. No way did she want to deal with soggy sandwiches or clean up olives a second time in one day.

Anita shooed her aside. "Go. Get a couple of wine glasses; I'll finish here. While you're at it, bring a dish for nuts, unless you want to eat them out of the jar."

"Docsn't matter to me."

Her best friend in all the world rolled her eyes. "This promises to be a session. Get the dish. Are we going to do our girl talking here at the kitchen table or in the den?"

Rachel headed for the china closet in the dining room. "The kitchen table," she called over her shoulder. "Look in the cupboard to your left; I'm sure you'll find something to dump the nuts into. There should be a basket on the first shelf. Use it, unless you specifically want a glass bowl. And I hope they're cashews— because I'm in serious need for a few. I've heard they're good for soothing nerves."

"A basket is fine." Knowing this kitchen as well as her own, Anita took sandwich plates from the cupboard, then grabbed a couple of napkins. "It must be significant if it's going to be a wine and cashew night. As to the tone of your voice, let's say I've never heard it crack like a fifth rate soprano in a third rate road show. I can't quite put my finger on what caused it, but I didn't need a college education to know you sounded seriously upset. I mean you didn't even wait until after Dave had his dinner and went to watch TV before calling. What's up?"

Rachel went to the refrigerator, took out the opened bottle of wine and poured a glass. She slipped the bottle her friend bought into the freezer to chill, then set Anita's glass on the counter next to her hand. "Remind me about the bottle in the freezer. As for Dave, no worries in that department. At least not anymore. Did you notice his truck isn't in the driveway?"

Anita almost dropped the jar of cashews she was dumping into a basket. "What do you mean? Was he in an accident? I didn't notice because I dashed through the back yards."

"Nothing as simple as an accident. I know you'll want to hear the whole story, and you will, but bottom line, Dave apparently doesn't want to live here...with me, anymore."

Anita took the tray to the table and set it in the center before she plopped down on the kitchen chair. "You've got to be shi—kidding me. No way would his lordship walk out on being king of the palace. You do everything but wipe his—brush his teeth, for heaven's sake. Of course, give him a few more years with all the sweets he garfs down and you may be doing that for him as well."

Rachel brought the wine to the table and handed one to Anita before taking a seat. "If that were the case why did I find this note under the table?" She pulled the crumpled note out of her pocket and handed it to Anita.

"Under the table?" Anita echoed as she glanced at the small yellow square of paper. "I don't have an answer to your question, but give me a few minutes and I'm sure I'll come up with something. I have to say the message is very short. Apparently he didn't want to waste any words."

"I think he meant for it to stick to the table." Rachel reached over and removed the note from Anita's fingers. "Maybe the stickum on the back was old and didn't work. Whatever the reason it was on the floor, under the table."

"Back to the note. What made you look there?"

Rachel massaged her temples with tips of her fingers. "Don't be obtuse. I didn't *look* there. I found it there by accident when the jar of olives fell out of the bag and broke."

Anita took the note back and smoothed it out with her thumb. "It sounds like I'll be here a while. Boy, am I glad Lyle's busy catching up on the medical columns in the daily paper. The latest ones deal with men. He's always checking to see if he has any new symptoms. Now, quit with those forty cent words, like *obtuse*. I don't have time to stop and look them up in the dictionary."

"Don't push it with the smart-assed quips." Rachel drummed her fingers on the table. "I came in with the groceries and the side seam on the canvas bag split. A jar of olives broke and the cans rolled. When I finally got down to gather the canned goods that's when I found this. I can still smell the olive brine; it must've soaked into the throw carpet by the sink. I should toss it into the washer."

Anita sniffed the air. "I don't smell anything. Sit still and please continue with the story."

Rachel took a big swallow of wine, licked the few drops from her lips and pointed to the note. "He wrote that he was leaving."

Anita looked at the note again and shook her head. "He could've at least given a couple of reasons for his decision. Gave you some options, like get a lawyer. Or don't do anything until you hear from me."

"Nope. You've read it. How could he go into detail on a piece of paper that size?" Rachel snorted. "I hope he's happy with what he finds."

Anita shook her head, grasped Rachel's hand and

squeezed it. She stared at the note again. "That surprises the hell out of me. I didn't think Dave could print that small. As far as I'm concerned, you're the poster woman of the old-fashioned wife. You stayed home and raised your kids, kept a neat house. Even though it was his business, you did all the painting in the house, along with taking care of the yard. If he'd had to shell out money to hire someone to do all the chores you've done around here, he wouldn't have been able to afford to leave. I wonder what he's expecting to find out there in the big wide world. The bigger question is how do you intend to get along financially now that he's gone?"

"I don't think there will be any problems, other than hiring an attorney. I'll have to dip into my savings to do that. Otherwise, I'm going to get along fine."

Anita shot her a suspicious look. "Have you been holding out on me…making plans, too? If so, my only question is why? Not that I'm trying to delve into your private life, but when couples have been married as long as you and Dave, most tend to stick it out until the end if only for financial security."

Rachel tilted her head back and rubbed her hands along the tense muscles in her neck. She'd had a suspicion this day was coming. All their friends thought they were the perfect couple. If they had only known about Dave's current behavior it would've shot that theory in the butt.

How was she going to tell Anita, without sounding bitter, or purposely didn't confide in her? "I didn't want to say anything because every marriage goes through a bad patch. You have your hands full with Lyle's hypochondria. As for Dave and me, we haven't been getting along for the past few years.

"He was starting to complain more about how I kept house, about my working, about the time I spent with the grandchildren, about everything. Maybe six months ago he started going off by himself, saying he was going fishing. Actually, other than to come by your place for a cookout, we haven't done anything together for a very long time." She massaged her temples again, hoping to ease the headache starting to form. "And, you know he didn't come with me the last couple of times."

"I didn't want to say anything about you coming alone because it was obvious you were upset, but, like always, I knew you'd tell me when you were ready. As for the fishing, Dave asked Lyle to go a few times, but you know my hubby, he's afraid he'll catch a cold rather than a fish. Dave stopped asking after a couple of refusals." Anita raised a questioning eyebrow. "Now that I think about it, it makes me wonder what he was fishing for."

"I don't think there's a woman in the picture, but I don't know for sure. You remember what a fuss he made when I decided to take a full-time job at the hospital. The frosting on the cake was when I set up my own checking account at a different bank. He wanted everything to be in our joint account. I told him I used that particular bank because it was on the right side of the street for me to use the drive-through lane to deposit my check on the way home."

"He bought that? I'm surprised." Anita held up her hand to stop Rachel from making a comment. "Wait a minute, I remember that night. We drank a whole bottle of wine and ate two bags of potato chips. Even I knew you had your paycheck sent direct deposit. How did you manage that?"

Rachel smiled, picked up a sandwich, and took a small bite. "After he finished doing his dickey-do dance and stormed out of the house for a couple hours, he never asked to see the check. All he was interested in was the W2 at tax time. If he'd been curious I could've always shown him the stub they give us. Anyway, I told him his name was on my account. What I didn't tell him was it was set up to be held in trust for him in case something happened to me. I'll have to go to the bank and take his name off."

Rachel became aware of whining coming from the laundry room—Miss Daisy. She forgot she put the dog in there after she heard Anita at the door. The pup hated being cooped up in the laundry room and especially did not like storms.

Raising a hand, she said, "Hold your comment, I'll be right back." She went to the laundry room and opened the door. The dog bounded across the kitchen floor and scooted under the table by Anita's feet. "You were about to say?"

Anita raised her glass and pointed it toward Rachel. "You fox. I have to say you don't appear to be as upset as I thought you would. I mean you're not crying or ranting. Except for your hands shaking when I first got here, you seem very calm. My curiosity is killing me so I have to ask again what made him leave today? For God's sake, it's Valentine's Day. Couldn't he have waited until tomorrow?"

Rachel shrugged, twirled her wine glass by the stem and blew out a deep breath. "We had a bang up argument last night. I'm glad the windows were closed so the neighbors couldn't hear. I'd decided to make something I liked for dinner. He didn't care for it."

"Okay," Anita reasoned, "but that shouldn't have led to something as major as this."

Rachel glanced around the kitchen. This room, where she had always felt cozy and comfortable, now reminded her of how her life was falling apart. "Like I said before, we haven't been getting on for the past several years. It seems like with each passing day we drifted farther apart. When he crossed his hands over his chest in that authoritarian way of his and *ordered* me to check with him before I cooked anything, I told him I'd fix what I damned well pleased and not to let the door hit him in the ass on his way out. Obviously, he took me at my word."

"I suppose he did, if you actually cussed. What do you plan to do now? Have you told the boys? What about your sister?"

"I haven't told Davy or Mike yet. I'll let them know tomorrow. As for Trina, she's on the road to Spokane. I'm sure she'll call when she gets there. As to the rest, I plan to do whatever strikes my fancy."

"That's rather vague. How about giving me some specifics."

Rachel ran her finger around the rim of the glass and grinned. "Well, let's see. I might learn to ice skate."

"In Florida?"

"They have indoor rinks." She tilted her head and tapped her chin with her index finger. "Then again, I may learn to play the piano."

Anita chuckled. "You don't have a piano."

"I'll buy one. I've also been thinking about taking up tap dancing. I used to tap dance when I was a little girl. I enjoyed it and it's good exercise."

Anita shot her an incredulous look at the tap dancing comment. "Are you going to start all this before or after you tell the kids? Wait a minute, trash that; you already said you'd call them tomorrow. I wonder how they're going to take the news."

"They will have to deal with the situation like I have to. My sons have their own lives; I intend to take mine back. I'll do what I please, when I please, with whom I please." She raised her glass in a toast. "To the future."

Anita clinked her glass against Rachel's. "I'll drink to that. What's first on your to-do list?"

Rachel rubbed her finger over her lips, taking time to digest the question. "A makeover at your shop. First thing in the morning if you have time."

"I'll make time. Don't you have to go to work?"

"I called my boss right after I spoke to you and arranged to take a couple of days off. Told her I had to take care of some personal business. Since I don't work weekends anyway, I'm off until next Wednesday. That should give me time to start getting my life in order."

"When do you plan to tell the boys?"

"When I get home from your shop, I'll call Davey and Mike and ask them to come over here. No, on second thought, I think I'll wait until Monday. There's no need to spoil their weekend."

Chapter 3

Her sons entered the kitchen through the garage.

Mike headed straight for the refrigerator, grabbed a can of Dr. Pepper and popped the top. "Can I get you one?" he asked, raising the can for his brother to see.

"Think I'll wait until I find out what this is all about before I have anything," Davy said. "I might need something stronger than soda."

"Are you holding back on me, man?" Mike asked. Although it struck his as strange that he didn't smell anything cooking when he came in the kitchen. His mom always had something going on the stove or in the crockpot.

Davy shrugged one shoulder, but didn't answer. Instead took a seat at the table and picked up the newspaper.

Something was up and his brother knew more than he did. He could tell by Davy's answer to the soda refusal and the fact the newspaper his brother held was upside down.

Mike joined him, turned a chair around and straddled it, resting his arms on the back. "I thought Mom was working today. She's usually off on weekends. I mean it isn't like her to call us over on a week day, even though she did say to come on my lunch hour."

"She told me the same thing, but it didn't matter.

Today's my day off."

Mike took another swallow of soda. "My gut tells me you know a lot more than I do, bro. I get the feeling I'm going to be mega pissed at you when I find out what it is. Add to that, Mom sounded pretty serious when I talked to her last night. Did she give you any inkling what she wanted to discuss with us?"

Turning the paper around, Davy picked up the sports section, stuck his face in it and kept it like that. "Not really."

Before Mike could ask his brother to explain what he meant by *not really,* their mother walked into the kitchen. She sported a shorter, bobbed haircut with the long front ends framing her chin, rather than wearing it long, pulled back and fastened at her neck. Not only that, Mike noticed she had definite red highlights in her usual plain brown hair. She also had some stuff around her eyes that made them look greener.

"What's up, Mom? You look different. Super sharp," Mike said as he slid his long lean form off the chair to stand and give her a kiss on the cheek.

Davy put the paper down, got up, went to the fridge and grabbed a can of beer. Without making eye contact, he said, "I agree with Mike. You're looking good, woman. Dad give you a day at the spa or something?"

"Oh, your dad gave me *something* all right." She paused for a split second and studied her sons' faces. "He gave me my freedom. You father left home sometime early Friday morning." She waved her hands in the air. "He left me a post-it note saying he hasn't been happy and he was going off somewhere to *find* himself."

Mike jumped up and snatched some paper towels from the roll on the counter to wipe up the soda he'd spewed all over the table. "What the hell? And you waited until lunch time on Monday to tell us?"

"Watch your mouth. I knew you both had big plans this weekend. Mike, you and Melinda were going up to Ormond Beach to visit with her family. Davy was working. There was no reason to cause a lot of upset by asking you to change plans. It wouldn't have changed anything."

"That's pretty cold, Mom," Mike said and looked at his brother. "You should've told us, we could have been here for you."

Davy didn't say a word.

Rachel opened the sliding door to the lanai and motioned for them to follow her outside. Miss Daisy was curled up in the corner, dozing in the shade. Was it her imagination or did the furniture look old and worn. She was going to have to work hard to get rid of this funky mentality. The plants looked in need of some TLC, but they were way at the bottom of the list. There were no song birds to be heard but she noted a couple of vultures sitting on the neighbor's roof.

"Don't get upset, Mike. Get another Dr. Pepper and come outside," she called over her shoulder. "I'll explain further once we get seated out here. At least on the lanai I'll be able to hose down your reactions rather than scrub the kitchen floor."

Rachel took a second gander at her sons. Knowing them as she did she was convinced that Mike was genuinely surprised. Davy, on the other hand, was not. He didn't even flinch when she dropped the bombshell.

"Okay, Davy, how long have you known about

your dad wanting to leave?"

He pulled out a chair for her, but didn't even attempt to make eye contact when he took a seat across the table from her. Staring at a spot over her shoulder, he asked, "What'd'ya mean?"

Unable to quell the simmering anger, Rachel set her jaw and narrowed her eyes. "I've known you since the day you were born, Davy. All I had to do was watch you while Mike was trying to lavage his lungs with soda to know he didn't have a clue, while you sat there cool as a cucumber. Your eyes gave you away simply by looking everywhere in the kitchen but at me. Just like you used to do when you were young and trying to hide something from me." She stood and leaned across the table, invading his space. "I'm only going to ask you one more time. How long have you known?"

She sat down again and watched Davy squirm in his seat like a five-year-old needing the potty, searching for the best way to spill what he knew without incurring her wrath. "For God's sake, spit it out before you choke on it."

Mike leaned in and gave his brother's upper arm a glancing blow. "Hey, bro, I'd answer if I were you."

Davy looked at his mother, bottom lip jutted out, his expression a hair shy of a pout. "I will if you don't call me *Davy*. I hate that nickname."

"Since when? I've called you that since you were born. Now quit beating around the bush or I'll call you something worse. Believe me; I have some doozies picked out. Want to hear them?"

He folded his arms across his chest and slid down in his chair. "No."

Rachel slapped her hand on the table. "No more

beating around the bush. Tell me what you know. And tell me now."

Davy took a deep breath and tugged on his ear. "Dad came by the house a couple of weeks ago. I was working in the garage when he stopped by. I was fixing the wheels on Susan's bike. She had hit the curb and...and..."

Rachel stood abruptly and threw her hands in the air. Keeping her voice low, she hissed, "I don't give a flying fu—fudgesicle what you were doing in the garage. I want to know what your father said when he came to see you."

Mike sat, glancing from his mother to his brother. "Watch it, Davy. Mom's really pissed. She almost dropped the 'F' bomb. Man, this is better than television." With a big grin on his face, he looked at his mother. "Is this the reason women like to watch soap operas?"

Rachel walked behind him and gave him a smack on the back of his head. "Quiet. This is no time for your warped sense of humor. Back to you, Davy, tell me what happened."

Rubbing his finger alongside of his nose he shook his head. "Dad said he wasn't happy, hadn't been for a long time. He said you had turned into a real shrew and it was getting on his nerves. He didn't know how much longer he could hang around."

"Oh, really? I presume he told you what an even-tempered paragon of virtue he had been."

"No," Davy said.

"I didn't think so. Did he happen to mention where he was going?"

"He said he would let me know so you could send

the rest of his clothes."

Rachel hit the side of her head with the heel of her hand. "Excuse me. I don't believe I heard you correctly."

Mike slumped down in the chair. "I think you did, Mom. He said..."

"I know what he said, Mike, I was simply making a point. Okay, Davy, since your father decided to confide in you, when are *you* going to take his things so *you* can send them?"

Davy shot up straight in the chair. "What do you mean, *me*? I don't have any extra cash. Jeesh, Mom, it costs a small fortune to take the family to the movies, not to mention keeping the boys in shoes. Seems like they need a new pair each week. And Susan, she..."

Rachel sat and leaned back in her chair and held up her hands with the palms out. "Stop right there. I don't want to hear your tale of woe. I know what it costs to run a house and raise children and have no intention of complying with your father's wishes. As far as I'm concerned I'll give everything I have to charity."

Davy jumped up. "Not his tools!"

"Everything goes, unless Mike wants some. I'm not playing favorites, you have plenty of tools."

Davy smirked, "Yeah, if Mike doesn't want them, maybe the new neighbor will."

That corked it. "Now I am sure you father came by your house more than once. I also know some of the things he told you. I'll say this one time and one time only. I met 'the neighbor', Mr. Dunn, once, when he asked which day trash was picked up. But, if I decide to give him your father's tools, that is my prerogative. Do you understand, Davy?" Rachel said, pounding her fist on the table and enunciating each word clearly.

The sound of her fist set the dog to barking and she came over to stand by Rachel's chair. She reached down and patted the dog on the head. Daisy plopped down by Rachel's feet.

"Yes, ma'am," Davy said, biting his lower lip.

Mike scooted his chair next to his mother and took her hand. "I can't believe what I just heard. I don't care what you do with Dad's stuff; I don't want anything. I don't know one end of a screwdriver from the other. I call a repairman or Davy. My main concern is you. How are you holding up? Do you need us to help you with anything?"

She sat back in her chair and shook her head. Leave it to Mike to be the concerned son. He always had a soft heart. "Do I look like I'm sad? Sorry, boys, but your dad and I have been having some major problems for quite a while. I was going to ask him if he wanted to go for counseling or did he want to end our marriage, but he took off like a thief in the night before I could even make the suggestion."

"Why didn't you say something?" Mike asked.

"You both have families to take care of; you didn't need me crying on your shoulder. The only thing I will say in my own defense is I didn't nag your father. Maybe I should have. Even though you know about Mr. Dunn, the funny thing is your father didn't say anything until the night before he left. We were having an argument and he accused me of flirting with the man."

"Flirting?" Davy asked.

"Actually, son, his exact words were I was *making goo-goo eyes*."

Mike guffawed. "Goo-goo eyes? Good one, Dave."

Rachel couldn't help it. She burst out laughing.

"I can't believe you two think this is funny." Davy snorted. "I find it pretty damn serious. What do you plan on doing now, Mom?"

"Son, I plan on letting myself go, wherever I want to, whenever I want to. I seem to recall a statement made by an actress of my time, Shelley Winters. She hit the nail on the head when she referred to a man she knew: 'We had a lot in common, I loved him and he loved him.' And, that about sums up my relationship with your father."

"I think you're going a bit over the top, Mom," Davy said.

"Think whatever you want. You haven't lived at home for many years."

Mike cocked his head and tugged on his ear. "I still can't believe what I'm hearing. Do you have a plan? Are you going to stay here? In this house I mean. I hope you're not thinking of leaving town."

"I'm staying put until things are settled. Besides, where else would I go right now?"

"You might go see Aunt Trina. Have you called her?" Mike asked.

"I was going to until I remembered she's on the road again. By the way, I made an appointment for tomorrow morning to see an attorney."

Davy gulped. "Aren't you rushing things a bit? Shouldn't you wait a while? See what happens."

Rachel knew her sons were upset, Davy more than Mike, but there was no way to make this situation easier for them. For her part, she should be feeling something more than relief, but there was no weeping or gnashing of teeth.

"In truth, I don't think I'm being a bit hasty. I have to learn how to protect myself and my status—as it relates to ownership of this house and any other assets—provided there are any. Your father could be very secretive. I'll have to go through his desk and file cabinet. I planned going through his desk this evening to see what I can find."

Mike walked around to her and squeezed her shoulder. "Don't know about my doofus brother, Mom, but I'm here if you need me."

"Look who's calling me a doofus. The king of doofuses," Davy snapped.

"Cool it with the name calling," Rachel said as she reached up and patted Mike's hand. She took in a deep breath of the cool morning air. "Thanks, Mike. Grandma always said that which does not kill us makes us strong, and I have no plans on dying any time soon."

Chapter 4

Rachel sat at the desk in the den, files spread from one side to the other. She had planned on doing this last night, but Anita came over again and they drank more wine, then talked until after midnight. By the time she left Rachel was too tired to do anything and headed straight for bed.

The new routine seemed to be having an effect of Miss Daisy. She had only destroyed one of Dave's shoes, and Rachel was not concerned. Let him buy a new pair. Then again he probably had no intention of using this pair because he left them behind.

One thing she had to give the man, he was super at record keeping. There were files for utilities and home improvement expenses as well automobile insurance and taxes for the past five years. For that, she was thankful. On the other hand, she noticed all the papers and files pertaining to his painting business were missing. He must have taken them in order to file his taxes. Or, maybe, since he was 'finding' himself, he was going to let the IRS search for him as well. Another possibility was he might have left them with Davy. She was bound to find out sooner or later.

That was another question she was going to have to ask her attorney, Mr. DeCarlo. Getting an appointment with him was not easy. Apparently he was in great demand and only saw people on referral. It was through

Harriet, a stylist who also filled in doing the pedicures at Anita's hair salon, that she got in to see him so quickly. He had handled Harriet's last three divorces.

Rachel checked all the file folder tabs looking for anything to do with the truck. She knew Dave paid it off last year. He had been talking about getting a new one. The folder was missing. The file with the title and papers for her old clunker were there. She would take it with her today. Who knows, depending on what Mr. DeCarlo had to say, she may stop by her local Ford dealer and buy a Mustang. She always wanted to drive a sexy, kick-ass, red convertible.

She found insurance policies for her car and the house. There was none for the truck, but then she recalled Dave's truck was insured through the business.

Thank goodness he never asked to see her bank accounts. All he ever wanted to see was her W-2 statement. She didn't have a lot of money, but she had managed to build up her savings over the past five years, not counting the twenty dollar bills she had been stashing each payday over the years. Had Dave been planning his exit during this time and why he didn't make a fuss? Only time would tell.

At least she wasn't in dire straits like one of her co-workers. When Marie's husband left he took everything they had. When Rachel had checked with the bank yesterday most of their joint savings had been withdrawn and there was only a hundred dollars in the joint checking. Dave's business account had been closed a week before he left.

Another point in her favor, Rachel realized, was she had a full time job. The house was paid for. She could make it on her own.

She glanced at the wall clock. It was about to chime eight o'clock. Time to hit the shower. Grabbing a canvas tote bag she stuffed the folders inside. Mr. DeCarlo would probably need more, but these might help get the ball rolling. Then again, he might not need this information at all, but at least she would have them with her.

She would have to hustle because Mr. Pesti was coming by this afternoon to give her an estimate for lawn care. He came highly recommended by Anita's husband, Lyle. Mowing lawns was one thing she refused to do. Dave pissed and moaned but did it. Ever since her encounter with the fire ants after Hurricane Charley, she gave grass cutting a wide berth. Flower gardening was okay because she knew what to look for when it came to the fire ant mounds. The little buggers like to hide in the grass and attack her ankles.

When she got ready to leave for her meeting with Mr. DeCarlo she sequestered Miss Daisy in the laundry room with a lot of chew toys, including the Dave's shoe that she'd munched on the day before. Too bad she was going to have to work on breaking the dog of the chewing habit. Dave left a closet full of shoes.

****

Mr. DeCarlo's office was quiet as a funeral viewing, complete with the fragrance of fresh flowers from assorted arrangements placed around the room. Oddly, there was no soft music. The reception area was empty. Maybe they scheduled time between appointments for client privacy. The paneled walls were decorated with Florida paintings. Rachel recognized two of Kelly McCabe's, a local artist. It was amazing how Kelly got her life on track after her first husband died. The furniture was deep cinnamon leather and the table heavy dark wood. The secretary took Rachel's name and invited her to take a seat.

Her mouth was dry, and her insides were writhing. She couldn't wait to have this over and done. She picked up a magazine, but was unable to focus on the article. Within a few minutes a door opened, and the secretary escorted her into the attorney's private office. He came around from the desk, shook her hand and indicated a wingback chair placed across from his desk.

The man was of medium height, slight build with warm hazel eyes. He had curly salt and pepper hair worn a bit on the long side for a man his age. Rachel didn't care how long or curly the man's hair was as long as he helped her straighten out her life.

"What can I do for you Mrs. Benton?"

Here she was, sitting across from a well-known divorce attorney and he wanted to know what he could do for her? It was most likely his way of putting her at ease. "I want to divorce my husband."

Mr. DeCarlo leaned back in his chair, resting his elbows on the arms and holding a pencil between his hands. "Since I'm a divorce attorney, it's a given. Give me the particulars in your case."

Rachel bit her lower lip. She had promised herself she would not cry. In spite of that pledge her eyes filled with tears as she told him the whole ugly story. "Everything in life has a beginning and an end. It's even in the Old Testament, I do believe, although I know I'm not quoting it word for word."

Mr. DeCarlo leaned forward to jot notes on a legal pad. "Close enough. Let's get started."

By the time Rachel walked out of the attorney's

office a short time later she was sure she would be feeling better, but she wasn't. Actually, she didn't know what she was feeling. The proceedings had been set in motion much faster than she had expected. She had time before heading home to meet Mr. Pesti.

In order to combat the blues she drove over to the Ford dealership and bought a car. They happened to have the one she wanted, a red Mustang convertible, and gave her a decent amount in trade for her clunker. They even took her picture standing by the car and said they would send her a calendar with the picture on the front. Maybe the day wasn't going to turn out to be a total loss.

The new car didn't take away the stress of the day, but it gave her sagging morale one hell of a boost. It was a whole lot better to tool around town with the top down, wearing huge Jackie O sunglasses, and her hair blowing in the wind.

If she hustled, she had enough time to get on home and get ready to meet Mr. Pesti.

****

Rachel barely had time to change into her jeans and T-shirt when a knock sounded on the front door. "Hold on a minute, I'm coming," she shouted as she slipped on her tennis shoes.

When she got to the door she choked back a laugh. Lyle should've warned her. The man standing there looked to be middle age…or older…or younger. He had one of those faces that made it hard to tell. His wilting brown eyes blinked constantly, as if he had something in both of them. Maybe it was a defense mechanism from stirring up gnats while working. The rest of his face was porcine, including his tiny pointed ears. She fully expected him to oink when he spoke.

"You Miz Benton?" the man asked with a snort.

Rachel bit her lower lip hard and stepped outside. Clearing her throat to hold back a gigglc, she said, "Yes, I am."

"Harvey Pesti," he said, taking off his cap with short stubby fingers.

Oh, my God, how am I going to deal with this man? Clearing her throat again she said, "I'm glad to meet you."

Mr. Pesti looked over the front yard and plopped his hat back on his head. "You must have allergies, Missuz, and that's why you need someone to handle the cutting. Yes, indeedy, the wife has the same kind of coughing trouble. Spends most of her time indoors during pine pollen season, she does." He glanced around the front of the property. "This looks to be a double lot. Not a lot of flower beds. Good thing. About the same in the back?"

Rachel nodded. "We can take a walk back there so you can check."

He followed her lead. "Well, I have a couple of different package deals. I have cut and run. Then there's feed and edge. I'll weed gardens, but I really don't like to mess in folk's flower gardens much."

"I think the cut and run along with the edge and feed for the lawn only." Major revamping of the garden would keep her mind occupied. "I can take care of the flower beds."

"Yes, ma'am. It sure looks like they need some tendin'." The man took a notebook out of the back pocket of his pants. Wetting his thumb with his tongue he flipped a couple of pages and hummed. "If the cut, run, edge and feed is what you want I can fit you in on Wednesday afternoons. Now, you realize that may change in the rainy season. Spend a lot of time catching up in the rainy season." He doodled with his pencil and quoted her a price.

"Sounds reasonable to me. Do you want me to sign a contract?"

"Won't be necessary, Missuz. I'll leave my bill on your lanai. You can put a check on the table or you can mail it to me. Makes no difference, but, just so's you know, if you miss one payment I don't come back."

He pulled a business card out of his shirt pocket and handed it to her. Rachel slipped it in her jeans pocket. "It's a deal."

Walking away he called back to her, "I also trim palm trees, but I charge extra."

****

The male voice that called to Rachel from the back yard did not sound at all happy.

In fact it sounded down right pissed. All she needed to make her day completely suck.

It had not taken long before Dave's absence became known. Calusa was a small town and news about him closing his business had tongues wagging overtime. Anita said it was the main topic of conversation at her beauty shop.

Over the past three weeks Rachel had fielded questions at work about her marital status. Her co-workers were as subtle as a Sherman tank when they tried to find out what was going on in her life. It was uncomfortable but not to the point she considered looking for another job. She might've considered a change, but she had too much seniority and was too close to retirement. To say her nerves were frazzled was an understatement. And the peace and quiet that awaited when she came home each night was worth a fortune…until today.

"Mrs. Benton, can you or your husband come out here a minute?" the voice said. "We have a problem to discuss. A major problem."

Rachel peeked out of her bedroom window and saw her new neighbor, Mr. Dunn. His baggy shorts and a knit shirt had seen better days. He held a plant in one hand, roots swaying in the breeze, and grasped Miss Daisy by a rope in the other. At least the rope wasn't around the dog's neck, but looped through her collar. The animal yelped and tugged piteously, trying to get loose. She'd better go out and see what the problem was before the other neighbors gathered, especially Floyd Patterson.

Didn't she have enough trouble this morning, trying to deal with a blocked drain in the bathroom sink? Apparently, she now had to face her irate neighbor. Why couldn't Daisy have annoyed someone who was used to her ways? Most likely she had and they shooed her away when they caught her up to one of her tricks. Betty Bradford once told Rachel she kept a spray bottle of water handy and used it liberally whenever Miss Daisy started digging in her garden.

The big question was how the dog had managed to escape the lanai. The last time Rachel glanced out the window the golden retriever had been dozing peacefully in the sun.

Rachel was not dressed to deal with this situation. Mr. Dunn was sure to think she was a frump in her old jeans, faded T-shirt and frayed sneakers and without makeup. Why did this have to happen when she was trying to deal with the problems at hand rather than impress a new neighbor? She plastered a smile on her face, went out on the lanai and saw where the screen had been pushed through. Miss Daisy's favorite escape route. What was she chasing this time? A bunny? A blacksnake? Or her favorite, a turtle.

"Thanks for bringing her back." Rachel opened the screen door and reached for the rope to take the dog. What was she going to do with the demon pet until her screen man could get here to repair the damage? "What seems to be the problem, Mr. Dunn?"

Jeremy Dunn set his jaw, held up a small hibiscus bush and pointed his thumb over his shoulder. "I spent the morning planting around the edge of my lanai. I was working on the other side when I heard something that sounded like digging. It was your dog. Are you aware there's a leash law in Calusa?"

Rachel directed his attention toward the torn screen, bit her lower lip and counted ten. No use getting off on the wrong foot. She had enough on her plate without getting into an argument. Did he think he had the market cornered on having a bad morning?

"I'll keep Daisy in the house until I get the screen repaired. I'll get to it right after I call the plumber to fix the bathroom sink. That is third on the list after I get a new belt for the vacuum cleaner," she said, trying to sound calm and dismiss the salty burning in her eyes. She shook her head. "Sorry, I apologize. I shouldn't take out my frustration on you."

"Why don't you get your husband to give you a hand? I'm sure once he gets home he'll have everything taken care in no time."

Rachel stared at the man's blue eyes and wanted to make both of them black. What gave him the right to interfere in her private life? It was none of his damn business if her husband was working or didn't take care of things. She was amazed he hadn't said one the neighbors told him Dave had split.

Before she could answer Mr. Dunn apologized. He held up his hand, palm out. "Now, it's my turn to say I'm sorry. I haven't seen your husband's truck in the driveway. He must be out of town. I assume that's why you have to call someone?"

She crossed her arms across her chest. What was she going to say? She wasn't one to vomit her life's story to a stranger. And, even though Jeremy Dunn was a neighbor, he was still a stranger. For all she knew he was a pervert who preyed on women living alone.

Her attitude must have sent a warning signal to him because once again he held up both hands, palms out. "I've got to apologize once again. You don't have to answer. Honestly, it's none of my business."

There was no need to go into all the sordid details, although she was sure one of the neighbors, most likely Elise Farrell must have mentioned Dave was gone.

Rachel simply said, "My husband and I have separated, Mr. Dunn."

"The name's Jeremy. I'm sorry to hear that." He scrubbed his hand over his face. "I seem to be telling you *I'm sorry* a lot."

"No problem, Mr., ah, Jeremy. Thanks for bringing Miss Daisy back. She's quite the escape artist. I'll try to keep a better eye on her. I'll call my screen company when I go back inside and see when they can get out here."

Jeremy glanced at his garage, then back at her. "Say, I have some spare screen and spline. I had to replace quite a few panels over at my place. If you want, I'd be happy to fix the screen."

"Since you want to be on a first name basis, mine is Rachel." But, she did not extend her hand. "As for fixing the screen, it's very kind of you, but not necessary. I'll add it to my round-to-it list."

"I don't mind helping you out. Let me go grab my toolbox so I can take a look at the sink after I replace the screen. I don't think I have a belt for the vacuum, but if you get one I can take care of that, too. There's nothing to it. In the meantime, I'll loan you mine."

Rachel gave a sigh of relief. It was almost impossible to get someone to come out on a Saturday, especially since it was a perfect March day for being outdoors. When the weather was good most of the guys in town were out fishing, having a beach day, or playing golf. That would mean she would have to take a day off from work next week and wait for a repairmen to show. No one she knew of would commit to a specific time anymore.

"Thanks, but I don't want to take you away from your yard work," she said, grateful for his offer.

"The yard work can wait. I'll set this plant in a pot and be right back. I think your problems are more pressing. Besides, we want to keep Daisy happy. I've watched her out here on the lanai. It seems to be her favorite spot."

"It is. She hates when the air-conditioning is on and she doesn't have ready access to the outdoors. This is her favorite time of year when she can go in and out as she pleases."

"Okay, then let's get it done. You may want to consider putting an inside fence around the bottom to keep her from running through. My brother-in-law did that at his house when he had a dog. Worked like a charm."

"What a good idea. As for taking care of the present problems, if you're sure you don't mind, I won't turn you down. I know there's no screening in my garage, but, if you need any extra tools there are plenty out there. Look around and help yourself."

Maybe it was a good thing she'd not been rash about cleaning out the garage and getting rid of Dave's tools. Most were brand new. Dave would buy them and not have a clue how to use them. Except for being a whiz bang painter, the guy was all thumbs. In retrospect, maybe he considered himself an artist. The last time she was out in the garage to take inventory she had counted twenty-four screwdrivers of various sizes. None of them for a Phillip's head screw, which is what she needed.

As for his clothes, she was still glad she had packed them in boxes and given them to the local homeless shelter. She had offered them to Davy, but he refused, saying even though he was the same size as his father, under the circumstances, he'd feel strange wearing them.

"Thanks anyway. I prefer to use my own." Jeremy gave her a quick two-finger salute and jogged over to his house. "Be back in a minute."

Rachel went in the house and opened the junk drawer in the kitchen. Dave used to complain about it, but she often found something she needed that saved her a trip to the mall or the hardware store. Looking down at the dog, she held a package with a vacuum cleaner belt. "Ah, ha, I had a feeling there might be a spare in here, Miss Daisy. Maybe this will turn out to be a pretty good day after all."

Jeremy soon came back carrying a tool kit and a roll of screening tucked under his arm. She came out on the lanai. "Can I lend you a hand with something?"

He knelt to repair the screen. "This won't take long. Why don't you clean out the cabinet under the bathroom sink and have a bucket ready. There's probably a lot of gunk and dirty water in the elbow joint. You don't want it to go all over the bottom of the cabinet."

"I'll hop right to it. Would you like something cold to drink? A beer? Soda?"

"Not right now. I'll take you up on the offer when we're finished. You might want to get the make and model of your vacuum so you know what kind of belt to get."

"While you were getting your stuff I found a spare one in the junk drawer. This isn't the first time I've had this happen. Miss Daisy sheds a lot so I try to keep a couple extra on hand. I simply forgot where I put them. When all else fails check the junk drawer." That was one of the few things Dave knew how to do. He was an ace at fixing vacuums.

Jeremy smiled. "Looks like we can get all the problems taken care of today."

Once he finished replacing the screen she showed him the way to the master bathroom. "It's the sink on the right. We never used the one on the left."

"Double sinks are the norm these days. Back in the day, we all shared one."

He grabbed a couple of wrenches and went straight to work. When she saw what he cleaned out of the pipe she wanted to gag and was glad she had removed everything from inside the cabinet. She opened the window, turned on the ceiling fan and liberally sprayed a scented deodorizer to get rid of the sewer-like stench.

Waving her hand in front of face while she sprayed, she commented, "Don't know how you worked under there without gagging or heaving."

"I've smelled worse." He picked up the bucket he had used. "Is there someplace I could wash up after I get rid of this gunk? I don't want to mess up your bathroom. After I finish, I'll change the belt on your vacuum, and you'll be all set."

"You can use the stationary tub in the garage. Follow me; it's on the other side of the kitchen. There's some towels on the shelf out there. You don't know how much I appreciate all you've done for me today. What do I owe you?"

"Not a penny. I'm glad I could help." Rachel noticed a mischievous twinkle in his blue eyes. "Let me take my statement back. You could give me a hand planting over at my place later this afternoon and we'll call it square. Unless you have other plans."

"It's the least I can do." She glanced at the clock. "It's way past lunch time. What do you say I prepare something while you're out cleaning up?"

"Now there's an offer I'm not going to refuse."

"Good. Any likes or dislikes?"

"As long as it's food, I'm fine. Unless you're going to go fancy with artichokes. The hearts are okay, but I'm not big on the peel and dip that goes with eating one of them. And I'm not crazy about avocado unless it's in guacamole."

"No worries there. Ham and Swiss on marble rye was more what I had in mind. I've got some potato salad, not homemade, from the deli."

"Sounds perfect to me. By the way, I'll drain the water out of the bucket and put the gunky stuff in a plastic garbage bag. Is the big trash can out there? No, I remember now, it's by the side of the house."

"There are some smaller trash bags on the shelf; you can use one of those."

She wanted to dance back to the kitchen. What could've been a very crappy day was turning out to be not so bad after all. Right now she didn't care if Al Kohn and Elsie Farrell were running around the neighborhood spreading rumors about her and Jeremy. Elsie was probably timing his visit. Rachel didn't give a damn. It was nice to have a handyman living next door.

****

She quickly fixed a couple of sandwiches and put out the potato salad. Did he like tomato and lettuce on a sandwich? Best to put it on a separate plate just in case. Same with the mayo, but she didn't get fancy, she set the jar on the table.

She had the table ready by the time he got back from the garage. "Have a seat."

"I didn't expect to get lunch."

Rachel took a seat across from him. "It's the least I could do."

During lunch, conversation settled on Calusa. She found out he had moved down from Tampa. She shared that she'd lived here most of her life but was originally from Missouri. When they finished he wanted to help her clear the table, but she shooed him out and told him she would meet him in a half-hour to help repair the damage to his garden.

****

Jeremy strolled across the yard and rcsisted the urge to shake his head. Why would a man leave a woman like Rachel Benton? Was he out of his friggin' mind or did this Dave character know something he didn't? So far that was not the vibe Jeremy was picking up. They had shared a very pleasant lunch. She gave him the low-down on the neighborhood, particularly the gossips. How Betty Bradford brought new neighbors a plate of cookies so she could get inside the house to see what the furniture was like.

He had already had a fair idea on the usual suspects, but it was nice to have confirmation. He didn't mention he didn't invite Mrs. Bradley into the house. He thanked the woman but told her he was diabetic and could not accept the cookies. After talking with Rachel, he figured there was a distinct possibility of Mrs. Bradley showing up with a plate of sugar-free cookies.

Now that he thought about it, since he'd moved in, it was always Rachel who was the friendly one. The night he asked about the trash pick-up she not only told him the day but the recycle rules. She had also filled him in about there only being one local paper. She'd said if he needed any help finding his way around town she'd be glad to help.

Over lunch, when she told him about the neighbors, she mentioned that if his wife needed to know about shops or hair salons to have her come over. Was that her way of finding out if he was married? Maybe. But the message he received was she was being a helpful neighbor and not on the make. He was right up front telling her he didn't have a wife and that he was divorced.

He didn't know if, in her case, Rachel had started proceedings, but he would be lying to himself if he said it had not occurred to him if she had, she would be available. Maybe not immediately, but in the future. The woman sure had a lot of plusses in her favor. Factor out the stress she was under earlier in the day, she had a pleasant personality. Knew how to say thank you. Not only was she easy on the eyes, she had fixed a great lunch.

Yes, indeed, she had a lot going for her. He was sure he would find out more when she came over to help him in the garden. Twenty-five years as a detective on the Tampa police force made him very good at asking the right questions in order to get the right information.

****

Rachel hummed while she finished cleaning the kitchen. There was no need to change clothes if she was going to dig in the garden. She was impressed when Jeremy offered to help clean up after lunch. Helping in the kitchen was a huge no-no in Dave's book. She couldn't even recall him offering to give a hand in all the years they had been married. As soon as a meal was finished Dave was nowhere to be found.

No, the big question was her first impression of Mr. Dunn...Jeremy. Since they had a shared a lunch in her kitchen she could not think of him as 'Mr.' If she had to pick one word to describe being around him it would be comfortable.

There was no attempt to be touchy-feely, which she

appreciated. He was polite, waited for her sit before he did when he came to the table. Conversation had not segued into anything personal.

Yet there was this fluttery sensation in the pit of her stomach. There was definitely a sense of camaraderie. Her dormant imagination surfaced and was busy creating a few scenarios dealing with forming a...a friendship...with benefits. She waved her hand in front of her face wondering where these ideas were coming from. Would it be possible in today's fast paced society? Only time will tell.

For now, it was a trip to the garage to get her gardening gloves, then over to give Jeremy a hand. As for Miss Daisy, she would put her in the laundry room with one of Dave's shoes and hope for the best.

****

She and Jeremy spent a pleasant time getting his garden in order. First they had a visit from Betty Bradford followed by Elsie Farrell who lived behind them. Rachel had to admire the way Jeremy handled the ladies. Always polite but in a tone that warned 'don't go there'.

She noticed his jaw tighten when Al Kohn came along and told him how to plant the hibiscus, when to water and how much to use at one time. She heard Jeremy utter something under his breath sounding like he'd already checked on Google, but once again the man kept his cool and told Al that he would keep his suggestions in mind.

Rachel wanted to pat him on the back when they were alone. Instead, she verbally congratulated him on the way he handled the neighbor's visits.

She returned back home with mixed feelings. She

was thrilled Jeremy had handled the ladies and Al with tact, but sad it had ended much too quickly.

Of course, she was sure both ladies and Al made a beeline for Floyd Patterson's place. It made Rachel wonder, since every dog has its day, when their turn would come.

Chapter 5

Sunday afternoon Rachel was trying to decide what to have for dinner. Cooking for one was not enjoyable but as it was part of her new lifestyle as a single, she'd have to get used to it. She knew she could go out to a restaurant but often felt conspicuous eating alone.

She stood in front of the open fridge door, trying to decide on scrambled or fried eggs when Anita came through the back slider, carrying a crock pot filled with something smelling delicious and probably full of calories. The aroma, of itself, raised Rachel's suspicions. The woman was a dear friend, but this had the appearance of turning into a gab fest rather than simply watching an old movie on TV, along with an adult beverage and popcorn.

"When I called earlier I wasn't expecting you to bring dinner. I simply thought if you weren't doing anything this afternoon you could drop down for a while after you and Lyle finished dinner."

Anita sat the pot on the counter then plugged it in. "Surprised the hell out of me when Lyle got up early this morning to go fishing with his buddies, Jake Sutton and Stuart Brady. Especially after he refused to with Dave on the river. They made arrangements to go on a charter boat heading out in the Gulf. Lyle is probably puking his guts out about now. If not *mal de mer*, he will come back with some new ailment. Anyway, I knew he wouldn't be home for dinner, so rather than waste a pot of my famous beef burgundy I thought we could share. Do you have any French bread in the freezer? If not I can dash home, get some corn meal and whip up some muffins."

"That won't be necessary. I have some tube crescent rolls we can pop in the toaster oven. Unless you have your heart set on corn bread." Rachel lifted the lid and sniffed the aroma. She took a teaspoon out of the drawer and tasted the sauce. "Mmmm, this is absolutely delicious. Tastes like more than one serving is in order."

"Crescent rolls will be fine," Anita declared, as she grabbed a wooden spoon from the large utensil crock and proceeded to stir the stew. "I'm so glad to be here. Lyle's been reading one of his doctor columns again so I don't even want to be home when he gets there."

"Good heavens, what is his malady this week?"

"He's convinced he's hypoglycemic even though the article said it rarely happens unless you're diabetic. He picked me up after I closed the shop yesterday and we went out for dinner. I had about all of him I could take because of the litany of symptoms he recited as he picked at his food. Let Stuart and Jake deal with him today. Actually, they'll probably tell him to put a sock in it. If my luck holds, he'll be so worn out when he gets home he'll go right to bed."

"If your luck takes a powder he'll bring home a good catch and ask you to help clean it." Rachel went to the cupboard. "Do you want me to put out bowls or plates?"

"Doesn't matter." Anita wagged a finger. "No worries about cleaning fish. He said if they do catch anything, it is scaled and gutted before they get off the boat. By the way, if we're going to have what you always refer to as an adult beverage, make mine red."

"Coming up." After Rachel put out two bowls, she got a couple of goblets from the china closet and filled them with merlot, then handed one to her friend.

Anita took a sip and let the wine roll around on her tongue. "This is good. Very smooth. So what's new with you?"

Rachel smiled. Here it comes. Subtlety was not one of Anita's long suits and she was sure either Betty or Elsie told her about working in the yard with Jeremy. She knew there would be more questions to follow, but she'd make her friend work for the answers.

"We're busy at work. The boss asked me to work a couple of evening shifts in ER admissions. I'm not so sure I want to. I told her I would think about it. Do you want me to put on a pot of coffee?"

"After dinner, provided you have that nice French blend we had the last time. For now I'll stick with wine. It goes good with the beef dish."

"I'll drink to that," Rachel said and raised her glass. She went to the cupboard and moved a few items around. "Ah, I do have the French blend. I'll put the pot on when we sit down to eat. Then it'll be fresh."

"That'll work."

"Do you want to drink your wine here or go in the den?" Rachel asked.

"The beef has to cook about an hour longer. Let's do the den."

Rachel sighed. She didn't like to go in there because the drab colors depressed her. "Nothing has changed there. I haven't even taken the time to get some bright throw pillows."

"The couch is more comfortable than a kitchen chair. They're too hard on my behind for a good chat."

Once they settled down, Anita curled up on the couch, Rachel in the arm chair, it didn't take long before, innocence dripping from her lips, Anita asked, "So what else is new?"

"I told you about work. Oh, no, I had an appointment with my attorney on Tuesday to sign papers to get the divorce proceedings started."

"You called me Tuesday night and filled me in. Remember?"

Rachel nodded. "Now you mention it, I did. And, I hired Mr. Pesti, the one Lyle recommended, to do the yard work for me."

"You told me that on Tuesday night as well."

"The only other thing I can think of is the new car, but I'm certain I told you about that on Tuesday."

"You did, and we made plans to christen it with a ride up old Englewood Road to Manasota Beach." Anita stirred in her seat. "Come on, Rach. You know damn well what I meant. I had the morning free yesterday so I decided to trim back some of those Mexican petunias around the lanai. They're getting very leggy, and Lyle claims they make him itch. I saw the new neighbor at your back screen door with a plant in one hand and leading the dog with the other."

Rachel groaned. "Unfortunately, the dog tried to redo his garden. It was not pleasant."

Anita cocked an eyebrow. "So that's why he went home and came back with his tool box?"

"What did you do, stand outside and keep watch?"

"Not keeping watch, but, hey, you're here alone.

And he lives alone. Then I saw him come over, tool box in hand and later when Elsie phoned me at the shop and said it was a couple of hours before he left your place but that you were working in his yard after lunch, a lot of things went through my mind. Like maybe you got lucky. Especially now that I know you two are on a first name basis."

Rachel burst out laughing. "*Got lucky?* I don't think so. He had extra screening in his garage and offered to fix the section that Daisy ripped through. When he was here, I happened to mention I was having trouble with my bathroom sink draining slow so he fixed it." She wasn't going to say anything about the vacuum. "He wouldn't take any money so I offered to fix lunch and help him finish planting around his lanai."

"Relax, Rachel. I wasn't asking for details. I'm sure the Fearsome Foursome will make up some pretty interesting stories based on their observations. I thought it was great you were making an effort to be neighborly. Especially when you were over at his place the same day helping him in the yard. I'll lay odds Betty was on the phone to Elsie before you had the first plant in the ground."

"Aw, come on, Anita, the least I could do was help replant what the monster dog had dug up. And, we had four plants in the ground before they walked over."

Anita waggled her eyebrows. "Play your cards right and things might warm up for the two of you. Of course, it doesn't hurt he's good a looking hunk. I think it's neat how his hair droops over his left eye. It makes him look so sexy." She snapped her fingers. "Kinda like that actor on TV. You know who I mean."

Rachel didn't want to guess which actor she was

talking about; there were so many in Anita's book.

"Don't you want to close your eyes, run your fingers through his hair, push it back it away from his eyes? Of course, you'd have to get close to do that. Maybe we can come up with a few more things around here that need to be taken care of…we could over-load the garbage disposal, break the—"

Increasingly uncomfortable with the direction Anita's brain was headed, Rachel said, "Hold it right there with the crazy suggestions. Nothing is going to happen. My personal situation is too complicated right now. No way do I have plans of getting involved."

She stopped for a second and thought about Jeremy's cute butt when he was working under her bathroom sink. "Does his hair droop over his left eye? I've never noticed."

"Of course you haven't. Not!"

Rachel took a sip of her wine and took a good long look around the den. It was so Dave with the different shades of brown in the upholstery, curtains and heavy dark end tables. "I think I'll paint in here, make it my own. It needs to be brighter. Maybe a nice cream, some bamboo end tables, change the curtains."

"The room sucks the way it is, but don't try to change the subject. Paint color is not as interesting as the subject of Jeremy and you."

"There is no Jeremy and me." She got up and lifted the curtain rod from the window to let some fresh air into the room only to find Betty Bradford staring back at her. She cranked opened the jalousie window. Plastering an insincere smile on her face she narrowed her eyes and said, "Hi, Betty. Want to come in so you can hear the whole conversation?"

"Well, I never," the woman answered and hot footed it across the yard.

Anita held her sides as she laughed. "Oh, my god. You shocked the shit out of Betty. Bet she doesn't tell Elsie she got caught. Do you want to move back to the kitchen?"

"No. If we stay here with the window uncovered we'll be okay." Miss Daisy came in the room and laid down by Dave's old chair. Rachel reached down and rubbed her ears. "By the way, I have to stop by your shop and thank Harriet for recommending Mr. DeCarlo. She said he was a tremendous help when she was in a miserable situation with her first husband."

"Yeah, then he helped her get rid of numbers two and three. She should get a discount rate if this current marriage doesn't work out."

Rachel grinned. "You would think she'd give up by now and assume marriage was not for her."

Anita took a sip of wine. "I don't think the whole problem is on her side, although she's terrific at picking losers. I think her real problem is she has some kind of a redemption complex. The first one was okay, but they were too young. The next two had a problem with alcohol; one had an ex-wife who didn't understand him. It turned out neither did Harriet. Poor Stan had a bad heart, but she was determined she was going to make him well. You knew him."

Rachel nodded and covered her ears. "Stop there. My head is spinning."

"The woman could write a book. Back to you. Have you had any word from Dave?"

"No, ma'am. I had hoped he would get in touch by now with some instructions. If not with me at least with one of the boys, most likely Davy since they were so close. Mr. DeCarlo told me not to be concerned about hearing from him as long as I intend to proceed with the divorce, which I do."

Anita shook her head. "Talk about being a gutless wonder. I can't believe he talked with Davy rather than you before leaving. That's positively cowardly." She slouched down in the couch. "Are you sure you want to get rid of this? It is soooo comfortable."

"I do. It's ugly. Now, to back to get back on topic, I imagine Dave felt it was the easiest way to handle it. Taking into account our last encounter, I honestly think I'm happier he did it this way. It's futile to get upset at this point. What's done is done."

"Since he walked out on you, I hope you're going for full ownership of the house and any bank accounts." She stood and picked up Rachel's empty glass from the end table. "Don't answer that until I come back with refills."

Rachel leaned back in the chair and waited for Anita to return. It would be tough for a while, but she would survive by taking life one day at a time. As for this room, she would figure out some way to make it her own.

Anita came back and handed her a full glass. "Took a few minutes to stir the stew and add a little more wine. Now, back to our conversation."

"Where were we?" Rachel asked.

Anita sat on the couch and curled her legs to the side. "I asked about the house and any bank accounts. You don't have to feel obligated to answer."

"You can bet the ranch I'm going for the house. As for the accounts, I told you we've been keeping our money separate for the past couple of years. I got the statement from his bank last week. It only had a small balance so he must've been planning this move for a while. The bank won't let me close it for thirty days to be sure there's no future activity."

"Didn't that tick you off, hon? I mean what a sneaky bastard he was…is."

Rachel took a sip of wine before answering. "As long as I'm not hung out to dry with unexpected bills, I'll don't give a damn. Dave may have left without facing me, but I don't think he's mean enough to expect me to pay his expenses. If that should happen, my attorney will handle it. I'm getting hungry, and I don't want to drink any more wine on an empty stomach."

Anita stood and started for the kitchen. "Glad to hear it…your feelings about Dave as well as being hungry. We can talk about your future while we eat. What do you plan to do now? And don't tell me you don't know. We all do that kind of dreaming once in a while."

"What do you mean?" she asked. She took a tablecloth with matching napkins in a bright buttercup pattern out of the drawer and proceeded to set the table. She was not lying to Anita. She was feeling better every day.

Anita brought the crock pot to the table and placed it on the padded mat before topping the wine glasses. "You know exactly what I mean. Especially after a tiff. The one that goes *if I were free I would take up sky diving* or something off the wall like that."

"No worries about me taking up sky diving. I'm afraid of heights. Besides, I think we already had this conversation the day I found out Dave left me." She took a fork full of food and sighed. "Man, this stew is delicious. Oops, we've been doing so much talking I forgot to make the rolls."

"Don't worry about it. We don't need them. There's a lot of potatoes in this, should be more than enough carbs." Anita glanced at her. "I hope you know I was teasing about the sky diving."

Rachel nodded. "I would love to learn to play the piano. And I think I already mentioned ice skating."

"Maybe, but right now you don't have a piano and you don't have time to practice. As for the ice skating, you'd probably fall and break your leg."

"Thanks for the confidence, friend."

Anita waved Rachel's statement aside. "Honestly, do you have any real plans? Something you would like to do or always wanted to do, but couldn't because Dave said no?"

"I can't think of anything right off hand, but I could probably come up with something if you give me a few minutes."

"I'll give you three minutes. The only thing I ask is you don't go around with a long face so the boys can tell Dave you're pining for him and can't manage without him."

Rachel took another small helping from the pot and mashed the potato with her fork, while she thought for a minute. "I haven't been pining or moping around and they know it. It seems to be bothering Davy, more than Mike. On the positive side, on my days off, I've been doing quite a few things. I've gone to the beach early in the morning for a long walk and a little shelling."

"That's a start. Do you have anything else planned?"

"Not really, but I'm giving a couple of things some serious thought."

"Like?" Anita questioned.

Rachel squared her shoulders. "Buying a red car."

"You did that already."

"Change the color of my hair," Rachel said.

"We've already taken care of that. Keep going."

"Buying some black lace underwear."

Anita started laughing. "In that order?"

Rachel grinned and shrugged. "Maybe."

"You go, girlfriend, just don't let your halo get so tight it gives you a headache. I can see you and Jeremy tooling down the Trail with the top down and you feeling all feminine in your new sexy underwear."

"Who said I'd let Jeremy in the car?"

"You never know what's going to happen in life. Jeremy is your handsome, ah, sensual neighbor. It's a possibility."

"I don't think so."

"Aw, come on. What if he asks you for a lift to the grocery store or the emergency room? You're gonna say no?"

Rolling her eyes, Rachel snickered, "Fat chance of that ever happening."

Chapter 6

Rachel picked up the watering can to give the plants on the lanai a much needed soak. She watched as the water swirled around the rims, pooling on the hard dirt before flooding the drip dishes and splashing onto the floor. One big attempt at soaking the dirt was not going to take care of the problem. Even loosening the dirt was not going to help—it was like cement. Being honest, she had to admit this was one chore she had let slide lately.

The bright yellow leaves on the philodendron were the first clue of ill health. She'd had this plant since her kids were toddlers. Now it looked mighty sad and in need of a serious trim. Not only a trim, it needed to be split it up into several pots. Philodendrons did well when root bound, but this was ridiculous. She would probably need a hatchet to break up the dirt ball. The geraniums were wimpy with leaves more brown than green. No use worrying about the Christmas cactus; it was past help and headed for the garbage can.

Looking at the lawn increased her gratitude for Mr. Pesti. Even though he had only been here once, the grassy area looked neat and healthy. She gave the plants another glance, not even Miracle Grow was going to help at this point. Dave had always been after her to let the flower beds go to grass so it would be easier for him to cut. Maybe that was why the present condition of the outside garden, as well as the house plants, bothered her. The garden and plants had been her job.

She would have to schedule time to get the garden back into shape. Make it in the early morning on the weekends, especially now that the warmer weather was waiting around the corner. She would either melt or fry to a crisp if she attempted to do gardening in the afternoon. She'd been soaked right down to her underwear the day she helped Jeremy with his planting.

Like old memories, maybe it was time to ditch all of this stuff and start over fresh. She wanted colorful flowers to cheer her. As he seemed to have a green thumb, she'd ask Jeremy for ideas the next time she saw him. She had enjoyed the time she spent helping to replant after Daisy's rampage of digging. Then again, she could always check on Google to see what grew well in this area at this time of year.

If one didn't take into account the visits to the attorney and the extra work hours she'd put in, she had been busy doing other things. More personal things that made her feel good. She now sported a stylish short hair cut in a brighter, more flattering shade of auburn. She was glad she followed Anita's advice and had a few subtle gold highlights added. Even her sons had noticed enough to make a comment. She wasn't sure whether or not to take Davy's reaction as a positive or a negative.

Her daughters-in-law had given her the two thumbs up gesture the first time they saw her new do. Looking down at her toes peeking out of her sandals, she could not believe she had actually picked a bright fire engine red polish when she had her pedicure. The glossy polish made her feel bouncy and...adventurous.

She smiled. Not a smile but a face splitting grin as

she thought about her new red Mustang convertible parked out in the garage. Dave would have had an absolute hissy conniption if she came home with a sports car while he was still here. She could hear him now telling her she was too frigging old to be driving a Mustang.

She didn't have to listen to Dave anymore. Not even in her head. She would never have chosen a sports car in the past because he always went car shopping with her and told her what she wanted, which model had a better resale value. Before the boys were old enough to drive, the vehicle had to be big enough to haul them, their friends and sports equipment. To keep the peace she had always gone along with getting a station wagon, then a minivan.

After the boys were married and out of the house, it was Dave who decided she needed a smaller, more economical car to drive around town. That was the one she'd traded for the Mustang and was happy to see it go. She had always hated the car but didn't want to make waves.

Going along to keep the peace was a behavior relegated to the past. Right now she didn't give a fig about resale value. She was having more fun than she'd had in years. Looking at her toes again she realized the color red was a big part of it. It was an element of the new, bright slant on life. From now on it would be her signature color.

She was intent on pinching off the dead leaves and blossoms from the geranium when she heard someone quietly call her name. Glancing up she saw Jeremy standing on the other side of the screen door. "Didn't want to startle you. Mind if I come in for a minute?"

Miss Daisy bounded out of the house and sat in front of the screen door, waiting for him. Rachel walked over and drew the latch aside while she held the dog by the collar. "Not at all. Come on in, sit and relax a minute."

As he bent over to pet the dog, he pointed to the geranium she was working on. "Hate to be the one to inform you, but that one is beyond help. Best thing you could do is put it in the trash."

Rachel shook her head, laughed and threw the plant in the green garbage bag hooked over the back of a chair. "You're on the money with that call. I haven't done much gardening lately, and I miss it. As a matter of fact, your yard puts me to shame. I was going to ask you for advice on bedding plants."

"Between me and the folks in the local garden center I'm sure we can handle that assignment. The reason I came by was I wanted to ask a favor, but it looks like you're busy."

"Not very." She picked up a small shriveled Christmas cactus and dropped it in the trash bag. "I used to think it would take an atom bomb to kill these."

"You may be thinking of palmetto bushes. It takes a miracle, along with super hard work, to clear those."

Rachel nodded in agreement. "I remember when we had a huge fire around here many years ago. All the vegetation was burned to a crisp but the palmettos came back in a matter of weeks." She picked up a droopy basil plant and tossed it in the bag. The plant stand was looking dingy but a good scrubbing with a wire brush and a coat of spray paint would do the trick. "All these plants have to go. I'll bag them and dump the dirt on the side of the garage later. What's the favor?"

"Stuart Brady from the repair shop called to say my car's ready. I was having a problem with the transmission fluid leaking. My buddy, Slick Hansen, was going to take me, but he got called into work. Would you have time to drive me to Brady's to get it?"

She glanced down at her dirt streaked shirt and shorts then held up her dirty hands. "I'll be glad to take you. Give me twenty minutes to shower and change."

"Take your time. I'll go back home and close up."

"Sounds like a plan. I'll meet you at my garage in twenty."

"Thanks." Turning around and walking backwards, he said, "Say, if you're not in a hurry to get back to the garden, why don't we stop for lunch on the way? Slick tells me the Captain's Net has great seafood."

Rachel glanced at the Minnie Mouse clock on the lanai wall. "I don't think we'll have time. Since he and Isabelle got married, Stuart's only open a half-day every other Saturday."

"You know Stuart?"

"Of course. Everybody in the neighborhood uses him for their car repairs. And, don't ever shorten his name to Stu. He hates it."

"So Slick informed me. I have a spare set of keys. I'll call and ask Stuart to put the set he has under the front seat, along with his bill and lock the car. My friend also said Stuart has a mail slot. I'll write a check and drop it in the slot. That way we can take our time and have a leisurely lunch first."

There was no way Rachel was going to turn down a free lunch. Especially at the Captain's Net. So instead of resisting she said, "Your plan sounds fine to me. On second thought, since we're going to lunch how about giving me twenty-five minutes?"

"Why don't you give me the leash and I'll take the dog for a short walk while you get ready."

Rachel opened the storage cupboard and took out the leash. "That will save me some time. Thanks."

She stood on the lanai for a few minutes, watching Jeremy jog alongside Miss Daisy as she lifted her face to the sun. The day was warm with no humidity; birds sitting on the phone wires called to her; and a handsome man was taking her out to lunch. What more could she ask for on a beautiful day like today? Not a cotton picking thing.

She hurried into the house and hit the shower. The warm water felt good sluicing over her body. She reached up and grabbed the melon and cucumber gel, squeezed a generous amount on the bath sponge and slathered her body. Taking in a deep breath she relished the fragrance. It had been a long time, a very long time, since she felt so feminine.

Come on now, Rachel, don't read more into this invitation to the Captain's Net. It's only lunch with a kind neighbor. One who came and helped me when I was having a very bad day.

I'm doing a random act of kindness. Go with that and have a good time.

She wrapped the bath towel around her body sarong style, padded into her closet and searched through her clothes. She finally took out a bright tropical print sundress she'd bought last week. After applying a little makeup she brushed her hair, then shook it and watched it fall into place. Anita had told her this style would be easy to take care of, now she had the proof.

She slipped on a pair of low heel sandals and went out to the kitchen. The dog was stretched out by the slider, pink tongue lolling out the side of her mouth. Jeremy must have given her a good workout. She brought her inside and lured her into the laundry room with a biscuit. So far, putting her in there was keeping her baseboard intact.

She went to kitchen, and grabbed her keys and purse from the counter before heading out the front door. She should've gone out through the laundry room but didn't want to risk setting Miss Daisy off since she was settled after her walk. She entered the code for the door opener, got in the car and backed out onto the driveway before pressing the control to lower the top on the convertible. Why waste such a beautiful day?

Jeremy moseyed up the driveway as she snapped the top down. He whistled, then pointed his thumb toward the street. "Going my way?"

She cocked an inquisitive eyebrow. Taking the time to change clothes was worth it. "Depends." she said, enjoying the banter. It had been quite a while since she had participated in this kind of conversation. It was fun. Her husband was never much in the banter department but now was not the time to be thinking about him.

Jeremy stood by the passenger door. "I'm open to any good suggestions."

She patted the nearside seat, then slipped on her sunglasses. "The Captain's Net is my destination. One of the neighbors told me they have great seafood."

He looked up at the clear blue sky. "It would be a great day to kick back and sit out on the patio." He paused. "Okay with you?"

"You twisted my arm. Hop in." Enjoying the moment she almost added *good looking,* but stopped. It was a bit too forward at this point in time.

As she turned the corner to drive out to the Tamiami Trail, Anita passed, stuck her arm out the window and waved. Not a discreet little wrist whip but a great big, flag-bearer show. What was the woman doing home at this time on a Saturday?

There will probably be ten messages on my answering machine by the time I get home. Good thing she left her cell phone on the charger or her friend would be calling her, demanding all the details as they happened. Let her stew for a while. Besides there was nothing to tell. Yet.

****

Lunch on the palm shaded patio with the old fashioned paddle fans was perfect. Despite the fact it was in season, there wasn't a crowd outdoors. Evidently most of the people had opted to eat in the air conditioned dining room. She like it out here because it was quiet, no noise from the kitchen. Though they were sitting outdoors, the aroma of shrimp cooking in vinegar and spices permeated the air, whetting the appetite.

Rather than have the peel and eat shrimp, they each had a bowl of spicy conch chowder and shared an order of fried calamari and vegetables along with a glass of chilled white wine. It had been a long time since she had dropped everything, buried her list of chores in the junk drawer and taken the day off. It was a pleasant change in routine.

No, it was more, it was absolutely satisfying to sit and enjoy the view of Charlotte Harbor. The tide was out and she could smell the wet sand and brackish water washing onto the shore. It wasn't an unpleasant smell, more reminiscent of her early morning beach walks. Pelicans were putting on a diving show; there was even a manatee swimming with her young calf. That, along with delicious food and comfortable companionship made it perfect.

"Do you come here often?" he asked.

"As often as I can." She took a bite of fried sweet red pepper. "Mmmm. I'd love to know how they keep the veggies from getting soggy. I asked but the chef won't tell."

"Has this place been here long? It looks new."

"The Captain's Net has been here since I've lived in Calusa. I've always liked it because not only is the food outstanding, it is classy. You don't have the noise of banging dishes or waiters calling to each other. Best of all, no TVs. Jack said if the people want to watch TV they can do it at home or a local sports bar. It took a pretty bad hit during Hurricane Charley. All the locals were happy when Jack Gardener decided to rebuild. He threw a whopping grand opening party to welcome his customers back. He's the third generation to run the place. Now Sonny, his son, helps manage the restaurant."

"You don't hear about family run places like this anymore." Jeremy leaned back in his chair. "I've been meaning to ask how things are going with you. I'm not trying to pry into your personal life. You don't have to answer if you don't want to, but I was working on the pool the day your boys came over and y'all were out on the lanai. I couldn't hear the actual conversation but from the tone one of them wasn't very happy."

"The understatement of the year," she snorted. "Davy, my oldest, isn't handling this very well. He and his dad were close. My husband seems intent on putting Davy in the middle of our split— and that worries me the most. I swear the man is playing his son like a fine violin."

"Unfortunately, it happens a lot," Jeremy said. "What about the other one?"

She took a sip of wine and closed her eyes listening to the island music coming through the speakers. What a perfect day. Jeremy looked sharp in dark blue shorts and white guayabera shirt. So laid back, so tropical. She'd bought Dave several, but he refused to wear them saying they weren't macho. Apparently that wasn't the case with Jeremy. "Mike is my younger son. I believe he is trying to remain neutral. Of course, I don't know exactly what his brother is telling him, but I think Mike is more able to refrain from taking sides."

"I hope so. It would be to his benefit."

"Sounds like you might've gone through something like this yourself."

He leaned forward to rest his arms on the table. "My case was the opposite. I came home from work and found nothing, I mean zip, nada, in the living room when I opened the front door. I had no idea where my family was. There wasn't even a note, like Lyle mentioned you had found.

"The strangest part was the crock pot was on and the smell of pot roast filled the house. The next day her lawyer had me served with papers. To this day I don't eat pot roast, but if it happens to be one of your specialties, I'd be willing to give it a try."

She was not going to mention pot roast *was* one of

her specialties. "I imagine you can appreciate what I'm going through."

"You could say that. So I know the last thing you need in your life right now is more stress." Jeremy stood and pushed back his chair. "If you will excuse me for a minute, I'll be right back."

Rachel was staring at the water searching for a sight of the manatee and thinking about their conversation. How coincidental that he had been through a similar situation. Of course, she wasn't the only person to go through a divorce. Otherwise the lawyers would be out of business.

Jeremy's deep baritone voice brought her back to reality. "A penny for your thoughts."

"They have to be worth more."

"Okay, how about a dollar? We have to take the present economy into account," he said in a serious tone along with a slight frown on his forehead that quickly disappeared to be replaced by a smile.

"A dollar sounds a whole lot better, but I won't charge you this time. I was simply thinking what a wonderful day this is. I mean sitting out here, enjoying a delicious meal, the view and your company." She glanced at her watch. "As much as I would like to spend more time here I think we need to get moving." She reached in her purse for her wallet.

"Put it away. It's been taken care of. You've been very gracious taking time out of what I am sure is a very busy day, to do this for me. The least I can do is treat you to lunch. How about we do this again next Saturday?"

"I'd love to, but I have to work evenings next Saturday. I'm covering for the admitting clerk in the

Emergency Room. I'll be happy to take a rain check."

He sat down. "Great. I know all about working different shifts. How about Sunday brunch? I hear they have several great spots over in Punta Gorda. We can make a day of it. Maybe take a cruise on the Harbor."

"I could do the brunch, not the cruise, I have to be back to work on Sunday afternoon as well."

Darn. She could kick herself for promising Joanie Thomas she would cover for her, but it was too late now. The McCabes were going to baby sit for Joanie so she and her husband could take their boat down to the Keys for a little fishing—and a much needed weekend alone.

"Do you always work the weekends?"

"I usually work days, Monday through Friday. This was a special request from a co-worker who has covered for me in the past. Anyway, I got a four day weekend out of it because she is going to work for me Monday and Tuesday next week."

"I understand. Like I said, been there."

Is he keeping tabs on me? If so, she wondered why. He hadn't done anything to upset her. To date, as well as being a great help when she was in a pickle, he had always been a gentleman.

"Most of the time I like to let things go until the weekend, depending on how busy it is at the hospital. Then again, there's not much to do when you live alone. I don't have to worry about cleaning up other peoples' messes. When my boys were still at home, it was a full time job. Most of the time they used the floor for a closet as well as their bureau."

Jeremy stood and came around to help her from her chair. "At least you always knew where to find their laundry. My mom was forever complaining about me and my brother only wearing one sock because she was sure we each had two feet. She used to say she was going to have good luck when all of the socks matched in a load of wash. I think she probably found a dozen pair in the back of the closet when Dan left home. It was different with my sisters."

"How many kids in your family?"

He kept his hand at the small of her back as they wove their way out of the restaurant. "There were six of us, four sisters and one brother."

"Do they live in Florida?"

"My sisters still live in the Tampa area. Dan passed away a couple of years ago. How about you?"

"One sister, she lives out west. I know what your mom meant about the socks not matching. I can look at it that way now; back then it was a different story. Now all I have to do is clean up after the dog."

"Ah yes. The delightful Miss Daisy." He shot her a genuine smile, the kind that even crinkles the corner of eyes. "Your dog and I are getting to be on good terms. She has actually stopped digging in my garden. If you ever need someone to let her out when you work evenings, let me know. I'll be happy to walk her."

The first thing that popped into Jeremy's head was: *what a lucky break*. The pesky animal who inadvertently set up their second meeting might be the one who helps him out as far as future dating. Miss Daisy wasn't all bad. Lately, he had been keeping biscuits on hand as bribes for the mini training sessions.

There was a down side to all this. The last time he talked with his neighbor, Lyle Scott mentioned that quite a few of the folks on the block had a pool going as to when Rachel's husband would show up at her door, hat in hand, begging her to take him back.

Jeremy declined the offer to join the betting. No way did he want to get involved, plus he was pretty sure Rachel would have a fit if she knew. Lyle said they were only throwing five dollars in the pot. Why waste the money? Jeremy hoped the guy never came back.

He wished Rachel would remain single and available. The woman took care of herself and was pleasant company. Didn't run her mouth ten ways from Sunday and from what he saw the day he fixed a few things at her place she was also a neat housekeeper.

Why would a guy with half a brain take off and leave a woman like Rachel alone to fend for herself?

****

When they got to the car he held the door for her before going around to the passenger side. "Are you buckled up?" she asked.

"Always. I've seen too many bad accidents where the people were thrown out of the car. At one of them, the driver was thrown out and the car ran over him."

"What kind of work did you do?"

"Until I retired, I was a detective with the Tampa Police Department."

She nodded. This information made her feel more secure. Plus, it explained why he noticed her routine. It was second nature for a cop to be aware of what went on in his surroundings. "That's good to know. I feel safer already having you as a neighbor."

She took the Tamiami Trail to the turn-off for Brady's repair and maintenance shop, pointing out various businesses along the way. After she pulled into Brady's lot, he got out of the car and leaned on the door. "See you later."

"Okay," she said and waved as she drove away.

Next on the agenda would be a phone call from Anita wanting to know where she had been going with Jeremy.

If she was really lucky, one of the boys would call and want to know why she was driving around, top down, with a man who wasn't related to them in the passenger seat.

Chapter 7

"Hey, Mom, where are you?" Davy and Mike called in unison as they came through the laundry room and into the kitchen.

Drat! Only one freaking week had gone by since she had gone to lunch with Jeremy. She had managed to avoid them all week. She should've kept the garage door closed and pretended she wasn't home. Of course, that wouldn't have worked because they both had keys. The least they could've done was call first. For all they knew she might have been cleaning the house in her underwear.

When Mike's wife, Melinda, called on Friday she mentioned she was going to Anita's for a haircut yesterday afternoon. Knowing Anita, she probably made a remark to Melinda about seeing her and Jeremy driving around in the Mustang. With the top down.

True to form Anita called last evening, wanting to know where Rachel was heading when she saw her Saturday. Rachel swore all she did was drive Jeremy to pick up his car, and, because she did, he treated her to lunch at the Captain's Net. Once something like that was repeated in a beauty shop, the story would mushroom with each telling.

As for her sons, she couldn't hide out in her bedroom for the rest of her life. Sure as God made little green apples, her boys were here to gang up on her. It wasn't like it'd been ages since they dropped by the house; they'd been good, *too good*, about checking on her since Dave left. By dropping in unannounced she could only surmise they, more so Davy, were trying to catch her doing something they felt she shouldn't.

Was she getting paranoid?

Her daughters-in-law called a couple of times a week, which seemed suspiciously like scheduled calls. That wasn't bad, and she wasn't going to make a fuss—as long as they didn't try to smother her with caring.

"Mom? Where are you?" the dual-voiced question came again. She closed her eyes and blew out a long deep breath. When the boys spoke as one, it always indicated trouble. It was one of those traits only a mother noticed. She might as well face the music. Davy would take the lead; Mike would follow.

"I'm in the bedroom getting dressed," she yelled. "I'll meet you in the kitchen as soon as I finish."

She slipped into white Capris and a red and white striped shirt. Damn, that was probably the wrong thing to say. If she didn't get out there pretty quick they'll think she had someone hiding under the bed.

Let them check. The closet too if they felt like it.

By the time she got to the kitchen Davy had straddled a chair and rested both arms across the back while Mike rocked back and forth on the back legs of the other.

"Sit properly in the chair, Mike; you're going to break the legs."

"Mom, you've been telling me that for years. Haven't broken a chair leg yet." He put all four legs on the floor and folded his hands on the table.

"There's always a first time. What are y'all doing

here today? Shouldn't you both be at work?"

The boys exchanged glances. The hesitation was obvious to her; each was waiting for the other to go first. As always, Davy, being the oldest, took the lead. "It's Sunday. We're both off. Mike's on his way to Sarasota."

Rachel glanced at the calendar and bobbed her head. "So it is."

"The reason we're here is we saw you driving out of the Captain's Net parking lot with some guy last Saturday," Davy said. "This is the first chance we've had to come by. Who is he?"

"Yeah, Mom, you were looking pretty cool zipping along in the '*stang* with the top down, wearing your big Jackie O sunglasses," Mike said. "The two of you were sure laughing it up about something. Davy thought the guy might be Mr. Dunn."

"It was Jeremy." She should have believed her when Anita said she wouldn't breathe a word to anybody. Hells bells, why should she bother? When a woman drove a screaming red convertible around town with the top down, she put herself on stage for everybody to see. She gave her friend a quick mental apology.

To gain a bit of time, Rachel went to the refrigerator and took out a container of tea. "What were y'all doing together on Saturday?" She held up the pitcher. "Want some?"

"No thanks. The question here is not what *we were* doing. What we want are some answers about what *you were* doing," Davy said in his new authoritative voice.

Mike held up his hand. "I'll pass, Mom."

She went to the cupboard to grab a glass and took

her time pouring the tea before joining her sons at the table. "Actually, as to what *you two* were doing, I don't give a darn as long as you don't ask me for money. Now, about what *I* was doing, what if I don't want to answer? You both need to keep in mind I'm old enough to do whatever I want whenever I want. Don't either one of you think because your father left you're allowed to run my life."

Davy took the lead. "We don't want the neighbors talking about you. You know Calusa is a small town and, and…" He scrubbed his hand over his face and stopped without finishing the sentence.

"Shove your *and's* in your ears or any other orifice that's handy. I don't give a crap what anybody thinks, including the neighbors. If they're talking about me they're leaving somebody else alone."

Mike leaned across the table and patted her on the arm. "Now, Mom, don't get upset. We're concerned about you."

"Yeah, *really* concerned," Davy snapped. "We don't want your grandchildren hearing anybody calling you a 'loose woman'."

Unable to hold back, Rachel burst out laughing. Somehow she could not picture her grandchildren, Chad, Matt and Susan using the term "loose woman" much less knowing what the words meant. Chad, the eldest, might, but at age twelve it was a stretch. "You've got to be kidding me. Mike, you and Melinda don't have any children yet, but do you have the same feeling?"

He merely shrugged and made circles on the table with his finger, The evidence further proving his discomfort was he didn't look her in the eye. She would have to get him alone later.

Glancing from one to the other, she prayed silently not to lose her temper. "If you *must* know, I was taking my neighbor, Jeremy, to get his car out of the shop."

Davy interrupted her and snickered, "I didn't know you were on a first name basis with the man or that the Captain's Net had a repair shop or you would drive someone to pick up a car all decked out in a low cut dress. At least I hope it was a dress."

Rachel reached over and grabbed him by the ear. "You're lucky I don't smack you up alongside your head. How can you dare question what I wear? And, if you must know, it was a dress. And, most of us in the neighborhood call each other by our first names, except for the Fearsome Foursome."

"Okay, but why did it have to be that bozo?" Davy snarled, pushing her hand away from his ear.

"You know, Davy, I'm sure I taught you better manners. Who gave you the right to talk that way and don't call my neighbor a *bozo*. That is rude and crude."

"Now, Mom, don't get upset. Davy and I were surprised to see you with someone...with a man." Mike soothed. "I'm sure he didn't mean to imply you were doing anything improper."

"Right. What Mike said," Davy said in a more contrite tone and rubbing his ear.

Rachel huffed out a sigh. Talk about role reversal. "Listen up because I'm only going to tell you one time. I said I would give my neighbor, Jeremy, a lift over to Brady's to pick up his car. He offered to take me to lunch for doing him a favor and I took him up on it. Do you have a problem with that?"

"Nice try, Mom," Mike said. "I happen to know

Stuart Brady closes early on Saturdays."

"I know. But, did you ever take into consideration some people have a spare set of keys and can call ahead and make arrangements?"

"Oops." Mike ducked his head as he shot her a sheepish look.

"Yeah, *oops*. Now I'm going to tell you both this only once. Oh, I said that, so I'll tell you for the second and last time: butt out of my life. If I have something I can't handle, I'll ask for help. Other than that, MYOB. Understand? Or, do I have to put it in writing?"

Davy and Mike stood up. "You're coming through loud and clear, Mom," Mike said, but Davy scowled.

"Good. Now do you want me to make you a sandwich?"

They both headed for the door to go back through the garage. Mike stopped, came back, and gave her a kiss on the cheek. "No thanks, Mom. Melinda called; she's waiting lunch for me."

"I thought you were going to Sarasota."

Mike grimaced. "Busted again."

Rachel folded her arms across her chest. "What about you, Davy?"

"Kathy's not making lunch. Since I have the day off, I promised to watch the kids while she went out to lunch and a movie with her sister. Keep in mind you're a grandmother, not some sexy ex-wife in Charlotte County. And, another thing, I've been meaning to ask, what made you dye your hair red?"

"My hair isn't red; it's auburn, my natural color. It was starting to look a bit dull so I had Anita add some highlights," she said, running her fingers through her hair and fluffing it. "I think she did a fantastic job. Do

86

you really think I'm sexy?"

Davy simply threw his hands in the air.

Mike smiled. "I think it looks great. Makes you look ten years younger. And, I thought you looked super foxy from what I could see of that dress you were wearing. If you got it, flaunt it."

Mouth taut in a straight line, Davy clenched his fists. "For God's sake, Mike, don't encourage her. She's our mother and a grandmother."

Before Rachel could say a word in rebuttal they quick stepped out through the garage. Good thing because her temper had reached the boiling point with Davy's last statement. There was no way he was going to influence her hair color or the way she dressed. If he thought she would tolerate him turning into his father or become her guardian, he had another think coming.

What would they say if they knew about Jeremy's helping out with basic repairs? There was no way they would notice because they had no reason to question her about plumbing. They might find out about her working with Jeremy in the garden last week if one of the Fearsome Foursome knew how to get in touch with the boys.

She whistled for Daisy before opening the slider. The pet slowly came around the corner from the den. Miss Daisy never could stand hearing people argue. Every time she and Dave had words the dog curled up in a corner and put her paws over her ears. Rachel took the leash she'd looped over the doorknob and snapped it on Daisy's collar.

"Pup, if my boys keep questioning me about my behavior, you're liable to spend a lot of time head buried between your paws. Right now, let's get some exercise so I can work off this temper."

****

With a bottle of wine tucked under one arm, the other swinging by her side, Rachel's pace was just short of a jog as she made her way down the street to Anita's place. If her family's behavior didn't change for the better—and damn soon—her brain was going to explode from overload.

She was so angry she didn't stop to chat when Floyd Patterson waved, she kept on going, knowing she'd have to pay the price somewhere along the way. Ditto on not stopping to chat with Elsie Farrell.

She loved her sons, but at this point she was ready to smack the both of them, the way she had threatened about an hour ago. Their wives weren't far behind in getting a taste of her temper as well.

Walking around to the back of Anita's house, like she always did, she spotted her friend on the lanai, stretched out on a chaise, reading a book and sipping a tumbler of iced tea. She opened the screen door, walked to the table and plunked the bottle of wine. "Tea is not going to cut it right now. Grab a couple of wine glasses, woman. I need to have some serious girl talk here."

Anita marked the page with a paper clip, got up and walked into the kitchen. Calling over her shoulder, "Do you want to drink out there or inside?"

"I spotted Elsie Farrell out for a walk on my way over. Out here's fine but I'll have to keep my voice down so she can't hear if she cuts through the back yards. I'm glad you have the fan going because I need to cool off."

Anita came out carrying a tray with glasses, a corkscrew and basket of mixed nuts. "From the sound of your voice you're obviously upset. I brought something to nosh on while you vent."

"If Lyle is home, you might as well call him out here so I don't have to repeat myself. Right now I'm too annoyed to have him listening in the kitchen like he usually does, but not catching everything I say."

Anita's eyes narrowed to slits. "This must be pretty serious. To answer your question, Lyle and Jeremy ran over to Home Depot to get a part for something Lyle's tinkering with out in the garage. You know how men are once they get into Home Depot, so you'll only have an audience of one." She uncorked the bottle and poured. "From the sound of your voice I might as well throw the cork away. What's up?"

"To be honest, I'm kinda glad your hubby's not here. Even though he means well, he loves to give advice and that's one thing I don't need right now. All I want is for someone to listen."

Anita picked out a few cashews and started munching. "I'm all ears and they're yours for the asking."

"It's the boys. They paid me a visit," Rachel said after a big swallow of wine. She started to cough, felt a tickle in her throat, grabbed a napkin from the holder and sneezed.

"Bless you." Anita rolled her eyes. "Oh, oh. They must've seen you with Jeremy last week like I did."

"Yes, and don't go jumping to conclusions like they did. I've already told you the whole story about taking Jeremy to pick up his car."

"And, his taking you out for a thank-you-very-much lunch."

"Plus, you know I like to drive with the top down."

Anita topped off Rachel's glass. "So, who gives a rat's ass if you're driving around town with a good looking guy in your new snazzy car?"

Rachel took a more lady-like sip before answering, checking out of the corner of her eye if Elsie just happened to be passing by. The coast was clear. "Apparently it's bothering the hell out of my sons. They walked into my kitchen and proceeded to double-team me with questions like why I was wearing what I had on. In fact, Davy wanted to be sure it was a dress. Did they think I would be out wearing hot pants or short shorts?"

"Careful there, Rachel. You're dating yourself using those words."

"So what?" she asked, drumming her fingers on the glass topped table. "Since when do my boys have the right to question me about anything? I'm three times seven and then some," Rachel hissed.

Anita leaned back on the chair. "Your present life style is a new wrinkle in the blanket, so to speak. I can see Davy getting all bent out of shape, because he's so much like his father. I'm having a hard time believing mild-mannered Mike also questioned you."

"Mike, for the most part, was his usual easygoing self. Davy was the lead inquisitor. For all I know he probably strong-armed Mike into coming with him. Then they had this cock and bull story about why they weren't at work. In all the excitement, I forgot neither one of them work on Sundays."

"Now that makes more sense, about Mike's attitude I mean. Davy probably got him all riled up on the way to your place. So, other than seeing you with Jeremy, what happened to cause their visit? Did they see you pulling out of a motel parking lot? If so you skipped that part when we talked."

"Don't even say something like that in jest. I was driving out of the Captain's Net parking lot. But from the way Davy carried on you would've thought it *was* a no-tell motel *and* that I neglected to take the time to put my clothes back on."

Anita tipped her head back and gazed at the ceiling fan as if gathering her thoughts. "Okay, so I can piece this all together, let's start from the beginning."

Rachel popped a Brazil nut into her mouth. After a few seconds of crunching she again related how Jeremy had asked her to give him a lift to get his car. "Damn, I feel like a kid who's been sent to the principal's office for misbehaving during assembly."

Over a dramatic waggle of eyebrows, Anita grinned wickedly. "Don't fret. I'm trying to get all the facts straight in my head. Sometimes you have to repeat the story a couple of times because there are particulars you may have forgotten to tell the first time out."

This woman was her best friend. Now she had a roiling in her stomach making her leery of confiding in her. Trying not to sound whiny, she said, "You're getting as bad as my sons."

Anita reached over and patted her hand. "Please don't get upset. I'm just so excited that you went out and that your sons are seeing you in a different light."

Recalling the day, Rachel closed her eyes. "Since the weather was perfect, we ate out on the new combination tiki hut and patio Sonny Gardener added after Hurricane Charley blew through. It's really cool with the thatched roof and fans."

"One of these days I may get to eat out there,"

Anita said with a mournful sigh. "Lyle always wants to sit inside in the air conditioning no matter where we go. Do they serve dinner out there?"

"Didn't really check. I know when Jeremy suggested eating there I was like *hey, let's go*."

"I would've done the same. It's one of my favorite places, except for breakfast, then I always stop by the Fork & Spoon to catch up on local gossip with Mandy Skinner. Anyway, sounds perfectly innocent to me. So what's the problem with the boys?"

"To hear Davy talk, I'm turning into a fallen woman. He wants me to think of my grandchildren. Doesn't want me to do anything to make them feel ashamed of me or embarrass them in any way. Then as a parting shot he made a comment on my *red* hair. You would've thought I was some kind of a flaming Mamie. Mike said I looked ten years younger."

Anita burst out laughing. "You've got to be shitting me. All this evolved because you had lunch with Jeremy and dropped him off to get his car? Before you go on, I'm going to have to have a serious talk with Davy about his hair comment. It's very flattering, even if I say so myself. After all, I picked the color."

"You hit the nail on the head with your comment," Rachel said before taking another sip of wine and gave Anita a wicked smile. "As for Davy's remark, I've already warned him he would incur your wrath."

"My heavens, what are they going to do if they do see you coming out of a motel?"

Rachel shot Anita a warning glance. "Don't even go there, because that's *never* going to happen."

"Careful my friend, *never* is a very long time. On the other hand, why waste good money going to a local motel when you two are neighbors? There are no security lights in the back yards. Who would know if you tiptoed through the grass one night? Should he invite you to go out of town, well that's another story, and again, who's to know?"

Rachel tossed a nut at her. Anita caught it and popped it in her mouth. "Good catch. Get your mind out of the bedroom. I'm still essentially married. I'm going through this process one step at a time. I can't have Davy contacting his father and saying I'm seeing the neighbor. If you recall, Dave had already accused me of making goo-goo eyes over the garbage cans."

Anita started laughing so hard she nabbed a napkin to wipe the tears from her eyes. "What is it with everybody these days? If you're friends with a man, the assumption is you're sleeping with him. Doesn't anybody believe in friendship between the sexes?"

"I agree with you…about being friends. You should very definitely cultivate a friendship before crawling between the sheets. In this day and age the boys should be mature enough to realize that as well."

"Speaking of the grandchildren, I haven't seen them over at your place lately," Anita said. "Don't tell me Davy isn't allowing them come over."

"He hasn't stopped them yet. Right now they're still in school and tied up with their activities. As for my sons, the way they're acting you would think I need a keeper. They even have their wives checking up on me. I'd have to be stupid, senile or both, not to realize what's going on. Melinda calls on Monday, Wednesday, and Friday, Kathy on Tuesdays and Thursdays. And—they always call at the same time."

"You mean they even have Kathy, wedding-in-the-wind, in on this?"

Rachel fingered through the basket, on the hunt for Brazil nuts. "You're never going to let my daughter-in-law forget, are you?"

Anita folded her arms across her chest and shook her head. "I'm not. Their wedding was different from the get-go. Remember how she couldn't make her mind up about what color to have her attendants wear? *Then* it was what color shoes. *Then* it was the style of shoes. *Then* it was the jewelry. Instead of buying the girls the earrings she wanted them to wear as a gift, she kept changing her mind and having them buy something else. I think they ended up going to about six different stores. Those girls spent a fortune by the time the wedding finally took place."

Rachel shuddered. "I know, but she meant well and she's come a long way since then."

"One could only hope so. Otherwise, she would be named queen of the dingbats. The most bizarre thing, other than the shoes and jewelry deal, was taking you and her mother, the prim and proper prude, to the male strip club for her bachelorette party. That had to be one for the record books."

"Yeah, I had the same opinion. I mean I was embarrassed...for her mother." Rachel couldn't stop the giggle that bubbled up from her throat. "I'm sure Pam wanted to slide under the table when the guy came to our table and did his best pelvic tilt so she could put money in his G-string. She actually got bug-eyed when he danced my way, and I slipped in a five. He was tasty enough to deserve a twenty, but I didn't have one."

With a grin, Anita raised her glass. "You are not a prude, there is hope for you and I am vindicated."

Rachel touched her glass to Anita's. "I'm working on it, just not going as fast as you want me to."

"Back to the wedding. Don't you remember, that Kathy insisted her attendants wear their hair loose and flowing?" Anita rolled her eyes and shuddered. "I tried to tell her a wedding in the park, by the water, in March, frequently involves wind. Would she listen? No. When it came time to take pictures, those poor girls looked like someone dumped dishes of limp spaghetti on their heads."

Rachel reached for her wine glass again and twirled it by the stem before running her finger around the rim, making it sing. "That's in the past and can't be changed. She's grown up a lot and having kids helped. I'm more concerned about what's happening now."

Anita saw Elsie and Betty standing together in Elsie's backyard and waved. Both women turned and went into Elsie's house.

Rachel turned around and glanced around the yard. "Why are you waving?"

"We had an audience," Anita said. "I'm positive they were not out there admiring the tangerines on our tree. No worries, they went inside after I waved."

"Thank God we don't have front porches or they would be walking up and down the street."

"As for your daughter-in-law, in my eyes she still has a touch of dingbatitis. Now Mike's Melinda is a different story. She has her feet firmly rooted to the ground. Mike was lucky to find her."

"You're prejudiced because she comes to your shop and Kathy doesn't."

"No, ma'am. If Kathy wants to walk around with hair as long as Crystal Gayle, it's her business."

"Come on now, that's an exaggeration, it's not nearly as long as Crystal Gayle's."

"Only misses by about six to eight inches. Back to our initial topic. My feelings in this case are your private life is none of their concern. They don't share theirs...do they?"

"No, and I don't want to share mine with them, either."

Inviting confidence, Anita leaned forward, elbow on the table, resting her chin on her hand. "By the way, have you heard anything from Dave since he left?"

"Nary a syllable. It's like he dropped off the face of the earth."

"I'm sure, in time, you'll hear from him, or about him. He's bound to want something. Maybe in his quest to find himself he'll meet someone and want a divorce?"

"Knowing Dave, if it's legal anywhere, he could've started proceedings already, and I wouldn't have a clue. And, since I've already started proceedings here, it could develop into quite the brouhaha."

"I'm sure, if he has decided to take the initiative, you'll find out soon enough."

Rachel slouched down in the chair and sighed. "Whenever Dave wanted something he wanted it done yesterday."

"To change the subject to a more pleasant topic, Lyle wants to have a cookout next weekend; how about coming by? Yes, Jeremy is invited; no, it's not a set up. A couple of the neighbors are coming as well as Roy and Joette Bradley."

Mischief gleaming in her eyes, Rachel said, "I'd love to come. I was supposed to work the evening shift this coming weekend for Joanie Thomas, but Mary Jo Harris asked if she could have the time. She and her hubby are buying a house and they could use the extra money."

Anita laid her hand over her heart and sighed. "Ah, it was meant to be."

Chuckling, Rachel smacked her gently on the shoulder. "Maybe Jeremy and I can walk down the street together and my boys, or their wives, will happen to drive by."

"Sure, and you could be holding hands, then he could stop in the middle of the street and waltz you to our door."

Rachel grinned. "Like an old Doris Day or Gene Kelly movie. I wonder if Jeremy knows how to tap dance?"

"You can ask the next time you see him. I don't think there's much chance of that happening—not dancing in the street, but someone in the family driving by and catching you. If you want them to know, I can always call Davy and ask him what's happening. Tell him I heard rumors around the neighborhood."

"Wash your mouth out with soap. With all that's going on I don't want to risk my son having a heart attack."

Chapter 8

Rachel spied Jeremy striding across the back yard, looking pretty tasty in dark blue cargo shorts, matching blue and white striped knit shirt and canvas shoes. It was a treat to be escorted to a neighborhood function. Dave usually went ahead of her, or not at all.

She was sure Mrs. Bradford, also known as Busybody Bradford around the neighborhood, was watching with the phone in one hand and a cup of coffee in the other. She probably had Jeremy's trips across the back yard written on her calendar and tallied them at the end of the week. It didn't matter which door Jeremy came to because what Mrs. Bradford didn't report from the back yard, old Mr. Kohn checked out from the front view. Between the two of them, they had all perimeters covered.

Rachel was sure Betty's nose was out of joint since the day Jeremy spied her on her lanai while he helped Rachel put in fire shrubs. Making out like she was watering her plants, after he waved hello and in a very loud voice asked how she was doing, Betty threw down her watering can and stormed into her house.

Later, Jeremy commented how Betty wasn't the only one of the neighbors who kept an eagle eye on him. The two men across the street, Al Kohn and Floyd Patterson, had also done their share of spying while sitting on lawn chairs in Al's garage which faced

Jeremy's house.

Neighbors she could ignore because she knew they would only be watching her until someone new moved in on the street or onc of thc established folks did something shocking. Once that happened, she'd be yesterday's news.

In light of the present events and her sons' concerns about her becoming a woman of questionable virtue, she found herself taking a closer look at Jeremy. She already knew the basics: over six feet and not overweight. While working in the yard with him, she realized his face was square shaped, then noticed his chin, which was nicely formed and kept his head from looking like a box. His wide set blue eyes were a striking contrast to his dark brown hair which appeared to be getting a bit thin at the crown.

These features were strong and kept him from being too perfect or too handsome. Perhaps the slight crook in his nose made him ruggedly handsome. His left upper lip didn't quite move when he smiled. As if he's been in a fight at some point in the past, maybe had some nerve damage or it didn't heal properly. She'd ask him about it someday.

Jeremy rapped on the lanai screen door like he always did before entering. Miss Daisy barreled through the house, barking and rocking back on her haunches until he opened the screen door and petted her. He strolled to the slider and called out, "Rachel, it's me. Are you ready?"

She quickly turned her head because she didn't want to be caught staring at him and his coordinated outfit. She made a speedy dash to the other side of the kitchen, opened a cupboard door and pretended to be rummaging for something. "Come on in, I have some things for you to carry. By the way, do you tap dance?"

"Are we performing at the cookout?"

She noticed the total look of surprise on his face and decided not to elaborate. She'd explain later...maybe. Pushing her hair behind her ears, she said, "Mmmm, no. Thought I'd ask."

"Come on now, Rachel, you've piqued my curiosity. Most folks don't ask a question like that out of the blue."

She tried not to blush, but could feel the heat creep up her neck. "It's nothing. A silly conversation I had with Anita. Forget it."

"Okay, if you're looking for a dance partner, I'm afraid you'll have to count me out for any fancy ballroom stuff. I manage okay with the slow ones." He tossed the dog a biscuit he fished out of his shirt pocket. "By the way, I thought you were working today and tomorrow."

"I was supposed to, but one of my co-workers asked if she could take it for extra money. I'm not fond of working evenings so I traded gladly."

Instead of pursing the dance topic, he resisted letting out a wolf whistle when he glimpsed Rachel's bright emerald green outfit. The below the knee pants showed off enough of her well-shaped calves and trim ankles to make his mouth go dry. He always appreciated the beauty of a woman's leg. Yes indeed, a whistle of any kind would be totally inappropriate at this time. But Miz Rachel was one gorgeous woman. It confirmed his opinion that any man who could still get it up and would leave a looker like this had to be a few bricks short of a full load. The way she wore her auburn hair showcased her green eyes and slender neck. Come to think of it the woman had nice ears as well. The kind a man could go crazy nibbling on.

Whoa here, fella. Time to put thoughts like that on the shelf for the moment, dwell on them later. All things considered, everything about her was inviting. A guy would have to be dead not to appreciate her.

Instead of getting all flowery, he opted to keep it simple. "You look nice."

She smiled. "Thank you."

"You're welcome," he said, giving her slight bow. "We're in luck as far as the weather goes tonight. No humidity, so it will be comfortable outside."

Clearing her throat and nodding, she walked to the fridge and took out a large glass pie plate and placed it in a carrier. "Thought I'd surprise Lyle and make his favorite dessert. It's a pineapple cream pie with slivered almonds. I'm keeping my fingers crossed he hasn't developed some kind of malady that would keep him from eating dessert."

"I don't think there will be a problem. His disease of the week has to do with rashes because his catch phrase has been *contact* dermatitis."

"Anita told me he's driving her bonkers getting her to switch from the detergent brand as well as the shower gel she's been buying for ages. She said she's changed the bed linens every day this week. In fact she brought me three different jugs of detergent because he won't let her use them anymore."

Jeremy sniggered, "We should be okay as long as he doesn't offer to show us where the rash is."

"Ugh! I hope not. Back to the dessert, maybe I should have asked you first if you like pineapple.

You're not allergic to nuts are you? No, of course not, you were munching some the day we went to lunch at the Captain's Net. How about the pineapple? I can fix something else."

"No worries there. I can't think of any food I don't like or doesn't like me. I'm not much on desserts, but I'll give the pie a whirl. As for nuts, they're one of my weaknesses. Never met one I didn't like. No pun intended."

"In that case, we're ready to go." She placed the pie in a large patchwork quilted case on the counter. "I packed everything in this insulated tote so it'll be easier to carry. Oh, sorry, I never thought to ask if you had anything you need to put in here?"

"No, ma'am. My contribution has been taken care of; I delivered some wine and beer this morning so Lyle could get it iced. If you're ready, let's go."

While they walked down the street the movie musical conversation she'd had with Anita started running through her brain again. She resisted smiling as she let her imagination run with a picture of her and Jeremy dancing down the street. Instead she asked, "So how do you like our neighborhood so far?"

"I like it fine. There are a lot of characters, like Betty Bradford and Al Kohn, but you'll always find that type in a small community. Floyd Patterson seems like he hangs with them for company. Elsie Farrell seems to find an excuse to come out in her yard whenever I'm working in mine. I'm surprised she didn't join the other three the day I moved in. The woman sure can ask a lot of personal questions. Is she a retired lawyer?"

"You're close there. She was a court reporter. You know, the person who takes notes during a trial. I assume she's had a lot of experience listening to lawyers."

He was well aware of what a court reporter did from his days on the police force and his appearances in court. "She appears interested on what's going on over at your place, always wants to chat when she sees me walking Miss Daisy." He ran his finger across his mouth. "I keep my lips zipped as far as offering any information. No way am I going to be misquoted on the gossip grapevine."

"Know what you mean. She stopped me when I was hanging out some wash the other day. She commented on not seeing Dave around lately, as if Betty hadn't been over to her place as soon as she heard, and the fact that she's seen you over at my house a couple of times."

"What did you tell her? Or would you rather not say." As he waited for her answer, Jeremy took in the neighborhood as they leisurely strolled to the Scotts. Old oak trees with Spanish moss dripping from the limbs and gardens filled with the bright colors of hibiscus, golden dew drops and bright red powder puff bushes flavored the scenery. Floyd Patterson kept two lion statues at the base of his driveway and enhanced his front garden with a bust of Venus. A wicked question crossed Jeremy's mind: did good old boy Floyd rub the statue's exposed breast for luck when nobody was looking?

Rachel's voice brought his attention back to the issue of nosy neighbors. "I told her Dave left me and I was filing for divorce. As to you being at the house, I said you were kind enough to lend me a helping hand whenever I had something that needed to be fixed. All she has to do is look out the window and see us working in the yard."

"Was her curiosity satisfied?"

She looked up at him and grinned. "Honestly, I don't care, but her eyebrows did shoot up to her hairline when I mentioned the word divorce."

"Atta girl. Keep 'em guessing."

"I meant to ask if you had another visit from Betty with a tray of cookies?"

"No, ma'am. She must have believed my borderline diabetic excuse."

"You stopped her cold with that one. Elsie told me Betty is very health conscious."

He tapped the side of his head. "I got her number her right away. Don't forget, I'm a retired detective."

When they arrived at Lyle and Anita's, Rachel noticed there were no cars parked in the driveway. She surmised they must be the first to arrive. Or was this Anita's plan all along? She was very good at organizing parties and couldn't resist doing the same with people. Her friend was the quintessential matchmaker.

Once they got around to the back of the house she saw Anita setting the table for four with her good china and flatware. This set off a series of five alarm bells in Rachel's head. She was glad Lyle had called Jeremy off to the side to help him with the grill. It gave her an opportunity to find out what was happening.

"What gives? I thought there were going to be two more couples," Rachel inquired.

"There were, but the other two canceled out at the last minute." Anita stood back and tapped her chin with her index finger. "Do you think I should put out table knives as well as steak knives?"

"Whatever you think best. Now back to your no-show guests. What happened? Nothing bad I hope."

Anita shot her a glance dripping with pure innocence. "Roy and Joette got unexpected company. His daughter, Nancy, and her hubby came down from Alaska with the three grandkids to surprise them. Roy's birthday is tomorrow and Nancy got in touch with Joette's son, Ned, and arranged a surprise party for tomorrow."

"That's nice," Rachel said. Not only *nice*, incredibly accommodating. "Were you invited to the party?"

"No. According to Joette, Nancy and Ned arranged a small family dinner at the Captain's Net. As for tonight, I invited all of them to come over, but Joette said it would be too much and asked for a rain check. She said the boys would be bored and that always ruins it for the adults. They were on the way out the door to go to Sun Splash, when she called me at the shop this morning."

"What about Harry and Celeste?" Rachel asked, tilting her head toward their place across the backyard.

"Celeste phoned me at the shop yesterday. Seems Harry forgot to tell her they were supposed to be at his boss' house for dinner tonight."

"How convenient."

Here we go, Rachel thought. Anita was at her best when it came to making up a story as to why other folks were not able to make it. She had seen the woman in action on this particular issue of matchmaking in the past. This was the first time it involved her.

"You shouldn't be surprised. You know she doesn't care for the boss' wife. She said the woman is too stiff and boring. Acts like she has a broomstick stuck up her butt. Trust me, Celeste would much rather be spending the evening with us, sipping martinis. You know how Celeste loves her martinis."

Rachel cringed internally. Maybe she had been too quick to condemn Anita as a matchmaker. She would have to rein in snap judgments and tread carefully. "You're right. She mixes up some of the best I ever tasted. James Bond would be thrilled with hers. I'll miss raising a toast with her."

Anita headed for the kitchen, calling over her shoulder. "No need. To make amends, she sent a shaker over. It's chilling in the refrigerator. She said all I have to do is put some crushed ice in yours. She also sent a jar of those queen sized olives you like, the ones stuffed with almonds. Now do you believe me?"

No use making a federal case out the present situation. For all she knew Anita put Celeste up to participating. She would take her friend's explanation at face value and not make waves. "Celeste is so thoughtful. Especially since I know she prefers those tiny sweet gherkins with hers."

Bending backward from the fridge, Anita handed Rachel the jar of olives. "You know, my dear, sometimes you have to believe me when I tell you people bow out at the last minute. As I recall, Dave was an ace in that department. No, actually, he rarely showed and never bothered to call. He always delegated you to make the excuses. What used to genuinely piss me off was when you wouldn't come over either."

Anita went to the cupboard, took out a couple of martini glasses and added crushed ice from the freezer. Rachel released the pressure on the lid with an opener and unscrewed the cap on the olives while Anita got the shaker out of the refrigerator and poured.

Anita raised her glass, "To the future."

"The future," Rachel echoed and took a sip. "This is really delicious. Back to our conversation about Dave in the past. I want to you to know I wasn't being a martyr. It was easier to handle it that way. He would start out by telling me to go and then want to know what I was going to fix for him to eat. By the time I prepared something at the last minute I would've been late so I stayed home. As for tonight, Anita, *my dear*, I'll give you the benefit of the doubt, provided you have four extra steaks in your refrigerator."

"You are a doubting Thomasina! Go see for yourself. I haven't even wrapped them for the freezer in case Lyle or Jeremy is extra hungry."

Rachel broke down and started laughing. "Okay, okay. I believe you. *This time*. So how is Lyle's skin condition coming along? If it keeps up much longer I won't have to buy detergent for at least a year."

Anita rolled her eyes. "Darned if I can see anything anywhere on his body, and believe me he's shown me all the places it's supposed to be. He swears he can see it and that it's pinhead size. I think he uses a magnifying glass because I couldn't see a damn thing. He's practically taken a bath in calamine lotion. I have it all over the towels and the bed sheets. So, if he looks a bit on the pink side you know the reason."

Before Rachel could reply, Lyle yelled from the grill area, "I already know how y'all like your steaks and they're almost ready, be sure to have the rest of the food on the table."

"All taken care of," Anita retorted as she carried

the large bowl of Italian tomato salad to the table. "This smells heavenly, Rachel, can't wait to have some."

Rachel watched as Jeremy carried the platters of baked potatoes and grilled vegetables to the table. It was rather sexy the way his dark brown hair hung over his left eye.

No matter how often he pushed it back with his hand it always seemed to go where it wanted. Overall, she had to agree with Anita; the man was easy on the eyes. Two big pluses were he was very comfortable to be around, and he could repair anything. Add to that he did it immediately instead of saying he would do it tomorrow or on the weekend.

Lyle snapped his fingers. "Hey, Rachel, are you still with us?"

"Sorry, my mind wandered for a second. What did you say?" she asked, then realized he was trying to pass the platter of steaks—and that his hand was very pink.

"I wanted to know if there was anything else I could get for you?" he said. "Do you want another martini? Looks like your glass is a few sips low."

"No, no, I'm fine. One is my limit when it comes to martinis," she said and took her steak before passing the platter to Jeremy.

"Then you only want to eat steak, nothing else. Right?" Lyle asked.

"Don't be silly. I want some of everything. Please pass the salad."

She watched Lyle and Anita exchange glances. What was going through their minds? Better she not know. Then again, looking at Jeremy's slightly crooked smile, all she could do was smile back. Rachel tried to steer the conversation back to things going on in the neighborhood. Bad move as it gave Lyle an opening.

"What's the latest on the Dave-takes-a-powder scene? Any idea where he might be?" he asked before taking a second helping of the tomato salad. "You outdid yourself on this dish tonight, Rachel."

"Thanks. As for Dave, I still haven't heard a word." Rachel concentrated on cutting her steak. "Would you pass the pepper, please?"

Jeremy knew it was time to change the subject. It had to be evident, even to Lyle; Rachel was uncomfortable with that line of questioning. She wasn't cutting her steak; she was slicing it with the precision of a surgeon.

"This is the best steak I've had in ages. Would somebody kindly pass the A-1 Sauce?" Jeremy asked.

Anita picked up the bottle and handed to him. Either not taking the hint or ignoring it, she asked, "Have your boys heard anything from Dave?"

Rachel concentrated on her plate. "To my knowledge, not a word. Unless one of them is holding back. I have to agree with Jeremy, Lyle, these steaks are exceptional."

Lyle took a sip of beer. "Thanks, it's my secret marinade. Speaking of the boys, I hear Davy and Mike came by and gave you the third degree about seeing you and Jeremy out and about in your spanking red convertible."

Jeremy did a double take at that announcement. She had never mentioned a word about it to him. "Didn't you tell them you were taking me to pick up my car?"

Rachel nodded. "Indeed I did. They didn't buy it because they saw us driving out of the parking lot at the

Captain's Net. When I explained why we were there they didn't buy that either. Davy said he didn't know Stuart Brady had a branch there." She picked up her martini glass only to find it empty. Did she drink it all without realizing? "I think I will have a glass of wine."

Jeremy drew the bottle out of the stone holder and poured a glass for her. When she motioned for him to stop at the half way mark, he asked, "Do you want me to give them a call and set them straight?"

Without giving it a second thought, Rachel reached over and patted his arm. She noted the look Lyle and Anita quickly exchanged and immediately removed her hand. "That's kind of you, but I can handle it."

She would have to be careful, or she wouldn't be able to walk home. All she needed to make life perfect was to have someone see her stagger down the street or worse yet, wake up with a hangover in the morning.

"They'd have gone ape if they knew about the day we met," Jeremy quipped. "I mean, about how we met."

"Pass the salad, hon," Anita said. "What do you mean the day you met?"

"I told you the whole story about Miss Daisy pushing out the screen and digging up Jeremy's flowers and how he ended up taking care of the plugged sink and replacing the belt on the vacuum." Rachel said.

Anita folded her arms across her chest. "Are you sure that's the whole story? You two aren't holding anything back?"

"Don't go jumping to conclusions," Jeremy warned. "Like Rachel said, she had some repair problems, I helped her so she fed me lunch, then came over to my place to help me replant the area the dog tore up. And before you go reading anything into it that is all there is to the story. Period."

Lyle stood and started stacking the plates and shot a crafty glance at Rachel. "Not a bad way to start. You left out the part about him helping you with your garden."

"Aw, come on, that didn't take place on the first day I met her," Jeremy said. "Where are you getting your information?"

"Floyd Patterson," Lyle snorted.

"How could he see me help Rachel? He lives across the street from us, not across the back yard. Ah, I know, either Betty or Elsie was spying on us."

On his way to the kitchen, Lyle said, "You got it. Anyway, as I recall, Rachel, you could never get Dave to fix anything even though he had a garage full of tools. Your newfound relationship could turn out to be the start of something nice, convenient. Hell, I'd say that's better than being picked up in a bar. As for the nosy ladies you could always plant a viburnum hedge or put a privacy fence across your backyards."

Jeremy and Rachel burst out laughing at the same time. He shrugged as she raised her eyebrows in silent questioning as to where their friend's mind was traveling.

Calling out the kitchen window pass through, Lyle chuckled, "Aw, come on guys. Give me a break. The mere fact you are neighbors is a big factor. Unless one of you decides to move, you'll most likely be seeing each other every day during which time the eyes of Calusa will be upon you."

Jeremy leaned back in his chair and rested his elbows on the arms. "Rachel, isn't it amazing how this man's mind works? Here we are trying to be good neighbors to each other and it seems like he's trying to move us to a whole new level."

"You're both adults. What do you care what your kids or the nosy neighbors think, Rachel?" Lyle asked as he came out of the kitchen carrying dessert plates. "Everybody ready for some pie? Oh, honey, I forgot the forks. Now, where was I? Oh, yes, what do you care what others think?"

Rachel laid her neatly folded napkin on the table. "Lyle, I don't *care* what the neighbors think. As for my sons, it's more a matter of constantly getting the third degree, more so from Davy than Mike."

Anita came out of the kitchen carrying the pie and forks. "Why would you expect more, sweetie? He's more like his father than Mike. I think we should do something to set them on their ear. Especially now that you're working on your new life, letting go of the old routine. Doing whatever pleases you."

"What else do you suggest? I thought I was doing pretty darn good with buying the convertible and getting a new hair style."

Anita cut four wedges of pie and served it. "That's a good start. One of my clients, Nikki Collins, teaches belly dancing. She also has a friend teaching line dancing over at Fisherman's Village in Punta Gorda. You could give that a whirl."

Without thinking, Rachel rubbed her belly. "I have enough here to do the belly dancing thing."

"Hey, Nikki says it's one of the best toning exercises you can do. She keeps telling me her students range from five to eighty-five. She dances someplace over in Port Charlotte on the third Friday of the month. What do you say we go check it out next month?"

"Sounds like fun. I have to get more active. This sitting and watching TV isn't doing it. I was thinking of joining a gym, but I'm not sure I'm up to making a commitment."

Anita nodded her head toward the men. "Good. Maybe if we're lucky we can talk the guys into doing the line dancing."

Lyle waggled his eyebrows. "If you play your cards right you might be able to talk us into going. What do you say, Jeremy?"

"Count me in. For the line dancing, that is. I wouldn't look too spiffy in one of those harem outfits."

Anita picked up her fork. "That's settled. Let's dig in before we decide we have to cut back on the goodies.

Chapter 9

Rachel arrived home after an especially busy day at work and kicked off her shoes as soon as she walked in from the garage. She wiggled her toes, allowing the cool tiles to soothe her tired feet. Usually her job involved sitting, but today they'd worked short-staffed. Every time she turned around, another crisis reared its ugly head. Doctors handed down stat orders so often she had to run requests from patient units to the lab or x-ray because the computer was down.

Mondays were always busy due to the high number of admissions over the weekend. Add to that, her supervisor wasn't happy because Rachel had told her she didn't want to work any weekends. She didn't have any future weekend plans per se; she simply liked to be home, especially on Sundays. To keep the peace she agree to work one Saturday a month. Seniority had to have some perks.

There was no way she felt like cooking tonight. Opening the freezer door she checked to see what was available and started moving containers around. Chili wasn't calling her name, neither did the vegetable soup. She pulled a large container of split pea soup from the back. Ugh! She detested split pea. It had been Dave's favorite. Whenever she did make it, she prepared two different meals. She'd ask Anita if she or Lyle would like it, or maybe Jeremy. She hated to waste food, but she would pitch it before she would eat a bite of thick green glop.

Nothing in the pantry appealed. She could always boil pasta, throw in a little garlic, black olives and olive oil but she didn't feel like doing all that now—maybe she'd be hungry later. After that, it was going to be an evening of TV and reading a book during the commercials. Not exciting, but not stressful either.

Anita was right. She had to start exercising more, keep the arteries open and burn up plaque. Besides, at her age, it was good for her bones as well. Maybe she would check the newspaper and see if there was an exercise bike or treadmill for sale. That way she wouldn't have to leave the house. She'd think about that next week. Right now all she wanted to do was change clothes, put up her feet and chill.

She and Jeremy, along with Lyle and Anita, had made tentative plans to go to Fisherman's Village in Punta Gorda tonight and give line dancing a try. Rachel was sure it would have been a lot of fun. Thank goodness there was a consensus to postpone going until next week, mainly because Lyle wouldn't be home from work in time.

She and Anita had discussed going to the Center Court to listen to music and dance. Rachel didn't have enough energy to get up out of the chair right now; if they had gone, someone would have had to carry her to the dance area. The mental picture of Jeremy hefting her in his arms gave her a chill. Not a bad one, more of a thrill chill.

She walked out of her bedroom after slipping into her old cut-off jean shorts and baggy T-shirt only to find her oldest son sitting at the kitchen table trying to act cool. The frown, as well as the set of his jaw, told her his efforts had failed miserably.

Heaven help me, here we go again.

"Hi, son. I didn't hear you come in. What brings you by today?" she asked, trying to act casual and keep the irritation out of her voice. Enough was enough. She was not going to put up with any of his nonsense.

Arms folded across his chest, a hint of authority in his voice and looking like he was sucking on a lemon, Davy asked, "Answer my question first. What's going on with you these days?"

Here we go again. "What do you mean? Nothing is *going on.*"

"That's not what I hear. First of all, I tried to call you all afternoon yesterday. All I got was your answering machine."

"I haven't checked for messages today. Maybe I didn't want to talk to anybody. You know it's nice to have a day of peace and quiet. Sunday is the perfect day for that. I like to take time having coffee and reading the paper."

"Nice try. And, you might have gotten away with it if Kathy hadn't run into Melinda this afternoon. Seems Melinda was down to Anita's to have her hair cut this morning. She was full of news about what a good time you had down at the Scotts' on Saturday night. She said Anita was all wound up about you coming with the bozo next door."

Rachel opened the freezer and stuck her head inside. She didn't want to take anything, only wanted a few minutes to cool off and count to ten. It didn't work. She took out a handful of ice cubes and put them in a glass.

Going over to the sink, she filled her glass. Turning around quickly, she held the glass to her cheek. "Now hold it a damn minute, Davy, I have had about all the interference I'm going to stand. Your attitude is too much. You are not my keeper; I'm not senile. I'm still competent enough to make decisions about my life and one is to give you my Hemorrhoid Of The Year award."

"Your what?" he croaked.

"You heard me. It's because you're such a pain in the ass."

"You may feel I am," he huffed, "but let me tell you, Dad doesn't like it."

That statement brought her up short. "What do you mean, *Dad doesn't like it*? Have you heard from him?"

She could tell by the way he cleared his throat and wouldn't look her in the eye he hadn't meant to let that one slip. "I'm going to ask one more time. Have you been in touch with your father?"

"He's called me a couple of times," he mumbled and stared at the ceiling. "So what?"

Rachel plopped on the nearest chair. "Stop looking at everything in the kitchen but me and keep a civil tongue in your head. Why did you neglect to tell me Dad's been in contact with you?"

"Because he didn't want me to tell you."

"But he wanted you to tell him what I've been doing? Well, isn't that too special for words."

"Don't go getting all snarky on me, Mom. He feels the same way I do about you seeing somebody."

"I haven't given either of you permission to be my judge and jury. Besides, he's the one who left." She pounded the table with her fist. "The gutless wonder didn't even have the balls to have a face to face discussion with me. The next time you speak to him, tell him when he left he lost any right to tell me how to live my life."

Davy drew back in the chair like he always did when he'd been reprimanded as a child and made no effort to respond.

"Did he happen to tell you where he's been? Where he's going? What his plans are? Where my attorney can contact him?" She took a big gulp of ice water. At the moment, she couldn't afford to give into rage. If she did, she might start throwing things. She stood abruptly, walked out onto the lanai, and started pinching dead leaves off her new plants.

Davy followed her. "I don't want you to get upset, Mom. He sort of told me where he's going, but he asked me not to say anything."

She turned toward her son. "You did upset me. *Big time.* Do you realize how utterly ridiculous you sound? Let me tell you something right now and you can share it with your father the next time he calls: I will see whom I please, whenever I please. I will run down the street naked, chasing twenty-six men if it suits me."

Davy stuck his hands in his pockets and rocked on the balls of his feet. "Come on, Mom, be sensible."

"How many times do I have to tell you before it finally sinks in? Repetition is getting mighty boring, but I'll give it one last shot: I do not have to account to you or your father for my behavior. You are to stop coming by without calling first. No more check-up phone calls from Kathy. I will tell Mike and Melinda the same thing. If anything earth shattering happens, I'll call you. Right now I am so angry I could smack the living crap out of you." She shook her finger at him. "And, in the future, if your father wants to know anything he can call me. I haven't changed the home number."

Face flushed, he remained seated rather than making a move to leave. "I bet you wouldn't be behaving like this if Aunt Trina lived closer."

"Where did that come from? Aunt Trina's been away from Calusa for more than thirty years. Besides, she's younger than me. She always came to me for advice until she married Uncle Pat. Once he was gone she's became a nomad."

"Yeah, but she's close family. I'm sure she would be able to make you see having a boyfriend at your age is not proper. Not right now anyway."

Rachel plopped in the chair across from her son and watched the blue jays outside vie for domination of the bird feeder. She was not going to admit Jeremy wasn't her boyfriend. Not in the way Davy was inferring. He was more of a male friend, a social companion and no way would she give that up.

"You've been married for thirteen years; you know marriage isn't always a bed of roses."

"I know. But you and Dad were..."

Enjoying seeing her oldest son actually squirm in his seat, she slapped her hand on the table to halt him in mid-sentence. "You *are* going to keep your mouth shut until you hear my side. When I'm finished you can speak. Understand?"

He flinched. "Yes, ma'am."

"For the past year it has been incredibly stressful here, more so for the last six months. I had no idea where I stood with your father. Time did not seem to be doing the job of healing it's purported to do. Also, the 'least said, soonest mended' axiom did not work."

"I had no idea," Davy muttered. "You two always seemed okay."

"Appearances can be deceiving. Dad and I finally came to a crossroads. One of us had to make a move. I didn't want to give up, but apparently he did. I had hoped he'd have enough of a spine to talk things out and see a counselor with me. He said I was crazy, there was nothing wrong with him; it was all me."

"You should have known Dad's wasn't the counselor type."

"Davy, I was at the end of my rope without enough slack to tie a knot and hold on. When I asked what I did that irritated him he'd walk away. Each time I'd ask him if he had a problem he wanted to discuss, he would get this far away look, like his mind was a thousand miles away, then he'd go in the den and close the door. Now, I ask you how you can resolve any situation, but especially a marital one, if one of the parties involved won't talk?"

Davy huffed out a long sigh. "I suppose you can't."

"You're damn right you can't. So I guess each time I tried to talk to your father he considered me a nag. Well, I wasn't nagging. While I was trying to save our marriage, he was looking for an excuse to get out of it. I wasn't going to say anything about what was going on between Dave and me. I never wanted you or Mike to feel like you had to take sides. I still don't want y'all to have to deal with that dilemma."

Davy cleared his throat. "I love you, Mom. I don't want to take sides. It's seeing you with another man makes me a little nuts."

"I am not going to live like a nun in a cloister. I want a social life. If a man offers to take me out to dinner or a movie or anywhere, I'm going. It has been a very long time since I had a social life. Your father was not exactly a party animal, you know. "

"Okay. Okay. I get your message loud and clear."

"Good. Next time your father gets in touch, be sure to tell him I'm fine and I can take care of myself."

Dave stood, gave her a two finger salute and headed for the front door. "Will do."

Rachel took another large swig of ice water and choked. She should've known better than to drink when she was so upset. Nevertheless, the air had to be cleared. "Good," she called after him and wondered how long it would be before they had another episode regarding her social life. Probably until the next time he spoke with his father.

****

The next afternoon Rachel was busy pruning the Mexican petunias in front of the house when a shadow moved over her work area. She looked up to find her son, Mike, standing there, and he did not look happy. Oh my God, must she have another mother-son confrontation? This was becoming tiresome. No, more than *tiresome*, it was becoming a royal pain in the ass.

"Do you mind taking a break? I need to talk."

"Sure, follow me." Rachel pulled off her gardening gloves and led the way around to the back to the lanai. She laid her shears on the table on top of her gloves. "Come on in the kitchen, I'll get us something cool to drink. Didn't I ask you to call before you came over?"

"Why, are you doing something I shouldn't know about?" Mike asked, raising a brow in question.

"Of course not. But keep in mind I wouldn't think of dropping by your place without calling first."

"Yeah, but this is home, I should be able to pop by anytime," he said, following close behind her.

They were already in the house when she realized she made a huge mistake inviting Mike in because the first thing he saw were two jeans clad legs sticking out from under the sink.

The next thing was a male voice saying, "I think you're all set here, Rachel. It should work like a champ. But turn on the water and hit the garbage disposal switch so I can check for leaks while I'm under here."

After she did as he asked, Jeremy said, "No leaks, You're all set," and slid out from under the sink.

"Mike, I want you to meet Jeremy Dunn. He was kind enough to install a new garbage disposal as mine died yesterday. Jeremy, do you want a glass of tea?"

"If you don't mind, Rachel, I'd prefer a cold beer."

"Me too, Mom, while you're at it," Mike said, shooting her a quizzical look.

She was not ready to say one extra word to her son about Jeremy doing her a favor. As far as she was concerned it fell under the category of need to know. Actually, she did not feel he needed an explanation of why Jeremy was doing the installation rather than calling an outside firm. So, instead of giving one, she went directly to the fridge and grabbed two long necks. Turning to face them she glanced from one face to the other and had no idea how this was going to play out.

Jeremy stuck out his hand and introduced himself. "Glad to meet you at last, Mike."

"Me, too, sir."

At least her son had not left his manners out in the car. Of the two boys, he was the most respectful. For some odd reason Davy seemed to carry a chip on his shoulder. She handed a bottle to each and asked, "Would you like a glass?"

"No thanks, this is fine," Jeremy said, and took a sip. "This sure hits the spot."

Mike shook his head and raised the bottle. "I'm good, Mom."

Rachel went to the cupboard and took out a glass. "Great, give me a minute to get something to drink. Then let's go sit out on the lanai and you can tell me what's on your mind, son."

"Maybe I should head home. You and Mike may want to talk in private." Jeremy started for the door.

Rachel loaded her glass with ice and tea before leading the way outside. "You might as well stay. You know the neighborhood. Talk will start now that Floyd Patterson is back from his trip. He will start putting two and two together and like always it comes out eleven. He'll add to the stories Betty Bradford and Al Kohn have circulated since Dave left. I'm sure by the time they're through I'll be designated the wicked woman of the neighborhood."

"Floyd is certainly a piece of work," Jeremy said and took a chair. "Don't forget about Elsie Farrell."

Mike laughed and scratched his head. "Are those folks still watching every move made in the neighborhood? It's true about some things never changing. They were doing that when I was a teenager. Especially, Miz Farrell. One night Davy was parking with his girlfriend on Miz Farrell's street. He shined his spotlight on her and waved when he saw her peeking out of the window."

Rachel rolled her eyes then nodded. "How well I remember. She must've had the phone in her hand to call me when he did. Well now we've discussed the inquisitive neighbors, Mike, what's up?"

Mike blew a long breath. He leaned forward and put his folded hands on the table. "As long as you don't mind Mr. Dunn being here it's okay with me."

"I don't mind. Get on with it."

"Well, Davy came over to our house last night. Told us you ripped him a new one. In case you're interested, he didn't get any sympathy from us or his wife. Kathy gave it to him with both barrels, told him to mind his own business and that he had no right to tell you how to live your life. Melinda and I agreed with her. To say Davy was not a very happy camper when he left our place is putting it mildly."

"Thanks for the support," Rachel said. "Now, I have to ask, what brings you here today?"

"I stopped by to let you know how I feel. You don't want us to take sides, but I think it stinks that Davy isn't keeping you updated on where Dad is headed."

"Honestly, I don't care where your father is. If he doesn't want to talk to me I can handle that, but it would make this whole divorce process so much easier if I could contact him or my attorney could contact his attorney. Then we could both get on with our lives. Right now I'm in limbo."

Mike ran his fingers through his thick, curly red hair, grabbed the back of his neck and flexed it. "I know where he is. In fact, he called Davy last week when I was over there. I talked to him. Talked to Dad, that is. He was in Oregon. From there, he was heading for a port in Washington State; I forgot the name already, and hopping a ship to Fiji or some other island in the Pacific. I mean I've heard of the middle-age crazies, but his behavior is beyond belief. Trust me, I'm not being disrespectful, but I think the man has lost his marbles."

Rachel grinned. "Oh, I don't know, Mike. We married young. Back in the day it was the accepted norm. Then you boys came along before we were married three years. In fact, folks used to think you and Davy were twins."

"But why? I have red hair like yours and Davy has dark hair like Dad." Then the light dawned. "Oh, I get it, not identical twins."

Rachel nodded and ran her finger along the side of her glass making patterns in the moisture. "I presume your father feels he missed out on some great adventure in his life. You remember how he always used to talk about his cousin, Bill, and how the guy traveled around the world working on cargo ships? I think your father was a little envious while he listened to Bill's adventures. I'm sure not all of them were glamorous, or true but all your father heard were the fun parts...the adventure."

"Wouldn't know, Mom. I never met this Bill guy."

"I doubt you would have," Rachel said. "The man was washed overboard during a storm on one of his voyages when you were only two or three."

She glanced at Jeremy to see if he was going to add anything, but all he did was take a long swallow of his beer and keep quiet. She was thankful he didn't reach over and try to hold her hand, even though she wanted him to. Not as a boyfriend or lover, but as one who had had similar life's experiences.

Who was she kidding? She *wanted* him to touch

her, to reassure her he was there for her.

She almost missed his quick wink before he made a comment. "Mike, if you don't mind my saying so, what your father did is not at all unusual in this day and age."

"I know, sir, but it doesn't make it right." He turned to face his mom. "Also, I don't think it's right that Davy won't let the kids come over to see you like they used to."

Rachel didn't think Mike realized what his brother was doing by withholding visits from the kids. Especially, her grand-daughter Susan. She missed their mall days together. It wasn't that she didn't enjoy Chad and Matt, she did, but right now they were at the age where they were involved in every sport that came down the pike. Then, during summers they were at camps. Miss Daisy must have picked up on her emotions because she came over and sat by Rachel's chair and rested her muzzle on her foot.

"That will take care of itself in a couple of weeks. I asked your brother to let me know the boy's sport's schedule, but he has conveniently forgotten," Rachel said. "As for time with Susan, I'm meeting Kathy, Melinda and Susan after work on Wednesday for a bit of girlfriend time at the mall."

"I believe Melinda did say I would be on my own for supper that night. As for the sports schedules, don't worry, Mom, I'll email them to you." Mike stood and bent over and kissed her on the cheek. "Well, I'd better hit the road. I have to pick Melinda up from work. Her car is down at Brady's getting a tail light fixed. Somebody backed into her at the grocery store." Jeremy started to stand. "Don't get up. It was nice meeting you, Mr. Dunn."

"Same here, Mike. And the name's Jeremy."

Mike nodded in acknowledgement.

Rachel reached up and grabbed her son's hand as he passed by. "Mike, I'm going to arrange a dinner, here at the house, with Jeremy, if he's agreeable, so we can get this nonsense straightened out in front of everyone."

Jeremy nodded. "No problem as far as I'm concerned. What about you, Mike?"

Mike smiled. "Sounds like a good plan to me. Now if we can keep Davy from copping a 'tude and making an ass out of himself, we might make progress."

After Mike left Jeremy took Rachel's hand, led her into the den, and pulled her down on the couch next to him. He slipped his arm around her shoulder and drew her close.

"Even though your youngest son supports your choices, it was a taxing scene. I didn't realize I was causing you a problem." He laid his finger over her lips. "Before you try to deny it let me say I can see the worry etched all over your face. From the frown to the set of your jaw, I can tell you're stressed to the max."

"It's not you, Jeremy. It's the whole situation."

"I'm a good listener, but first we are going to start out with a few minutes of cuddle time. Strictly on an adult, friend-to-friend basis. No hanky-panky." He pointed to the clock the end table. "Now let's be quiet for two minutes."

She started to wiggle away after a minute but he held her tight and she rested her head in the crook of his arm. He watched the minute hand sweep away two minutes. "Okay, now we can talk about what's happening. You can tell me as much or as little as you want to. Maybe I can help."

Rachel stretched her legs out and rested her feet on the coffee table. She took a deep breath and snuggled against his side. "Life hasn't been the same for the family since Dave took off. His leaving has created a schism, more so with Davy. I'm aware Mike is trying to play peacekeeper, but it is not an easy job. Then again, I don't want the boys to hate their father. Intellectually, I know Davy doesn't dislike me, but he is resentful." Stopping for a second, she said, "No, when I take the time to give it serious thought, I suppose he is more disappointed than resentful."

"Why would he be?"

"Maybe it's because he's so like his dad in nature. Or, maybe it is because someone has to be the bad guy, and since I'm available, I'm selected."

Jeremy rubbed the side of her arm. "I take it Mike is very much like you."

"In a lot of ways, I think he is. Keeping peace at any price is not always easy. Anyway, I know they didn't want me to file for divorce. They felt I acted too quickly, but there was no way I could dangle in the wind of no-man's land. I had to get on with my life."

"Somehow, Rachel, I can't picture you as the kind of woman who would 'dangle in the wind' or pine away. You are much too vibrant."

She slipped out from under his arm, moved to the end of the couch, and faced him, banding her bent knees with her arms. When she moved, Miss Daisy hopped up between them and laid her head on Jeremy's thigh. "You know how it is. Our kids think we're old."

"If they only realize the freedom we have at our age, they would be mega jealous." He sat sideways, facing her, with his arm resting on the back of the couch. "So now you're planning to have a family gathering. Are you sure you want me here? I won't be offended if you change your mind."

"Absolutely. Unless you prefer not to. I don't want to put you in an uncomfortable situation."

"No problems there…unless someone arrives carrying a gun."

"Right, you were a detective. This should be a walk in the park. I want you to know exactly what you're dealing with. I'll invite Anita and Lyle so you don't feel totally outnumbered."

He reached over and patted her on the knee. "It's up to you. If they can't make it, I can handle myself."

She shot him an impish grin. "There's not a doubt in my mind you can. Jeremy, I don't want to lose your friendship."

This was his opportunity, and he didn't want to blow it. There was nothing wrong with friendship, and it was an opportunity she presented and he was going for it. He would be stupid to push for more in the present situation. He wasn't in a hurry to go to the next level.

"Nor me yours. It seems your oldest son is making more out of our relationship than exists. Having been in your situation, I know you're not ready to get involved with anyone at the moment. Nevertheless, I don't see anything wrong with us dating occasionally. What do you say?"

"I agree. We did have a good time the couple of evenings we went out. And, as long as you don't mind helping me in a pinch when things break down or go wrong, I don't give a rat's ass what Davy thinks."

He raised his eyebrows and in a soft voice, said, "You say that now, Rachel, but I think you do."

"We'll see." She rested her chin on her bent knees and maintained eye contact. "What did you mean about you've been in my situation? Come to think of it, other than the fact you're divorced and a retired police officer, I don't know much about you."

He rubbed the dog's ears. "I was married for ten years; although everything wasn't super, I thought it was okay. Like I told you before, I walked into an empty house. The wife took everything but the kitchen table, one chair, a fold-up chaise on the lanai and a blow-up mattress. And there was a note. "

"Sounds familiar."

He shook his head in agreement. "Yeah, it said I would hear from her lawyer the next day. I spent the night on the chaise on the lanai trying to figure out what happened. She never did like the fact I was a cop and worked all kinds of shifts."

"I know the feeling, I mean about finding a note." She considered getting up and closing the window in case Floyd or Al were taking a shortcut on the way over to Elsie's yard. But all she saw were some robins kicking the mulch out of Elsie's flower bed so the window could stay open.

"Anyway, there was no waiting to hear. The next day I was served with papers the minute I got home from work. I didn't care that she took all the material things, but I did fight like a demon for shared custody of our daughter, Melody. I have never regretted that decision."

"Do they live here in Calusa?"

"No, Patsy lives in Atlanta. Melody lives in

Charleston. She's married and has two children. Ann is ten and Kate twelve."

"So you've kept in touch with your daughter?"

"Sure have." He smiled. "You might say Patsy's and my song was ended, but Melody lingered on."

Rachel snaked her foot around Miss Daisy and gave him a poke in the ribs.

He grabbed her ankle. "What? I was making a play on words."

"I know. It was funny. I imagine what you're trying to tell me is that I will survive," she started humming and moving her arms to the disco beat.

Jeremy burst out laughing. "That's exactly what I'm trying to tell you. Melody and I talk at least once a week and visit whenever we can. She's a nurse and her husband, Rob, is a cop; so far they're doing okay. Maybe it's because she's my daughter and was used to the crazy schedules we keep."

"What made you move to Florida?"

"I didn't move to Florida, I was born here. My entire career on the force was spent in Tampa."

"How did you end up in Calusa? We're not exactly what you would call an exciting metropolitan area."

"Believe me, I've had enough of living in a city. I used to come down this way to go fishing with a buddy. You've heard me mention my friend, Slick. Calusa was exactly the kind of place I was looking for, so here I am." He stood and reached out his hand to help her stand. "I do believe you've had enough to deal with today. What do you say we get dressed and go out for dinner? Your choice."

"Sounds fantastic to me. Give me twenty minutes and I'll meet you outside. Want to take my car?"

"Don't think so. Your son, Davy, will probably be on the lookout for your convertible. He'll never be looking for my SUV. How about we go down to Ft. Myers? I know a great crab place on the water."

"See you in twenty."

"You're on. I'll let Daisy out and then go home and get ready." When he stood so did the dog. The dog stretched and jumped off the couch and followed him to the back door.

He grabbed the leash draped on the back of a chair and snapped it on her collar. "We're definitely making progress here, Miss Daisy. You give going to the dogs a whole new meaning," he said as he ambled to the screen door and waved to Betty Bradford on his way to the front walk.

****

Rachel was ready and waiting when Jeremy pulled up in her driveway. He hopped out of the SUV to run around and open the door for her. This time he gave an audible wolf whistle when he saw her decked out in a bright blue Capri outfit and killer wedge sandals.

He wanted to say *you look gorgeous* but once again opted for, "You really look nice in that color."

"Thank you. Are you going to take US 41 to Ft. Myers or the Interstate?"

"I thought we'd go 41. We may have to deal with traffic lights, but mileage wise it's shorter."

They were driving over the bridge to Punta Gorda when Rachel turned toward the window. "I always get a feeling of peace...well-being whenever I ride over this bridge." She waved her arm toward the water. "The view of Charlotte Harbor is amazing. Have you ever watched the sunset from this area?"

"Not yet."

"I know Key West is supposed to have the most spectacular sunsets, but I believe they would have to go some to beat ours."

He would have to add drinks at Fisherman's Village to watch the sunset on his things-to-do list for the future. "Have you ever been to Joe's Crab Shack?"

"Not in years. The last time we were there was for Mike's twentieth birthday."

"The saving feature about the place is, it doesn't change. Do you like to pick crabs?"

"I've never tried. I always went for the seafood combo platter, but I'm willing to learn."

"Good. I'd love to teach you."

****

The lights along the pier and aroma of spicy seafood made her mouth water. Loud up tempo music greeted them the moment they drove into the parking lot. Despite that the place was rocking by the time the sun set. The hostess led them to a table facing the water.

"You still good with sharing a bucket of steamed crabs?" he asked.

"Absolutely. I hear cold beer goes great with them."

Jeremy did a double take. "You like beer?"

"With certain dishes like pizza or brats or…"

He laughed. "I get the message."

Their server came and Jeremy placed their order, the Classic Steam Pot, along with a pitcher of beer. After the waiter left, he asked, "What are some other things you like?"

She pursed her lips. "Let me think. I like to read

books with happy endings, movies that make me laugh, music…any kind but heavy metal and watching a garden blossom. What about you?"

The waiter came with their pitcher of beer along with two mugs. Jeremy poured a glass for her. When the man left, Jeremy said, "I'm with you about the garden. Somewhat with the music, I favor country-western. As for the books and movies, I prefer the action kind, but I do like to read biographies."

Rachel lifted her mug and clinked it against his. "To our differences and similarities."

"I'll drink to that," he said.

There was no problem with peeling the shrimp. At first the tang of the spice the crabs had been cooked in burned her lips, but a few swallows of cold beer took care of the sting.

"I'll do the first one for you and then you are on your own."

Rachel was having such a good time she didn't care about her finger nails or creating a mess. After the third crab she got the hang of it to the point where Jeremy put in a second order.

She swept the crab shells into the bucket that sat in a hole in the table and wiped her hands on a wet napkin. "This is a lot of fun. Thanks for suggesting it."

****

On the way home, Rachel turned her head to look at Jeremy. She wanted to reach over and brush her fingers along the side of his cheek, but held back. What would he think if she did, especially since he was aware of what she was going through with her oldest son?

Still, her fingers itched to follow through with her desire for a small gesture of intimacy, but she resorted to words instead. "That was exactly what I needed. To think peeling a shrimp was my forte until now." She rested her head on the back of the seat. "The first time my brother-in-law tried boiled shrimp he ate it shell and all. He was from a small town in the Midwest so we had to forgive him. My sister, Trina, and I had to show him how it was done. Once you showed me how to crack crab I was fine. Thanks for teaching me."

He reached over and patted her on the knee. "My pleasure. I usually order Joe's classic steam pot when I go there because you get a good variety. The Dungeness crab is probably my favorite, but the sweet snow crab runs a close second. I noticed you didn't eat any sausage."

"I'll give it two thumbs up but passed on the sausage. Why eat meat when there was good seafood?"

"Now you know I'm a carnivore. As for trying something new, we'll do it again soon."

The remainder of the trip home was spent in companionable silence and listening to sixties music on the radio. He reached for her hand before they reached South Punta Gorda and held it all the way to her driveway. When they got there he ran around to the passenger side, helped her out of the car, then walked her to the front door.

He ran his knuckles along her jaw line and felt the softness of her skin. "See you later."

She stood on tiptoe and kissed him on the cheek. "Until later."

He watched until she was safely inside and went back to his car. The big question now was, could he hold out until later? It was getting more difficult every time he was near her.

Chapter 10

I am going to make it through today. I am going to make it through today.

The words darted through Rachel's mind like an old forty-five record stuck in a deep groove. There was no way this meeting could start or end soon enough. It felt like traveling an unpaved country lane after six weeks of hard rain.

She dreaded the impending family gathering, but deep in her heart she knew it was something that had to be addressed before relationships became damaged beyond repair. Damn Dave's spineless hide! She wished he was here so he could see all the havoc his abrupt departure had triggered.

Wednesday night, Jeremy took the dog over to his place so she could meet with her daughters-in-law at the mall after work and not come home to a minor disaster. It was getting to the point that she didn't think she could get along without his support. He had become part of her life…a good part. Even in her uncertain, pre-divorce state she didn't want him too far away.

The meeting at the mall was strictly a time to enjoy shopping and dinner. They shopped until they dropped, then ate dinner at her granddaughter, Susan's, favorite pasta bar in the food court.

As for today, Kathy made arrangements for the kids to be at her sister's place down in South Punta

Gorda. They loved to go there because Sari had acreage and a lot of animals. The kids would spend the night, eliminating any excuse from Davy that he had to pick them up as a way of weaseling out of facing facts.

The next bump in the road was Jeremy. Yesterday Davy called her at work and informed her he wouldn't sit in the same room with the man, let alone talk to him. To which, Rachel *informed* him he had better show or he would not want to meet up with her in the near future. The tone of her voice must have conveyed the seriousness of her message because he said he'd be here. She would see how that scene played out after thirty minutes. She knew her son better than he thought she did. Davy was too curious not to cross examine Jeremy about his intentions as they related to her.

To hear Davy rant and rave yesterday, one would think she and Jeremy were about to elope and she was turning all her personal finances over to him. Telling him the ink wasn't even on the divorce papers only set him off more. She was very thankful when Kathy took the phone from him and told him to go take a flying leap in the pool and cool off.

Time to put those thoughts aside and concentrate on this evening. She almost jumped out of her skin when she heard Jeremy's voice call her name. Miss Daisy scooted in front of her trying to get to the screen door to greet him. She had to grab hold of the counter to regain her balance.

If that dog causes me to fall, I'm going to...I don't know what I'm going to do, but it will be something. "I'm in the kitchen," she called.

Daisy danced in circles until he came through the door. The dog was becoming attached to the man. It was a positive pairing because Jeremy was teaching the mutt manners. One hand signal from Jeremy and Miss Daisy sat on her haunches and waited for his command to move.

Jeremy carried a huge glass bowl of diced mixed melon, kiwi, and pineapple, in one arm. "Where do you want me to put this? If you don't have room in your fridge, I can take it back home and bring it over later. Since Anita and Lyle couldn't make it I thought I'd come early, see if I could help with anything."

"Too bad they had to go up to Orlando. Anita said Lyle was going to spend the day at Disney, while she attended some kind of beauty convention."

Jeremy shook his head. "I can't wrap my mind around the fact he likes to go there by himself. Or he doesn't mind being in the crowds."

"Me either. He's bound to pick up something…a cold or rash. But, knowing Lyle he probably has some kind of bacterial wipe stuck in his back pocket. He'll want to share the details with us. You know we're going to get the third degree about what happens tonight, when they get back."

"Maybe, if we're lucky, we can get them to treat us to dinner to hear all about it. You know, tell them it'll cost them to hear the whole story."

"Sounds like a good plan to me. By the way, the fruit salad looks beautiful. I didn't have a clue you were a whiz in the kitchen. You must've spent all morning cutting up the fruit."

"Not me. I probably would've chopped off a finger within five minutes. I let the nice ladies over at the Publix Supermarket do the hard work. I dumped it in this bowl when I got home. I think it looks better that way rather than the big plastic container it came in."

"The next time you see the ladies at Publix, you let them know I thought it was beautiful that you gave them the credit for doing the work. There's room in the refrigerator out in the garage. When you come back let me run some ideas past you." She sucked in her lower lip as she checked the clock on the microwave. "We have an hour or so before Davy and Mike get here with their wives."

When he came back from the garage, she leaned against the counter, hands folded. "I'm at my wit's end trying to decide where to set the table. It's a lovely evening. Should I keep the windows open and the fans going, or should I turn on the air conditioning? I'm afraid if the conversation gets too heated we'll be the entertainment of the neighborhood or someone may end up calling the cops."

Jeremy rested his hands on her shoulders and planted a quick kiss on her forehead. "Relax. I doubt that will happen."

"Which statement are you answering? The heated one or the cops?" She reached up and placed her hands over his. "Mr. Patterson is always looking for an excuse to call them. I think he has 911 on his speed dial."

"Both." Jeremy leaned his forehead against hers. "Woman, you're whipping yourself into a state over this gathering. First of all, don't let Davy set you up for an argument. Nothing diffuses an argument like one person keeping quiet. That makes it difficult for the other person."

Rachel tilted her head back to look into his eyes and blew out a deep sigh. "Especially when Davy hops up on his soap box and starts preaching."

"If he does, we can let him go for a while and hope he runs out of steam. As for the cops, no worries there. I was one. I've had some experience along these lines. I doubt anything will happen today that will be classified as domestic violence."

Rachel's eyes glistened as she sucked on her lower lip. "Oh, my God, I certainly hope not."

"Turn around."

"Turn around?" she asked.

"Don't give me grief. Please, do it."

She did and felt the pads of his fingers massage her neck and shoulders, finding all the knots the present situation was causing. She reached up and patted his hand after a few minutes.

"Thanks, I think I'll make it through this meeting. I'm going to set up in the dining room. But, I will keep the windows closed. Will you give me a hand with the tablecloth?"

"Lead the way."

****

Mike and Melinda were the first to arrive. Melinda set a bottle of wine on the counter. Her husband introduced her to Jeremy, then asked, "Where's Mom?"

"She popped into her room to powder her nose," Jeremy explained.

Before he could go on, Rachel walked into the kitchen. Melinda came over and gave her mother-in-law a hug. "How's it going, Rachel?"

"Not bad. I take it you've met Jeremy?"

"Sure have. Mike introduced me. Can I give you a hand with anything?"

"I think we're set. You can help with getting the food on the table when Davy and Kathy get here."

"Fine. By the way, there's a bottle of wine on the counter," Melissa said. "Do you want me to put it in the fridge in the garage?"

Before she could respond, Rachel heard the front door open, signaling the arrival of her other son and his wife. Feeling the tension rise in her belly, she wished for a couple of Celeste's martinis, but wine would have to do. "On second thought, Mike, why don't you open it now? We can put it in the wine crock you bought me for Christmas last year."

Mike grinned, obviously aware of his mother's discomfort. "You mean the one sitting here on the counter?"

Rachel returned a weak smile. "The very one," she admitted, then turned to Jeremy. "Are you going to have wine or do you want a beer?"

"Think I'll have a beer."

Mike nodded. "Sounds good to me. Why don't you go get a couple out of the fridge in the garage? Might as well get one for Davy, too, while you're out there. I'll pour the wine for the ladies."

When Davy and Kathy entered the kitchen, he simply glanced around the room, said nothing, didn't even smile.

"If you're looking for Jeremy," Mike said as he uncorked the wine, "he in the garage getting beers."

The mood in the kitchen was tense by the time Jeremy came back with the beer. He handed a bottle to each of the boys.

Rachel cleared her throat. "Why don't we sit on the lanai for a few minutes? Kathy, there's a tray of cheese and crackers over there on the counter. You can take it out. Melinda, you take the dish of mixed nuts."

Once they were seated outside, silence reigned. Jeremy was not about to be the first to break the ice. He sat back and observed as they looked at each other, each waiting for someone to say something. Even Miss Daisy lay at his feet under the table without begging for something to eat.

Finally Mike asked, "Do you think the Rays are going to the Super Bowl?"

Jeremy smiled and rubbed the side of his nose with his index finger to hide a smile. "I don't think so. They might make it to the play-offs for the World Series."

"Oh, right. I meant the Bucs. Do you think they'll make it to the Super Bowl?"

Davy grabbed a handful of nuts and started to munch. "Okay, let's cut the small talk and get to the real reason we're here. What's this big get-together all about, Mom?"

Rachel took a deep breath. "Okay. I'm going to give my talk and I don't want to be interrupted. Promise?"

They all raised their right hand, except Jeremy. He didn't think he had any say in the matter. Best he maintain his role as an observer and support for Rachel.

"Good. First of all you know I filed for divorce. Actually, I did it weeks ago."

"Why didn't you wait until it was final to have a celebration dinner?" Davy snarled and pointed a thumb toward Jeremy. "Does he have to be here?"

Rachel narrowed her eyes. "Yes."

Mike gave his brother a back-handed slap on the shoulder. "You promised Mom you would keep your mouth shut until she finished talking."

Rachel continued, "My attorney explained what my

options were and I instructed him to proceed. There was no problem with the residency requirements. The biggest difficulty is going to be getting the house solely in my name. It'll take a while, but it can be done.

"Next," she went on, "I love the four of you, but you have to give me some breathing room. And, Davy, you have got to stop being my judge and jury. But then, we have already had this discussion. Too many times." She noticed Kathy and Melinda exchanging looks as if they would rather be in Sarasota window shopping…any place but here. "Ladies, I know you and your husbands discuss my situation over dinner and pillow talk, get a new subject.

"Finally, y'all seem to have some concern about me seeing Jeremy. Get over it. He happens to be a very nice gentleman who is also good neighbor, as well as a friend. To date we have no plans to elope or take a world tour together." She looked Jeremy in the eye and caught the smile hovering at the edge of his mouth and swallowed hard. "Unless you're keeping something from me."

He shook his head, "No, ma'am." He almost made a smart remark about asking her if she would take a couple of days off from work so they could spend the weekend away from prying eyes, but he held his tongue. He couldn't, even in jest, because the shit would surely hit the fan. He had to hand it to her, when the woman decided to take a stand she went at it balls to the wall.

"Good," she said with a brisk nod, "because I don't have clothes for a trousseau, nor do I have the time or the money to buy one. If plans should change I will keep my family updated. Any questions?"

Davy's jaw noticeably tightened. "When is the divorce final?"

"I'll let you know. Since you're the one Dave keeps in touch with, you can keep him apprised of what's happening. If he wants more information or wants to contest it, let him contact my attorney because I don't want to speak with Dave."

"Sounds to me like you have everything in order, Mom," Mike said, grabbing a square of cheese, then popped it into his mouth. "When do we eat?" He rubbed his stomach. "Cheese and crackers are okay, but I'm hungry for some real food."

Melinda shot her husband the hairy eyeball, stood, and started gathering the empty plates. "Honestly, Rachel, I don't know how you have the patience to deal with these two. I think you deserve a medal."

Kathy gathered the empty glasses. "Amen to that. Why don't we ladies go inside and start putting out the food." She turned to her husband. "Try not interrogate poor Jeremy in an attempt to scare him off before we call you to the table. Also, keep in mind you're outside and all the neighbors have their windows open."

"Don't worry, Kathy," Jeremy said, taking a sip of beer. "I can handle myself."

It got very quiet after the women left. Mike fiddled with his beer bottle, wiping the moisture from the side and peeling the label. Davy slouched in his chair and scowled, but didn't look Jeremy in the eye.

When he was sure they were alone, in a low voice Jeremy said, "Okay, fellas, it's time you start acting like adults and cut your mom a break."

Davy straightened up and leaned forward, elbows on knees, with the obvious intention of getting into

Jeremy's personal space. "I think you need to butt out of our family affairs. When we want your advice we'll ask for it. Right, Mike?"

"Count me out of this conversation," Mike said, narrowing his eyes. "Jeremy, I'm sorry you have to put up with my asshole brother. Since Dad left, he thinks he's in charge of the family. More so than our father ever was."

Davy turned his head and glared at his brother. "Dad was laid back, too laid back."

"Exactly my point," Mike said. "You need to take a page out his book."

In a nonthreatening tone Jeremy said, "The way I look at it, boys, your mother is perfectly capable of making her own decisions. Having been down the divorce road, I know it is not an easy one to travel. Your folks were married a long time. Your mom has a lot of emotional baggage to deal with right now. She needs your support, not your interference."

Davy slowly leaned back and slumped down in his chair. "I assume you've appointed yourself to help carry her *baggage*?"

"Only if she asks me. And, by the way, Davy, next time you refer to me as *bozo* you and I are going to have a serious man-to-man discussion."

"Who told you I said that?" Davy countered.

Jeremy washed his face with the palm of his hand and shook his head. "Man, you were raised in this neighborhood. You have a lot to relearn about living on this street. Especially when the weather is cool and the windows are open."

After Jeremy called Davy on his *bozo* remark silence once again hung heavy in the air, like a dense smog, as each man waited for the other to say something...anything.

Jeremy leaned back in the chair and consciously worked at relaxing his muscles, curious as to which one of her boys would break the silence. He'd just have to wait them out. Funny how that always worked. It was one of the best lessons he had learned during his years as a detective.

There was no way he was going to let these two young men intimidate him, nor was he about to let them off the hook. What he had observed from the short time he knew him, Jeremy's gut told him Mike was more a wait and see kind of guy and would not jump to Davy's defense. On the other hand, Davy was an unknown. No, the best move was to sit back and wait them out. Thank goodness the ladies didn't take the bowl of mixed nuts away. He took a hand full, sat back and bided his time. This encounter could turn out to be very interesting.

He glanced at Davy. The guy's jaw was fixed and a pulse beat in his neck. His eyes darted all around, but avoided looking at Jeremy. The man was a powder keg of emotion and distrust. Jeremy had met more than his share of *Davys* over the years; they were the kind whose short fuse got them into a lot of trouble. Their main problem was shooting off their mouth before they engaged their brain. They counted on bravado to enable them to walk away from a situation a winner.

Since he couldn't walk away right now without upsetting Rachel, Jeremy was sure Davy would bite his tongue in half before he'd admit he was interested in her relationship with regard to him. And it would not stop Davy from swaggering and trying to bully. If intimidation was the game plan, Davy wouldn't win.

Jeremy was light years ahead of him in that field.

Sure as shit, Mike leaned back in the chair and folded his hands on his mid-section. Jeremy picked out a cashew and popped it in his mouth. *Come on, Mike, don't be afraid to go for the gold.*

Tugging on his ear lobe, Mike asked, "So, Jeremy, where do you come from?"

"Tampa," he said, keeping his answer short and to the point. He was surprised it was not a more personal question. Like how many times had he been married or divorced or did he have kids.

"Did you always live there or are you a northern transplant?" Mike asked.

"Always. Four generations. One of my great-something grandfathers came down on a mail boat." Jeremy wasn't going to make it easy for him, even if Mike was a nice guy. "I'm not big into tracing the family history so I don't know exactly when."

"Do you have family up there?" Mike asked.

This was getting to be fun, but he maintained a poker face. "Sure."

Mike continued, "Any brothers or sisters?"

Before Jeremy could answer, Davy sneered. "You said you knew about going through a divorce. How many ex-wives do you have?"

Enough was enough. Jeremy elected not to string this out. He leaned forward and rested his elbows on the table. "I have four sisters, Sylvia, Arcadia, Gerry and Maria. I have one ex-wife, one married daughter, a great son-in-law and two fantastic granddaughters. Do you want names and addresses for reference?"

Mike's face flushed in obvious embarrassment as he shot his brother a put-a-sock-in-it look. "No, no that's not necessary. How did you end up in Calusa?"

He grabbed another handful of nuts and popped one in his mouth, taking a couple of seconds to chew before answering. "Came down for a red fish tournament."

With a curled lip and an obvious edge to his voice, Davy asked. "Do you always give such short answers?"

"Hey, Dave, I'm the guy on the hot seat here. I'm simply answering your questions as you ask them." He knew Davy was dying to ask where he thought Jeremy's relationship with his mother was headed, but was afraid to ask right out. Good, let the guy stew.

"Okay, what do you do for a living?" Davy inquired.

"I'm retired," Jeremy said, still smiling inside, as Davy shot him a look that clearly said cut the shit. Then again, the present situation seemed to be tickling the beejeebers out of Mike.

Huffing out an exasperated sigh Davy snapped, "Retired from what?"

Deciding it was time to let the man off the hook, Jeremy said, "The police department. Was on the force for thirty-five odd years. Retired as a homicide detective. Does that answer your question?"

"Almost. It appears you live alone so I assume, since you said you're divorced, you don't have a steady girlfriend."

"You could assume that, Dave," Jeremy said. He wanted to add the old adage about the word assume making an ass out of you and me, but held his tongue.

"Oh, for pity's sake, Davy, let the poor guy alone. He's entitled to his private life," Mike said.

"To a degree, little brother, but not when our

mother is involved. Like Grandpa Benton used to say, we need to know if his intentions are ancient and honorable.

Jeremy was unable to suppress a laugh. That was the last statement he expected to pop out of Dave's mouth. "Don't know about ancient part, but you can count on the honorable. As your mom said a while ago, we're not planning to elope. Since we do enjoy each other's company all we have in mind right now is go out to dinner every now and then, maybe take in a movie, spend an evening with friends. Do you want me to call and request your permission before I ask her?"

For the first time Davy actually looked embarrassed. "Of course not."

"Good, because I had no intention of doing that. Going back to the divorce question, I've walked the walk, so I know what your mother is going through. As for interviewing somebody you want to put on the hot seat, you both have a lot to learn about the art of gathering information."

Mike smiled and stood. "Davy, Mom's old enough to make her own decisions. I'm sure she'll keep us posted if anything crops up she feels we need to know. I'm going in to grab another beer and check on how the ladies are coming along in the kitchen. Who wants another?"

"I do," Davy said.

Jeremy gave Mike a slight nod of agreement. After Mike went inside, Jeremy said, "Dave, trust me, I understand your concerns, but keep in mind your mother is under a lot of pressure right now."

"So she keeps reminding me."

"She shouldn't have to remind you. There's a lot of

strain involved in the break-up of a marriage, especially one lasting many years. Your mother has crucial decisions to make, ones that will affect her the rest of her life. Keep in mind she's holding down a full time job to boot. You might cut her some slack."

Davy slouched down in his chair. "Oh yeah, well she doesn't seem to be having any problem making these decisions."

"Don't kid yourself. Your mom is a woman with a lot of personal dignity. She wants to do the right thing and at the same time protect her interests. She is also a very strong woman."

"What makes you think you know so much about my mom?"

"Dave, I wasn't a cop all those years without learning something about human nature. Believe me, I could tell you stories that would make your hair stand on end, especially in the area of domestic violence. Until you've experienced what she's going through, and I hope you never do, don't make any judgments about her behavior or any determinations she makes right now. She was wise enough to get an attorney and start proceedings rather than let herself sway in the wind."

"So you're putting me on notice you know everything there is to know about people, especially my mother?"

"Nope. That wasn't my intention. But, let me give you a piece of advice. Until your mother asks for your counsel don't give her any. She is still your mother. From the short time I've known her I don't think she tells you how to run your life."

Davy stared at something over Jeremy's shoulder. Jeremy would swear the man was trying to get his thoughts in order before making another statement. He couldn't blame him. The guy was torn between his parents, a terrible place to be at any age. Patsy had been an ace at trying to turn Melody against him when they were going through their divorce. Luckily he had managed to diffuse his ex's vitriol through exercising patience and example. He never once bad-mouthed Patsy to Melody.

He had driven to Atlanta on his days off and made it a point to spend as much time as the courts allowed with his daughter. It had been a pain in the ass, literally, doing that long drive, but it paid off in the end. As far as he could determine, Rachel was trying to do the same. He could only hope her about to be ex had enough sense to follow her example.

Before either one said another word, Kathy stuck her head out the door. "Come and get it. Mike's already at the table and has a fresh beer waiting by your plates."

Davy pushed his chair back and stood. "We're not finished with this topic, Jeremy, so don't think everything is copasetic as far as I'm concerned."

"Fine with me. I'm not going anywhere; you know where to find me and my phone number is listed. Let me know when you want to play twenty questions again."

****

As Rachel got ready for bed she said a prayer of thanksgiving the dinner went as well as it had. The conversation mostly centered on the food, the roast pork was perfect. Davy didn't complain about any of the side dishes like he usually did. Over dessert the topic was things to do in Charlotte County. Mike offered to help Jeremy with any computer problems he might have. Davy didn't offer to help Jeremy with anything, but at least he remained civil.

Her experience told her time would be Davy's healer, but she also prayed she had the patience to stay the course without alienating him in the meantime. She knew she could count on Kathy's help in that department.

As for Jeremy, it appeared he was able to hold his own with Davy. He even made major brownie points by referring to him as Dave. Her last prayer of thanksgiving was that tempers hadn't flared to the point Mr. Patterson called the cops.

****

Jeremy kicked back in his easy chair and thought about *The Dinner*. It had been a very long time since he'd had a family experience like that. In fact it had been at Melody's wedding when he had to be nice and polite to Patsy for their daughter's sake. His ex-wife had pitched a fit because Melody wanted him to give her away when Patsy wanted her new husband to have the honor. When he offered to step back for the sake of keeping the peace, his daughter made her wishes known and Patsy backed down.

Melody was much easier to deal with than Davy. Was it because she was a girl? Or because he made the effort to be part of her life? How would she have handled it if he and Patsy had stuck it out and separated now? He would never know.

He sensed Davy was not going to change his behavior without a fight. Since his father had opted to travel rather than stay in town, Rachel was going to have her hands full trying to convince her oldest she didn't need or want a keeper.

Chapter 11

Rachel padded barefoot into the kitchen wearing an oversized sleep shirt. It was her favorite, the one that reached past her knees and displayed a slightly faded teddy bear. Dave used to shake his head and ask her when she was going to throw the *damn thing* in the rag bag. She hated to get rid of it because the fabric was soft against her skin and sagged in all the right places. Now she was glad she hadn't tossed it out.

Glancing out the window she noticed there were a lot of dark clouds in the sky. That usually indicated rainfall within the hour. If it did materialize rather than scoot out to the Gulf of Mexico, she would not have to water the plants. She stretched and yawned. That would be one less chore she had to do today.

Thinking back to the past few years, it hadn't mattered if she wore a sexy nightie or one of her comfortable sleep shirts; it made no impression on Dave. His main concern was she stay on her side of the bed and make him pancakes on Sunday mornings. He didn't like to be touched. His mother had been the same way. The only hugger in the family was his Aunt Mary who died the first year after Rachel and Dave married.

In his defense, the man made the best coffee she ever tasted. She would miss that. In fact, she did miss waking up to the smell of freshly brewed coffee. She would have to get an automatic timer the next time she went to the store. She opened the cupboard, grabbed a mug, and poured a cup. Taking a sip she took out the sugar bowl and added a teaspoon to her cup. She still hadn't gotten the measurements right. This brew was strong enough to walk out of the pot and into her cup.

No matter which way you looked at it, life was full of adjustments. Some good and some, well, not so pleasant. But as her Uncle Tom used to say, you had to take the shit with the sugar. She smiled as she recalled her mother reprimanding him for having a dirty mouth. Of course, kids would remember that phrase because a parent disapproved.

Her musings were cut short by the ringing of the telephone. She checked the caller ID before answering. It was not a good motherly attitude to avoid speaking with her son, but she was not feeling particularly motherly with regard to Davy. This time it was Melinda. Rachel would keep it short and to the point.

"Good morning, Mel."

"What did we ever do without caller ID, Rachel?" Melinda asked.

"We took our chances and answered to find out who was calling. To what do I owe the pleasure of your call?" Rachel was hoping she was not going to regret asking that question.

"Actually, I was surprised to hear you pick up the phone. I thought you were at work today so I was going to leave a message asking if you wanted to come over for dinner tomorrow night. Feel free to ask Jeremy. Mike and I like him."

"I'd love to. If I happen to see Jeremy, I'll ask if he has any plans and let you know. What time?"

Melinda gave her a time. "And, don't worry. Davy

and Kathy won't be here. They're going down to her sister's place for one of the cousin's birthdays."

No way would Rachel admit that seeing Davy was a concern. She'd have a peaceful meal with Mike and Mel and hope they'd steer clear of asking about the divorce.

"See you tomorrow," she said and hung up.

She checked the clock. She still had time before she had to head for the shower. It was nice not to have to rush this morning. She had taken the day off to take care of personal business. Business she hoped would soon be resolved. Mr. DeCarlo wanted her to drop by his office today and sign some papers. He said everything was going smoothly. The situation with the house was another matter, until that was resolved she could not get her final decree. As she had no plans on moving, there was no rush to resolve this dilemma.

If push came to shove and she had to give up the house she could always search for a rental. Or she could move in with Jeremy. Where in the world did that thought come from? No matter, just the thought of living with him made her mouth go moist and nerve endings swirl. She would have to put those thoughts on the shelf for another time.

She set her cup on the table and went out through the garage to get the newspaper, thankful it was up against the garage door so she didn't have to grab a robe and walk out to the street to get it. Must be a new delivery person.

Scanning the headlines of the *Calusa Times,* she walked inside. There was nothing there she hadn't heard on the eleven o'clock news last night. She took a quick glance at the local section and checked the obituaries. Dave used to give her a hard time about doing that. But, since she worked at the hospital she knew quite a few of the people who had passed. There weren't any names she recognized so she pulled out the crossword puzzle to do later.

Noting the time on the microwave clock she decided she would read the comics after she got home from the attorney's office. Depending on what she had to do there she might be in need of a good chuckle.

She picked up the warm coffee cup and took time to gaze out the kitchen window thinking about the family dinner this past Saturday. It was an experience, but it didn't go as badly as she had anticipated. Best part was, no left overs. The men had demolished a whole pork roast, vegetables and five pounds of mashed potatoes.

At one point, when Jeremy was out on the lanai with the boys, she was concerned she might need to rescue him. Or at least put on the fan so the smell of the roast would calm the waters. No worries there. According to Mike, Jeremy had no problem handling Davy. Mike confirmed Jeremy made minor brownie points by calling her son Dave.

She couldn't decide whether or not to be surprised at the way her daughters-in-law stood with her. Well, not Melinda, she had been close to her from the get go. Independent Mel would give Mike a run for his money and, to date he seemed to be enjoying the race. It was a plus that they liked Jeremy. It was one less dilemma she had to worry about. Handling Davy was enough right now. What a shame she couldn't turn him over to Mr. DeCarlo.

Kathy was the flip side of the coin from Mel. Early

on in the marriage she'd been a bit of an air head. She had always echoed and agreed with whatever Davy said, at least in front of her. As the children grew older, Rachel noted Kathy had changed for the better. Nothing like raising kids to ground you. For her to take a stand against her husband was a miracle in itself. Rachel had to wonder what was going on there. Maybe the woman had finally developed a spine. Rachel had to do that early on, or her two boys would have walked all over her when they were growing up.

When she thought more about Saturday she recalled that when the guys came in to eat, Jeremy had a smile on his face. She had assumed he'd had the situation well in hand.

Mike was his usual placid self. Davy seemed to have had the wind taken out of his sails. About bloody time. Yes, indeed, altogether the dinner had gone much better than she had anticipated. No arguments or zingers at the table. Maybe civilization was not dying after all.

Her thoughts were interrupted when the phone rang. It was Jeremy.

"Hi, Rachel, at dinner on Saturday you mentioned you had to do a lot of running around today. I was wondering if you needed a chauffeur."

"I don't think so, but thanks anyway. I'm going to see the attorney. He called and there are some papers I have to sign. I don't think it would look too good if I show up with a male escort, especially at this point of the proceedings."

"If you're going to be gone for a while, what do you say I come over and get Miss Daisy? You know how wild she gets when she's been cooped up all day.

She can run around the yard and keep me company while I work out there."

Rachel was not so sure Jeremy was worried about Miss Daisy being cooped up all day. He enjoyed having the dog to play with and then send her home. Sort of like having grandchildren. If they started to misbehave you could always send them back to their parents.

"As long as you don't mind, I'd appreciate that, but I think the pup would appreciate it more. It looks like rain and the newspaper said sixty per cent chance, so I don't know how much you'll be able to do outdoors. By the way, I have to take the car in for an oil change. Don't know how long a wait I'll have before they can do it. I'll probably think of a few more things while I out and about."

"No problem. We'll get as much yard time as we can. It sounds like you have a lot on your plate today. How about I fix dinner tonight? You can come over here for a change."

Two dinner invitations in one day. She would ask him about going to Mike and Mel's when she saw him this evening. Without hesitating for a second, she accepted. "Sounds like a plan. What can I bring?"

"Your lovely self. See you around six. Bring the dog out on the lanai now and I'll come get her."

She ran to her bedroom and grabbed a bathrobe and slippers and whistled for Miss Daisy. "Come on, girl. You're going to get to spend time out doors with Jeremy."

At the sound of the man's name the dog bounded into the kitchen and sat waiting by the glass slider, tongue lolling out of the side of her mouth and whining softly. Rachel shook her head. It didn't take Miss Daisy long to become attached to Jeremy. He was good with her and spent a lot of time training her, breaking her of bad habits. Rocking back and forth on her haunches the dog lifted her paw and scratched on the glass when she saw Jeremy open the screen door.

Rachel opened the slider to let him inside. "I'm beginning to get the idea my dog likes you. And, I have the feeling it's because you spoil her rotten. Her leash is on the back of the chair, I didn't put it back after I walked her last night. Do you have time for a quick cup of coffee?"

Jeremy squatted and rubbed the dog's ears while she tried to lick his face. "Coffee sounds good. We have a good time playing catch together. I'm on to her now. I have two balls."

He stopped abruptly at the end of his comment, his eyes wide at the innuendo. He even blushed to the roots of his hairline. "I mean…"

Rachel held back a smile as she poured him a mug and handed it to him. It was refreshing to see a man blush when he felt he had made a suggestive comment. "No worries, I know what you meant. Come sit for a minute."

He pulled out a chair and sat. "Thanks. What I meant to say was otherwise I'd have to chase her all over the yard to get the ball back. I'm getting a little long in the tooth for that kind of work out. Once the weather gets warmer I'd probably pass out."

She went back to the counter and topped her mug. "Don't worry. I'd call 911 if I saw you stretched out on the grass."

"You're too kind, but what if you weren't home?"

"You've got me there. I'm sure one of the

neighbors would notice."

"I'm *sure* it would be a toss-up between Floyd or Elsie."

"Like I said before, Floyd has 911 on speed dial, so he'd probably be the winner. By the way, I have to admit since you've been working with Miss Daisy these past weeks, her manners have improved considerably. Trust me, I'm exceedingly grateful. She was getting to be downright obnoxious."

"Glad to hear it. Not that she is obnoxious, but that she is making progress in behaving. Now she comes the first time I call her." He drained his cup, rinsed it and put it in the sink. He grabbed the leash and whistled. The dog followed as they headed for his place. "See you later. Keep your chin up. It will all be over soon."

"It can't be too *soon* for me. It seems like it has been going on forever."

Jeremy stopped and turned to face her. "Trust me, Rachel, before you know it, it will be a memory. The only time it will be around is when you invite it back."

"I'll have to take your word."

****

Walking out of the attorney's office, Rachel breathed a sigh of relief. To date, Dave had not made any attempt to contest the divorce, and Mr. DeCarlo followed all the usual procedures. He had even called Davy and tried to get a number or an address where he could reach Dave or his representative.

Davy maintained his dad always called him and said he was moving on and would call from his next stop. Since his father did not have a cell phone he had no idea how to contact him. She sincerely hoped her son was telling the truth and not playing games.

When she got to his office Mr. DeCarlo had told her, in spite of their son saying his father did not have a cell phone, Dave did have one. Mr. DeCarlo managed to reach him in American Samoa, and they had had a long conversation. Dave even gave Mr. DeCarlo a fax number where he could send the papers because he claimed he was anxious for the divorce to proceed.

Dave always said he wanted to travel the Pacific and go island hopping. More power to him. Maybe he found a girlfriend. If so, she hoped he was happy.

Rachel left her attorney's office in an upbeat mood. It was as if someone had removed a thousand pound weight from her shoulders.

At this moment all she was going to think about was getting her car serviced, afterward she would stop by the package store at Walgreens and buy a nice bottle of wine for dinner tonight. She never thought to ask Jeremy what he planned to make. Should she buy red or white wine? She could play it safe and get one of each.

It was a lucky day for her. When she got to the dealership there was no one ahead of her. Sitting in the waiting room she took out her cell phone and hit speed dial for Anita's shop. It was time for a bit of pampering.

****

Rachel walked into the Hair Lair and found Anita at her station, wiping the countertop and rearranging containers. The woman motioned for her to come over and sit in the chair. Rachel knew this might turn into a question and answer session, but it was okay.

She glanced around the shop. It was only Anita and her co-worker, Harriet, and realized she was among friends. Besides she would only give out information she was comfortable with sharing because anything said here would only be repeated in the strictest confidence to everyone they knew. It was much different when she and Anita had a girlfriend session outside of the shop. What they told each other in confidence when they were alone did not go out to the general population.

After fastening the cape around her shoulders, Anita ran her fingers through Rachel's hair. "What do you have in mind? It must be something special because it isn't time for your regular appointment."

She scrunched her shoulders and held up her crossed fingers. "We do have something to celebrate. Keep *your* fingers crossed too. Mr. DeCarlo finally located Dave and faxed the papers to him. If all goes as well as it did today this whole divorce will be a thing of the past by the end of the month."

Anita's reflection in the mirror showed her holding up her crossed fingers confirming she got the message. "Gotcha. I'd hoped you were going to say something different like a hot date weekend out of town with somebody special."

"Maybe someday, but not right now," Rachel replied, grateful Anita refrained from mentioning a specific name.

"That's okay; I know putting this all behind you is your first priority. Wish I had some champagne or at least some wine in the shop so we could celebrate. You'll have to settle for coffee or iced tea."

"I'll have the coffee. If anything this good happens again you won't have to worry about wine, I'll bring champagne."

Before Anita could turn around, Harriet was handing a cup to Rachel. She raised her own cup in a toast. "Congratulations are definitely in order. I know this has been a rough time for you, sweetie. Like I told you, been there. Three times. The not knowing when the end is coming is a royal pain in the ass, but it comes eventually. Thank goodness nothing last forever, it merely seems that way."

Rachel nodded. "I'll add an amen to your statement."

"So Mr. DeCarlo is doing right by you?" Harriet asked.

"He is. Thanks for the referral," Rachel said.

Anita started running her fingers through Rachel's hair again. Pulling it back on one side, lifting it to the top of her head. "Do you want to keep a long bob or look at some of the magazines or do you have something in mind? If not, do you want to tell me the occasion? You can try to deny it, but I've known you a very long time girlfriend. It's more than getting the legal stuff settled."

"I know you're very perceptive, but don't go reading more into this visit than there is." She shot Anita a smile, eyes sparkling with mischief. "Jeremy did invite me over to his place for dinner tonight."

Anita bounced on the balls of her feet. "I knew it, I knew it. So you're here so we can make you look exceptionally glamorous and sexy."

"Don't know about the sexy part, but I think I'd like to try a new style. How about something short and shaggy? Summer's here. I don't want to spend time fooling around with this longer style. I'd like a *wash and go* but chic."

Anita tilted her head, squinted, and did some more rearranging and some back combing with her fingers. "So it's nothing special. You want to get ready for summer. Mmmm, like maybe spending time in the pool over at Jeremy's? Don't answer. We'll say that being the case, I think we can handle it. No problem. I have a couple of short wigs here if you want to try one on and see if you want to go short."

"Sure. Why not? Let's give it a try," Rachel said.

Harriet brought three wigs and laid them on the counter. Anita had started doing this because the client left much happier *knowing* how she was going to look, rather than *assuming* how she was going to look, when she walked out the shop. So Rachel cooperated and let Anita fuss.

After trying on the third one, Rachel turned her head from side to side and checked the back through the mirror Anita held up behind her. "I liked the shorter, shoulder length bob I've been wearing. It's been easy to handle. On the other hand, today I feel like doing something radical. I like this gamin style."

Anita took the wig off and put it on the stand. "I never could understand why you wore your hair so long in the past. You have the facial bone structure to wear this style. Something women don't think about is, if they have nice ears they should show them. She pulled the hair away from Rachel's ears. "See what I mean."

Rachel turned her head from side to side and nodded in agreement. "I never thought about having nice ears."

Harriet walked up beside Rachel. "Add some sexy hoop earrings along with a scooped neckline that enhances your cleavage and you'll look fabulous. I think it's going to work great for you. Let's get you shampooed."

Rachel had worn her hair long because Dave liked

it, but she wasn't going to bring up any topic that ended with discussing him. Looking around, Rachel followed Harriet to the shampoo chair. "If you have time, I'd like to gct a pcdicurc."

"I have to run to the bank. I'll be back before Anita finishes cutting your hair. Right now we have to concentrate on getting you looking stunning for tonight."

Rachel let out a long sigh. "Now that I'm almost through the divorce tunnel and found out the light isn't on the engine of a very big freight train, I feel ready to start letting go of the old ways. Let's get started."

Anita sat in the empty chair by the shampoo bowl while Harriet washed Rachel's hair. "About time, but I think the dinner with Jeremy has more to do with your coming here than what went on at the lawyer's office today. I mean you could go home and take a nice long bubble bath and indulge yourself that way. What you have planned to do now portends something else entirely. By the way, if you decided to go for a swim after dinner don't worry about getting your hair wet and doing any damage to the color. There's more chlorine in our tap water than in a pool."

"Will you put the brakes on it, woman? I have no intention of doing the midnight swim thing. Don't make me sorry I even mentioned the invitation. Jeremy knew I had a lot to do today, and he simply invited me for dinner so I wouldn't feel rushed."

Anita shot Rachel a sly smile as Harriet wrapped her head in a towel and led her back to the chair."

Harriet grabbed her purse. "Be back in a few."

Pumping up the height with her foot, Anita rested her hands on Rachel's shoulders. "So things *are* going well with the neighbor? Lyle says he's a great guy."

"You should have the same opinion. After all I understand you've had him to your house for dinner a couple of times." Rachel was sure it was all part of Anita's match-making scheme as well. Jeremy had mentioned he felt he was under scrutiny when he was there and Anita started asking him personal questions.

"He and Lyle get along. Jeremy even listens to Lyle's latest malady. You have to admit the four of us did have a good time the night y'all came over. Then again, a lot of water has flowed over the dam since then, including the big meet with the family. You've been around him a lot more, now I'll get your opinion. Unless you're holding out on me."

Rachel tried not to squirm so she used the excuse of getting more comfortable in the chair. "How did you find out about the family dinner thing? I haven't had a chance to talk to you about it."

Anita raised an eyebrow. "Don't fidget or you'll be getting a haircut you won't like. Too bad I had to be in Orlando. Have you forgotten about our neighbors? Betty couldn't wait to fill me in the minute she saw us pull up in the driveway. Al Kohn cornered Lyle Sunday night when he was putting the garbage can out for the morning pick up. Jeremy dropped by for a few minutes when he was taking a walk last night."

Busted. She meant to call Anita last night when she got home from work but put it off because she was tired of the subject. "I wasn't going to call you in Orlando, and I was planning on stopping by here today. Besides it's only been a couple of days. I had to work yesterday. I took today off because I was doing legal stuff and had to get my car checked. So what did Jeremy tell Lyle?"

"I assume he gave Lyle the abbreviated guy version. Jeremy said he and your sons talked and everything was going good. Now, why do I find that hard to believe? If it was only Mike there I would agree, but since Davy was there, well that's a horse of a different color."

While Anita cut her hair, Rachel filled her in on the unabridged version. "So when they came in to eat they all seemed to be getting along fine. I wouldn't say they're buddy-buddy, but they weren't glaring at each other either."

Anita grabbed the can of mousse, squeezed some into the palm of her hand, and then massaged through Rachel's hair before grabbing the dryer and a circular brush. "This is getting very interesting. Now all we have to have is Dave walk back on the scene. Then we would have the makings of a good soap opera."

"Bite your tongue, woman. Besides, I don't think that is going to happen. I understand he's in American Samoa, but I didn't ask Mr. DeCarlo exactly where because I didn't want to know."

"Dave was always such a tightwad. I recall he'd ask you to pay for your own food when you ate out. What did he do...rob a bank?"

"Who knows?" Rachel said. "Remember I told you Davy said his dad was going to work on a freighter."

Anita quirked a brow and harrumphed. "At his age? Give me a break. Dave doesn't know a bloody thing about working on a ship. Hells bells, I can't ever remember him ever going on a cruise ship, much less working on one. Don't you have to have some kind of papers to work on a ship?"

"I don't have a clue. All I know is what Davy tells

me. The last he told me was Dave was going to be working his way around the South Pacific."

Anita finished styling Rachel's hair and gave it a light spritz with spray net. "I find that very hard to believe. He's more likely to have paid his way to get there. I understand they have a few cabins they rent out. It's cheaper than going on a luxury ship. Come to think of it that would be right up Dave's alley."

"Whatever. As long as he didn't ask me for the money, I don't care." Rachel breathed an internal sigh of relief as she contemplated her last statement.

How *was* Dave managing to take this trip? She knew neither Davy nor Mike had any extra money to float their dad a loan. Did Dave sell his truck along the way? How much of his savings did he have left? The bigger question was how much had he managed to squirrel away while he was making his plans? She always felt he did under the table jobs for cash, but she never had any proof.

No, she would stick to her guns. If the man did ever contact her for money she would say sorry, you should have managed better.

As for the dinner tonight...was she trying to seduce Jeremy with the new hair style? She didn't think so. At least not on a conscious level. Jeremy was...was...she didn't know what category to place him in. He was a good neighbor. He was becoming a good friend. He was thoughtful. He was fair but fearless when dealing with Davy and didn't take any of her son's guff.

Yes, indeed the man had a lot of good qualities she admired. Still, it was too soon to do more than admire him as a good neighbor and friend. Then again, why did she look forward to being with him?

Now that the legalities were in process and about to end, she would be free to pursue a deeper relationship with Jeremy. The question was, did she have to courage to do it?

Anita handed her the mirror and spun the chair around. "What do you think?"

She gave Anita a thumb up with her free hand. "It's what I was hoping for."

Anita winked and let the chair down. "It never hurts for a lady to look her best when someone is fixing dinner for her."

Chapter 12

Depending on the time of year, Florida often went long spells without rain. Even when dark clouds filled the sky, threatening torrential downpours, they often floated out into the Gulf of Mexico, or over to the east coast, if the prevailing winds so dictated, without shedding a drop. She hoped it would be that way today.

As soon Rachel got home she headed straight to the slider to see if Jeremy and the dog were in his yard. On her way there she found a big note on lined yellow paper, written in red marker, anchored by a vase of flowers on the kitchen table. It was from Jeremy, telling her he took Miss Daisy to the pet park for some exercise. The next line said she should kick back and rest a while, but before she did she should look in the refrigerator. The last sentence said dinner was at seven o'clock. If she wanted to mosey over earlier she should feel free to do so. It was simply signed with a large capital J.

What was it with men? Did they have a problem with signing their whole name? Dave always did the same thing when he left a note. As she reread the note her curiosity got the best of her. She kicked off her shoes and went to the fridge. Inside she found a stemmed glass of white wine along with a dish of peeled shrimp on a bed of ice and a small container of cocktail sauce covered with plastic wrap.

What a delightful surprise. A woman could get used to this kind of pampering very quickly. She was coming to believe Jeremy had a strong romantic component to his personality, and it made her smile and feel all warm and gooey inside.

No sooner had she addressed that thought when she found herself focused on the niggling question of why was he being so nice? Did he have an ulterior motive? She shook her head as if to fling the negative thought out of her head. She had to stop looking for reasons and simply enjoy the gesture.

She took the treat into the family room, turned on the CD player, kicked back in her recliner and took a sip of the cool wine. She let it roll around on her tongue. It was a very nice pinot. Munching on a shrimp she realized it had been many years since someone had done something this thoughtful.

Dave wasn't much for this type of cosseting, unless it was for him. Then he could soak it up, but don't ask him to reciprocate. His was more the occasional lunch out, but at *his* favorite place. Or asking her to go to a gun show when he knew she had no interest in guns. She fooled him the last time he had asked and she went. As she recalled it had been several years ago and was the last time he had asked her to go anywhere.

She took another sip of wine followed by a shrimp coated with cocktail sauce, enjoying the piquancy of horseradish on her tongue. Maybe Dave wanted to head for the South Seas because they no longer had any common interests. Perhaps he hoped to find a native woman who'd wait on him hand and foot. Rub his back. Feed him figs—or whatever kind of fruit they had there.

No, wait a minute, she had done that for years and

it hadn't helped. Well, she didn't peel fruit and feed him, but she had done the rest. Lately she had stopped dropping everything to do for him.

She glanced at the clock. It was four-thirty. She took another piece of shrimp and listened to George Strait singing an upbeat song about dancing and romancing and falling in love.

She closed her eyes and thought about tonight's dinner. If shrimp and white wine was her appetizer, what was the main course? Dessert? She also had to wonder if the nice ladies from Publix were preparing the meal or if Jeremy would actually be doing the cooking. It didn't matter as long he didn't ask her to clean the kitchen.

She must have dozed off for a few minutes because when she heard Miss Daisy's yapping she awoke with a start. It sounded like it was coming from outdoors. She checked the clock on the mantel, it read six. Stretching her arms over her head got up and went into her bedroom. She was about to slip into a pair of sandals and let the dog in before heading on over to Jeremy's when the phone rang. It was him.

"Wanted to let you know we're back. Guess I didn't have to because Daisy's barking probably woke you. I tried to keep her quiet but she saw our resident grandfather turtle, and, well, you know how that goes."

"Do I ever. Don't know what a turtle ever did to her. How did you know I dozed off?"

"Because you left the slider unlocked. When we got back I stuck my head in the door and called your name. You didn't answer so I came in the kitchen to see if you were home. I checked the fridge and the treat was gone. I saw your purse on the counter. Thought you might be in the den. Went there to check and saw you kicked back in your chair. You looked too peaceful to wake up. So I brought Daisy over here. By the way, I fed her when we got back."

"I appreciate that. Thanks for not waking me. I was more worn out than I thought."

"Come on over any time," he said.

"I was on my way."

"See you in a few minutes."

Come to think of it, this would be a new experience for her as she had never been any further than his back yard. Even though she knew he had a pool she hadn't been on the lanai since he moved in. The day he arrived she had been working so she didn't have a clue what it would look like on the inside.

His furniture must not have been remarkable or the Elsie and Betty duo would have spread the news all over the neighborhood. They were always looking to see if a new neighbor had anything kinky. The rental a couple of doors down the street had kept them busy for weeks. Floyd had the cops out there at least twice a week. He must have been on to something because the last time he called them the man and woman were taken out in handcuffs.

When the owner came to clean out the house there wasn't much in the way of furnishings, just a mattress, couch and a couple of chairs. Rather sad when you thought about it. Floyd Patterson said he read in the paper that the couple was selling drugs.

The only thing she did know about Jeremy's was he was not renting. The people who owned it previously were not very friendly, as far as sharing information. It was like they were here one day and gone the next.

They had kept to themselves and never bothered to socialize. Then one day there was a for sale sign on the place. Word was they had moved back north. Lyle said it was because the husband had been transferred. There was no way she could make a comparison. Why would she want to?

She turned on a couple of lights in the living room and kitchen so she wouldn't be coming back to a dark house and made sure the front door was locked. She took the unopened bottle of white wine out of the refrigerator, picked up the red from the counter and placed them in her wine tote before heading out the back door.

Jeremy waited on the lanai and held the screen door open for her. She handed him the tote. "Thanks for the chilled wine and shrimp treat. It was a lovely surprise and made me feel very spoiled."

He bowed. "My pleasure, ma'am. I was sure today was going to be a bit stressful and you could use something unexpected." He peeked in the bag. A big grin split his face. "Thanks for the wine. Why two? Do you plan on some heavy drinking?"

"No, but I didn't know what you were serving so I got one of each to cover all bases. The white is cool so you may want to put it in the fridge."

"Or we can open it now and share a glass. Come on in the house where it's more comfortable. Or, if you prefer, we can sit out here by the pool. I can turn on the overhead paddle fans. I'll even unroll the blinds so Betty can't spy."

The lanai was cozier than she expected. There were a lot of areca palms in crockery pots. There was also a round glass topped table, but instead of the usual PVC constructed furniture he had wicker with big red and white striped comfortable cushions. She wondered if he'd had a professional decorator. Maybe she would ask him later, depending on what the inside looked like.

"Good heavens, don't do that. Blinds being lowered will make her doubly suspicious. She might even show up carrying a plate of cookies for dessert." Rachel glanced around the area. "This is lovely, very tropical, but I think I'll opt for the air conditioning. Maybe we can sit out here later after dinner and have coffee."

"Your call."

They went in through the sliders to what the builders now referred to as a great room. It was amazing what you could tell about a person by the way they furnished their homes. It was also a lesson in preconceived ideas. She had expected to find a room of mismatched secondhand furniture or at least dark leather. The lanai should have been her first clue. The room was definitely masculine, no frills and clean lines with a plasma screen TV mounted on one pale green wall. It was a good size but did not dominate.

A large U-shaped hunter green sectional filled the center of the room, balanced by a low, square tile topped coffee table, accessible by all sides. There were a few pictures on the bookcases that bracketed the TV. She assumed they were family.

As if reading her mind, Jeremy took her hand and led her over to them. Pointing to one, he said, "This is my daughter Melody, her husband, Rob, and their two daughters, Ann and Kate." He pointed to another photo. "The four women are my sisters."

"Four sisters? Didn't you have a brother, too?"

He nodded. "Dan passed away several years ago. We were the youngest. My sister, Arcadia, is the oldest. She has all the family pictures."

"You must have been spoiled rotten when you were growing up." Did his sisters help him with the decorating? She didn't think so because she had not heard any gossip about a woman being in his house for any length of time. Joette Hannifin Bradley had plenty of stories about the neighborhood buzz when her ex-husband moved into her place. After tonight things could change as far as she and Jeremy were concerned.

He held his thumb and index finger almost touching. "Maybe a little, but they sure worked hard to teach us how to treat a woman. Dan never married. Apparently, it didn't take with me because my ex wasn't very happy."

"Don't beat yourself up, my friend. I'm still recovering from that particular journey."

Jeremy shook his head. "Right, but now you're on a smoother road. Come on into the kitchen while I finish dinner. I have a stool over by the sink."

On the way to the kitchen she noticed a small dining room table set with candles, two place settings on a white table cloth and matching napkins. Another lesson from his sisters she surmised. In contrast, the kitchen was a different matter. It was small galley style and cluttered. There were pots and pans everywhere along with wooden spoons.

She took a sip of wine. "Looks like you, ah, went to a lot of trouble cooking. What's for dinner?"

Jeremy topped her a glass. "I'm definitely not a gourmet cook, but I do have one specialty, chicken and vegetables simmered in white wine. If you don't like chicken you're out of luck." He looked around the kitchen. "Don't worry I'm not going to ask you to clean up any of the mess. I'm an ace at kitchen clean-up duty. My ex had the rule of the cook not cleaning the kitchen, so I've had plenty of practice."

"Don't know how she got away with that rule. It never worked at my house. Oops! What an insensitive remark to make under the circumstance. I apologize."

"No worries. Why don't we go into the great room and enjoy our wine? Dinner will be ready in..." He glanced at the stove timer. "...about forty-five minutes. Do you want to grab the tray of cheese and crackers from the counter and I'll bring the wine."

Once they were settled on the couch he asked, "So how did the meeting go this morning? If you don't want to talk about it, there's plenty of other topics."

"No, I don't mind. I don't have any secrets." She took a sip of wine and proceeded to fill him in on what happened from the time she got to the attorney's office until she spent some time with Anita. "It was a relief to hear Mr. DeCarlo say he was able to contact Dave.

"There's no way Davy can convince me he didn't have a way of reaching his father. As it was Mr. DeCarlo found him. I thought Davy understood I have no problem with him staying in touch with his dad."

"He'll come around in time. If you ask me, and you haven't, but I'll say it anyway, most children don't want to see their parents split. It doesn't matter how old they are, they still have a difficult time handling it. Too often, especially when they're young, like my daughter was at nine, they feel it's their fault. It took me a very long time to convince Melody she wasn't to blame which is one of the reasons I never remarried. My life was too complicated. Not only did I have a child, but I was a police officer. My first marriage suffered because of my job; eventually the relationship died."

"I wondered why you were single."

"You should've asked me. Your sons had no problem."

Rachel scrunched her eyes closed and grimaced. "Please tell me they weren't rude."

Jeremy waved her comment aside. "They were curious. Anyway, now you know the reason why I never remarried. As for your boys, deep down they think they should've been more aware of what was going on. As for Davy, he'll come to grips with the situation. You have to give him more time."

"That is essentially what I tried to tell him. The other thing I'm having a problem with is convincing them I can have a life without Dave. Mike isn't the difficult one. Speaking of Mike, he and Mel invited us for dinner tomorrow night. Are you up for it?"

"Sure. What time should I pick you up?"

Rachel gave him the time. "Back to the subject of Davy. Sometimes I feel so sorry for him."

Jeremy nodded. "Even though he and Kathy have been married a long time, it's a bit different at our age. We're further down life's road. You might say we've been there, done that. We're lucky because we have our priorities straight. Not to change the subject, I meant to tell you, I think the new hair-do is spiffy."

"Spiffy? I haven't heard that term in eons." She smiled and raised her glass. "Here's to spiffy." After taking a sip she asked, "So how did your day go?"

Miss Daisy sauntered into the room and curled up by Jeremy's feet, let out a long sigh and looked at him with pleading chocolate brown eyes. He reached down and scratched her long silky ears. "We had a very busy day. She loves to ride in the car. She ran so much down at the park I thought I was going to have to carry her out. Actually, I thought they were going to have to carry me out, too. When we got home I had to give her a good brushing because she picked up quite a few burrs in her coat."

"I'm sure she loved every minute of your attention. Don't let her wear you out. She's still an adolescent dog. Hasn't figured out her mistress is not as young as she once was."

Jeremy cocked his head to the side. "Her mistress looks pretty damn good to me."

Rachel blushed with pleasure. "Thank you, kind sir. You made my day."

"You're very welcome. As for spending time with the pup, that won't be a problem. Miss Daisy is high strung. Like most retrievers she needs to run." He patted his midsection. "And I can use the exercise as well. So we're helping each other."

The view from where she sat made Rachel realize he looked perfectly fine to her. Was it genetic or was exercise part of his daily routine? There was a lot more to learn about him, and she was anxious to get started.

"Good. I'm sure Miss Daisy is enjoying herself immensely. I tried to tell Dave she wasn't a lap dog when he brought her home. I do feel sorry for the pup. Especially when I'm working, and she's cooped up."

"I think I have a solution. What do you say we time share her? I'll unlock the screen door and you can leave her on my lanai before you go to work."

"I tried leaving her on my lanai, but she tends to

bark if nobody's home. The neighbors complained. One left a nasty note taped to my screen door but didn't sign it. Why don't I give you a key?"

"Whatever you're comfortable doing." The timer on the stove went off. He put out his hand to help her off the couch. "Now I think it's time to eat."

"Can I help you bring anything to the table?"

"No, but you can light the candles." He reached in his pocket and took out a book of matches and handed them to her. "Have a seat, I'll be right back."

****

Dinner was delicious. The chicken was seasoned to perfection with garlic and marjoram. The vegetables were not over-cooked and the wine was chilled.

When dinner was finished she wanted to help clear the table. He refused. "Trust me, I have a method. Why don't I make some coffee and we'll take it out on the lanai. I bought a chocolate cake for dessert. I knew once you saw it you would know I never made it, so I had better own up."

Rachel beamed. "Once again you called on the ladies at Publix I take it?"

"The head baker and I will be on first name basis pretty soon." He handed her two plates and forks and opened the door to the lanai. "I'll be out with the coffee in a few minutes."

"Don't forget a knife," she said.

"A knife?" he echoed.

"To cut the cake."

Rachel slid down in the chair, resting her head on the cushion and stretched out her legs. It had been a long time since anybody had pampered her. Actually, nobody had ever pampered her the way Jeremy did…does. She could get used to this very quickly.

Within a few minutes he came out carrying a tray with the cake. "Be right back with the coffee. You take yours black as I recall."

"Yes, sir." She watched him walk back into the house. Yes, indeed, this could be the start of something wonderful, and she had no intention of letting anybody screw it up.

****

Rachel pulled into the employee parking lot at SAM's Club and parked next to Davy's car. She wanted to open both windows so she could enjoy the warm breeze as she tilted the seat back and waited. She couldn't do that because she wanted the element of surprise. She had to keep her fingers crossed he didn't recognized her car. It wasn't easy to hide a red Mustang convertible.

She knew if she went into the store her son would make a beeline for his office and use work as an excuse not to meet with her. This was going to be a mend the fences day. Davy was her firstborn, and it hurt her heart to be constantly bickering with him.

Earlier that day, Kathy came by the hospital to visit a friend and popped by the admitting office as Rachel was leaving for her break. While they were walking to the cafeteria for a cup of coffee, Kathy let it slip about the pictures Dave emailed from Pago Pago and how beautiful they were. When Kathy realized what she said she gulped and sputtered like a damp sparkler on the Fourth of July. Her daughter-in-law tried to apologize, but it was too late. Now the question was how to approach Davy without getting Kathy in trouble.

She slid down in her seat when she saw him

walking toward his car. When he got to the driver's door she turned the key in the ignition, lowered the passenger window and called his name. She could tell by the way he jumped she had startled him. Good. He needed some shaking up.

"Get in, son." She smiled. "You and I are going to take a ride and have a happy hour talk. It's been long time since we've done that."

Unease evident on his face, Davy stammered and pulled out his keys to unlock his car. "I'd love to, Mom, but I can't. Not today. I promised Kathy I would take the kids to karate lessons."

"Davy, my dear, that is a big fat whopper. I spoke to Kathy when she stopped by to see me at the hospital today."

"Hospital? Was she in the emergency room? Why didn't you call me? Is she okay?"

"Settle down; Kathy's fine. She was visiting a friend and we had an informative chat over coffee. That's when I checked if you had anything to do when you got home. She said you had nothing planned other than a dip in the pool. I promise I won't keep you long. I have plans tonight."

He opened the door and slid in the front seat. "Where are we going?"

Rachel kept her eyes on the road as she drove out of the parking lot. "To the Captain's Net."

He sat staring out of the window and didn't attempt any conversation, neither did she, until they were seated in a booth for two near the bar. She was thankful they were there because the noise and loud music would drown out their conversation should it become intense. They placed their order and since it was happy hour the service was quick.

"How long were you going to wait before you told *me* where your father was?"

Davy picked up his beer mug, shrugged his shoulders, and didn't say a word for a couple of seconds before he grumbled. "Your attorney found him. What more did you want? Kathy must've spilled her guts to you over coffee."

"She didn't do it maliciously. She was simply excited to tell me about Pago Pago and what beautiful pictures you father sent you and how happy he seems."

Davy snorted, "Sure she was. She probably couldn't wait to tell you and create more trouble. Wait until I get home."

Rachel reached across the table top, and took his hand, holding on firmly when he tried to pull away. "Davy, if I hear you said one cross word to her, and believe me, I will find out, you will not want to deal with me." Abruptly, she let go of his hand. "I don't lose my temper often, but when I do, it's-Katy-bar-the-door because I'll take you on."

He slouched down in the booth. "Are you going to call Mike and get him and Mel to back you up? I heard you and your neighbor were over at their place for dinner and feel like I'm being double teamed."

"No more double teaming. We're family. This includes your father, even if he is enjoying life in the South Seas. As for you and Mike, I love both of you but this discord is upsetting me."

"I don't want to upset you but I'm having a hard time with this divorce situation. Plus it seems like you like Mike better because he's sucking up."

Rachel reached for his hand. "Because your brother

invited us for dinner? And, by the way, we had a very pleasant evening. If you invite Jeremy and me, we'll be happy to come over to your place." She gently rubbed her thumb over the top of his hand. "Trust me, Davy. I understand some of what you're experiencing. Mike isn't sucking up. He's only trying to deal with life the way it is. That's all I want from you as well. I don't care if you talk to your dad ten times a day."

"Don't hold your breath waiting for me to invite the neighbor to our place."

"Your choice. Nonetheless, he has a name, it's Jeremy or Mr. Dunn, if you prefer, and you should have the good manners to use it."

"Okay, bottom line, I choose not to invite your neighbor, Mr. Dunn. If Mike and Mel want to, it's their business. As far as Kathy is concerned, I promise not to get out of line, but I will have a talk with my wife about betraying confidences."

Rachel leaned back and took a sip of wine. "There's no *betrayal* here. Deal with it and get over it. Do you remember Jean, your father's aunt?"

"Can't say I do."

"I think you were two or three years old when she died. I recall how she used to tell me about working through her blindness with her macular degeneration. How everyday living was changed for her. She had gone from being a meticulous housekeeper to doing the best she could under the circumstance. She was quite a lady. I used to drive her to the place where the visually impaired people met. On the way home she would tell me what she did during the day. What she had accomplished.

"I particularly recall the day she told me about

learning to sew a button again. It wasn't easy because she couldn't see what she was doing but she could feel the fabric and the needle sliding through the button hole. She was so proud when she accomplished any kind of a small task.

"I can empathize with her now, even though it has been many years down the road, because that is exactly the way I feel. These days it is like I'm feeling my way through life, but I know if I persist to the end, I'll be okay."

Davy gave her a weak smile. "On some level I realize you and Dad are not getting back together, but Dad keeps in touch with me. Maybe he does that because I don't ask him a lot of personal questions."

"You're not making any sense. You don't ask Dad any personal questions but don't hesitate to ask me."

"You're my mom."

Rachel raised her eyes to the ceiling. "I realize this divorce has not been easy for you. You were close to your dad, especially the last couple of years, and I don't want that to change. On the other hand, I don't want to find out from my daughter-in-law what I should've heard from my son."

"I asked Dad's permission to give Mr. DeCarlo his email address and he said yes. I gave it to Mr. DeCarlo the next day."

Since things were going well she was not going to tell Davy that with a little investigation the attorney had found Dave's cell phone number. Apparently Dave hadn't let on either. "Mr. DeCarlo said your dad was cooperative and gave him the name of his representative. I don't want these proceedings to get mean. I'm sure your dad is as anxious to have this settled as I am."

"Mom, I don't want to hurt your feelings, but before Dad left he told me he had some money stashed. Said he was going to live his life the way he wanted to, not the way you thought he should." Davy's voice was choked and tinged with sadness by the time he got to the end of the sentence.

Rachel twirled her glass and swallowed the egg-size lump in her throat. She felt her eyes burn with tears. She grabbed a tissue from her purse and blotted her eyes. It was the first time she had cried in front of her son.

"I'm truly sorry your father felt the way he did. He should have told me, and we could've dissolved this relationship more amicably. I want you to keep in mind what he did when I want to live *my* life from now on."

He picked up his beer mug and took a long swallow. "It's easy for you to say now that he's gone and you have someone else in your life."

"Now that statement was totally unreasonable because your father may have someone new in his life. I hope he does and he's happy." She chose her words carefully. "Did Dad tell you why he left the way he did??"

"He was afraid you would explode, and he wasn't up to facing that."

"Let me ask you, son, did I explode?"

Davy started playing with the coasters, turning them on edge and letting them fall. "No. When he asked, I told him you simply started proceedings and got on with your life."

"And his reaction?"

Davy ran his fingers through his dark hair.

"Honestly, from the sound of his voice, I think he was disappointed. I imagine he thought you were going to fall to pieces or maybe you would beg him to come back and try again."

"That will never happen."

"I told him the last time we talked. When it finally hit him you weren't going to have a nervous breakdown, he was on the west coast. That's when he made the decision to hop the freighter and go to wherever it was headed."

"Thanks for finally telling me the truth. I hope he's happy. I mean that."

"Me, too, Mom, but somehow I don't think he will be and that has me sincerely worried."

Rachel sighed and reached across the table and squeezed her son's hand. "Don't waste your time worrying. My mom always used to say that worry was the interest we paid on death. You have a lovely family and a lot of living to do."

"Okay. I'm sorry if I came across as to too controlling or too demanding. I love both of you and I want you both to be happy. I've never been in a situation like this before and I didn't know what to do."

"You don't have to do anything. We'll hang tough and take life one day at a time like everybody else."

"Sometimes that's easier said than done."

"I know, Davy, but we're family and we're strong. Together we can handle anything. Your dad will eventually find happiness."

"I'm glad you think so," Davy said.

"Trust me, a year from now this will all be a bad dream. And, who knows, maybe your dad will end up staying on one of the islands and invite you and the family to come for a visit. Now tell me what all is happening with you and the family?"

Davy took a sip of beer and laughed. "Sports, sports and more sports. Except for Susan. With her it's ballet and riding lessons.

Rachel raised her glass of wine. "Davy, my love, you have been blessed with a lovely family. Enjoy every minute. Take it from one who has been there. These years fly by much too fast.

****

When she got home Jeremy called and said Lyle and Anita would meet them at the Captain's Net for dinner because Anita was running late at the shop. Had Rachel known, she could've stayed there and waited for them. She dismissed that idea because she was still in her scrub uniform from work.

She hurried up, changed and was ready when Jeremy pulled up in the driveway. She grabbed her purse and ran out to meet him just as he was getting out of the car. He left the engine idling as he got out, then went around to the passenger side to open her door.

"You must have had a busy day," he said as he got in, put the car in gear and backed out of the driveway. "You were later than usual getting home from work."

"I met Davy after work and had a drink with him at the Captain's Net." She fastened her seat belt and sat her purse on the floor by her feet. "It was time to have a one on one session with him."

"Do you mind going back again or do you want me to call them and meet somewhere else?"

"I don't mind going back. I could really go for some of their crab cakes."

"Okay. How did it go with Davy?"

"Fine. We resolved some issues. He's really a caring guy; he just goes about showing it the wrong way. But I know his heart is in the right place."

"He'll come around."

Rachel rested her elbow on the arm rest and glanced at the familiar scenery of strip malls and gas stations as they made their way to the restaurant. It was comforting to see the familiar. Was Dave enjoying the newness of his surroundings? She hoped so. It would be terrible to make such a life changing decision only to discover it was a mistake.

After Jeremy pulled into the parking lot of the Captain's Net, Rachel scanned the area. "I don't see Lyle's car."

"I told him we would wait for them in the bar," Jeremy said, not making a move to get out of the car. "Unless you prefer not to since you were here earlier."

"No problem. We can order appetizers while we wait."

Jeremy took Rachel's elbow and ushered her through the door. "Sonny said he'd hold a table for us."

It was much quieter than when she'd been here with Davy. The lights were still dim but the music was more subdued. Sonny must be targeting the dinner crowd, who tended to be older. One of the doctors at the hospital told her a table of eight got up and walked out one night because the music was so loud they couldn't hold a conversation.

"Now we are on first name basis with the owner?"

Jeremy smiled and shrugged. "What can I say? You get to know people quicker in a small town. What'll you have? Wine?"

She shook her head. "Tonight is a martini night."

She ducked her head and grinned. "I know you'll see I get home safe and sound if I get a bit tipsy."

"You'll be fine as long as you eat. If you do get a bit wobbly, I'll take care to see you get tucked in."

She gave him a wicked wink and took a chip from the complimentary bowl. "No doubt in my mind."

By the time their drink order came they saw Lyle and Anita wave hello from across the room and make their way through the small lounge tables to join them.

The first words out of Anita's mouth were, "So how did the latest chat with Davy turn out?"

Rachel looked at Jeremy and raised her eyebrows. "You are absolutely right about the small town thing." Turning to Anita, she said, "It worked out great. I think this will be the last time I have to *chat* with Davy on this subject. How did you find out?"

"One of my clients is a server here. She broke a nail and stopped by to have Harriet fix it for her. She said it looked like you were crying. Did that boy of yours upset you that badly?"

"No. She must've seen me when I was happy everything was resolved," Rachel said.

Jeremy laid his arm across the back of Rachel's chair to massage her shoulder. "I think the conversation tonight should be Davy-free. What do you say?"

"I'll drink to that," Rachel said raising her glass.

"Me, too," Lyle and Anita said in unison.

"Good, because here comes the hostess to take us to our table."

Chapter 13

Giving Jeremy the key to her house meant a lot of stress reduction in her life. She no longer had to dash home from work to take care of the dog, then turn around and go back out to run errands. All she had to do was phone him if she was running late. When she said she didn't want to impose on his time, Jeremy said he wasn't in the least bit shy. He would be up front and let her know if he wasn't available. Sounded fair to her so she agreed.

She was surprised when he handed her the key to his house, saying he wanted her to have it in case she needed something when he was out of town visiting his daughter in South Carolina. It always seemed something happened if you were out of town, so he would appreciate it if she would check on his place while he was gone. That way he wouldn't come home to any surprises, like a flood from a broken pipe or a busted water heater.

Another benefit to having Jeremy in her life, she now had a *real* social life, the kind where you got dressed up to go out. They went to dinner at least once a week, mainly on Friday nights. She appreciated not having to cook at the end of a long work week. Sometimes they drove down to Ft. Myers or up to Sarasota or Venice. Lyle and Anita regularly joined them if they were going to Captain's Net. Lyle swore that was the only place where he never had an allergic reaction to the food. Rachel had to resist rolling her eyes when Lyle made that comment.

Jeremy scared her because he was so easy to be around. More and more she found herself looking forward to being with him. She enjoyed lunches with Anita and the ladies at work, but there was definitely a plus side for having male companionship. Especially male companionship where she didn't have to be constantly on guard, watching every word she uttered. Before he left, Dave had become very good at reading his own meanings into her side of any conversation.

The last time they had gone over to Davy's, a week before he took off, Dave had spent the entire time putting her down in front their son's family. Rachel made light of the comments rather than create a scene.

She had to admit Dave had never been much for the social scene. Actually, Dave hadn't been much for anything for the past couple of years, including conversation. For a man who now claimed he wanted to see the world, he never expressed that desire to her. She would've loved to travel.

He would sit and eat dinner staring at the plate or the wall behind her head. When he finished he would fold his napkin, get up, head for the den, close the door and that would be the last she saw of him until the following morning.

At breakfast he would read the paper in silence. When she tried to share a topic or article she thought would be of interest, he shot her an annoyed frown, folded his section of the paper and left the room. She was not missing that aspect of her life one iota.

He gave up taking Miss Daisy for her morning

walk, passing off the chore to her. If he could only see Miss Daisy now, how well behaved she had become. Would he be proud? Surprised? Since Jeremy had been working with the dog there was a world of difference. All of it for the better.

Maybe Dave had been making plans for a long time and, in doing so, purposely pushed her away. That was silly on his part because all he had to say was he was unhappy, wanted out, let's sell the house and split everything fifty-fifty. Would she have agreed? Maybe. Maybe not. Like her dad always told her, hindsight is always twenty/twenty. Also we always feel we had all the answers *after* the event. She was fairly certain they could've worked things out without him running away.

There was no use mulling over what-might've-beens. She walked into the living room to close the blinds against the late afternoon sun when she saw Davy pull in the driveway. The two boys and their wives were in the car...without the kids. No one was smiling.

A sinking sensation slammed her in the pit of her stomach. Something was up. She prayed it wasn't another go round with Davy trying to arrange some kind of reconciliation. Could be he might have presented a new strategy to his brother and included their wives.

Last week Davy had asked if she wanted Dave's email address. She had declined for the present. A year or so down the road she might be ready to get in contact with her about-to-be-ex, but not right now.

Rachel opened the front door as they came up the walkway. "Hi, come in. To what do I owe the pleasure?" She looked at the clock. "Aren't you supposed to be working Davy? Mike?"

Before they could answer she heard Jeremy's voice call hello as he came through the back sliders into the dining room. He wasn't coming to bring Miss Daisy back because the dog was stretched out under the kitchen table. Something was definitely wrong, because even the dog didn't make a move to greet Jeremy. This scene made the hair on the back of her neck tingle. Something was amiss.

Her throat dried like a desert; her hands shook as her anxiety level increased. If something had happened to one of the kids Kathy wouldn't be here.

She hugged herself as her eyes darted from one to the other. "Somebody say something because y'all are scaring the crap out of me."

Mike took her arm led her to the couch. "Mom, I think you better sit down." He nodded in Jeremy's direction. "Thanks for coming over, Jeremy. Davy, I think it will sound better coming from you."

Davy squatted down in front of her and took her hands in his. Looking her square in the eye, he said, "It's Dad. He's dead. I heard a little over an hour ago."

"Dead?" she parroted. Cocking her head to the side and furrowing her brow, she repeated the question, "Dead? Like in not breathing?"

The first thought that flew through her mind, one she dare not express without sending Davy ballistic, was why now? Why couldn't he have done it before she spent money on an attorney?

Davy got up and sat next to her. "I got a call from an official in Pago Pago. Seems Dad loved it so much he had decided to stay there. Against advice from the locals, Dad went swimming like he usually did, in spite of the red flag warnings. There had been a lot of shark sightings, but he insisted they were dolphins and he would be fine."

Rachel bit her lower lip and grabbed Davy's hand. "Please don't go into any gory details, but how did they know it was him?"

Davy winced. "Someone identified him when...after he'd washed up on shore. They also found his shorts on the beach with his wallet in the back pocket."

In a very subdued voice, she asked, "The one who identified him, was it male or female?"

"He was living with a woman." Mike sat down beside her and laced his fingers with hers. "She gave Dad's personal information to the police."

"I hope he enjoyed his time with her." She noted the surprised look on her sons' faces, but oddly both of her daughters-in-law smiled faintly. She couldn't see Jeremy's face because he was standing behind her with his hands firmly resting on her shoulders.

"Boys, don't look surprised. I'm not being generous because he's passed. It's time for some honesty here. Davy, you keep telling me your father left because he was unhappy. You're up to date concerning our situation since I have openly admitted we had grown apart over the past couple of years. If he found some pleasure in the past few months, so be it."

Mike simply squeezed her hand while Jeremy massaged the back of her neck with his thumbs. Davy got up and walked to the chair across from his mother and sat. "That's mighty big hearted of you, Mom."

Kathy perched on the arm next to her husband and leaned her head down to rest on his. "Davy, now is not the time to be cantankerous or make any judgments about your mother. Rachel, I think I know what you mean. Don't get all upset, Davy, I can feel you fuming. You don't have any idea what the day-to-day relationship between your Mom and Dad has been the past few years, like they don't know ours on a day-to-day level."

Rachel was taken aback. So much for thinking she and Davy were on the same page. It must be the shock of hearing his father was killed in such a horrible manner. As for Kathy she never realized the woman had such insight. Good for her.

"Thanks, Kathy. I appreciate your support," Rachel said. "And in case you're wondering, I don't want to know about your personal life. Ever. That goes for you two as well," she said, angling her head toward Mike and Mel.

Melinda snuggled next to Mike on the couch, "Count me in as far as Kathy's opinion is concerned."

Davy glanced at Jeremy. "You haven't said a word, but I assume you're with them. I know when I'm out numbered."

Jeremy nodded. "Having dealt with unexpected tragic death, I'm well aware of what your mother is trying to say. She's merely being honest about her feelings as they relate to your father. I'm sure she's sincere when she says she hopes he found some happiness. I know there's more for you discuss as a family. Why don't I come back later?"

Rachel reached up and grasped the hand he was resting on her shoulder. "No, please stay. The family must have wanted you to be here; otherwise, they wouldn't've called you to come over."

"Okay, but what do you say I go to the kitchen and get a pot of coffee started?" Jeremy asked.

Kathy and Melinda jumped up to follow Jeremy to the kitchen. "We'll give you a hand."

Rachel called after them, "I don't think coffee is going to cut it. There's several bottles of chardonnay out in the garage fridge. If anybody wants red they'll have to make a run to the store." She heard both of her sons gasp.

Davy fixed his jaw. "I can't believe my ears. You're going to celebrate?"

Mike came to his mother's defense. "Davy, you're sounding like a first-class ass."

Staring Davy in the eye, Rachel said, "Thanks for your vote of confidence, Mike. As for you, Davy, don't be stupid, we're not celebrating. My reason for suggesting wine is it will have a better calming effect on all of us. The caffeine in the coffee will only hype us up. On second thought, get a pot of coffee going *and* open the wine. Might as well cover all bases while we're at it."

When she was alone with her sons, Rachel glanced around her little used living room gathering her thoughts. Strange she should receive the news about Dave in this more formal setting than in the kitchen or den where they had spent most of their time. She folded her hands on her lap and concentrated on the picture of a huge red hibiscus that hung on the opposite wall. "So, did his lady friend have any idea what your father's final wishes might be?"

Davy sighed. "Her name is Nafauna. She sounded awfully nice on the phone and, needless to say, she was incredibly upset. Dad must've leveled with her about his marital status because she said she would do whatever the family wished. I told her we would get back to her as soon as we discussed it with you."

There was probably more to the story than Davy was relating. That was usually his way when he was uncertain, feeding only bits and pieces of information. Rachel would discuss Nafauna with him later. She wasn't ready yet. "What do you have in mind?"

Davy got up and moved to sit on the marble top coffee table, facing his mother. "I talked it over with Mike." He nodded toward his brother. "We decided to make arrangements for Dad to be cremated there. I didn't think you wanted his ashes sent back here. Nafauna said if we decide on cremation, there's a man on the island who has a boat he uses for folks who want to have their ashes strewn at sea. He also conducts a service. She said she and the few friends Dad made during the short time he lived there would attend."

Mike added, "We thought since Dad spent his last days on the ocean and in it, it would be an appropriate way to handle it."

Eyebrow arched, Rachel pressed, "You found out all this information and made preparations in an hour?"

"Cut me some slack, Mom, it might've been a little longer. It wasn't my day off. I had to get someone to cover for me, then I had to track Mike down at work, he was out on a call. He got in touch with Melinda. Then Kathy had to contact her sister so she could take the kids. It was at least a couple of hours ago."

"Okay, that makes more sense. As for the arrangements, what she suggested sounds like the right thing to do. Actually, if I am reading between the lines, I do believe everything has been set in motion already.

Am I correct?"

"Yes, ma'am," they said in unison.

"Let me know the cost and I'll take care of it. We'll have to put an announcement in the local paper. I'm sure some of your father's friends and clients will want to know, if they don't already. The Calusa telegraph is very efficient."

"Mike and I are going to handle the financial part, Mom," Davy said, obviously stunned at his mother's offer. "I told the official we would send a bank transfer to cover the cost."

"That's very generous, boys, but it will be an important part of my closure to my relationship with your father. As you know I was very hurt when he left the way he did, but I'm not bitter. It's more like I felt stupid because I didn't recognize how unhappy Dave was. Do you want to have a religious service here?"

Davy washed his hand down the front of his face. "Mike and I talked about that as well. Dad wasn't a church goer. Do you think it's necessary?"

Rachel sighed. "Let me think about it. I can give Reverend Moore a call and run the situation by him and see if he has any suggestions. Perhaps we can hold a private memorial service for the family and a few close friends, followed by a dinner."

"Sounds like a good idea, Mom," Mike said.

Davy reached down and pulled out a large manila envelope from the side of Kathy's tote purse and handed it to his mother. "Before Dad left he asked me to give you this if anything should happen to him."

Hands shaking, Rachel took the envelope and tore the flap. She pulled out a folded document and flipped through the pages. It was an insurance policy. She frowned at Davy. "Did you know about this?"

Davy raised his right hand. "I swear I didn't know what was in there. It was sealed when I found it propped up by the front door the day he left. Besides, it was addressed to you. There was a note attached saying I should hold on to it in case something happened to him. I saw it when I went out to get the newspaper."

They both glanced at Mike. He held up both hands, palms out. "Don't evil eyeball me. You both know Dad didn't talk to me very much, much less confide anything important. Davy was his favorite. Dad always referred to me as Momma's boy."

When Rachel slipped her hand in the envelope to check what was inside she felt a loose piece of paper as well as a plastic sleeve. She pulled out the paper and unfolded it. It was a handwritten note. She immediately recognized Dave's scrawl. This time it was on a bigger piece of paper.

Rach, if you are reading this I have gone to meet my maker. Don't be sad. Or maybe you'll be doing a happy dance. Either way I wanted you to know I didn't hate you, never did. I was restless and unhappy. Who knows the real reason? Maybe I felt we married too young. I hope this policy will help you to have a nice life. On the other hand, I hope you're an old lady and it keeps you out of a nursing home.

It was simply signed with the initial D.

She pulled out a document, scanned the amount and gasped. $250,000. She collapsed back on the couch, mouth agape, absolutely flabbergasted. Choking back a sob she passed the policy and the note to Davy.

Mike slid his arm around his mother's shoulders and pulled her close. "I guess we didn't know a lot about the man."

Davy cleared his throat, got up and walked back to the chair. "Looks like I had more faith in him than the rest of y'all."

With a tight voice Mike warned, "Now is not the time to start with that. We each knew the man differently and we're all entitled to our opinions. If they are to be discussed at all, we'll do it later."

Melinda walked in the room carrying a tray of glasses. Jeremy followed with the bottle tucked in the marble cooling tube. "What will be discussed later?" Melinda asked.

Mike patted the couch cushion next to him. "Y'all better take a seat. Babe, put the tray on the table and come sit next to me."

Kathy perched on the arm of the chair next to Davy. "Rachel, we can't leave you alone for a minute without something major happening. What gives?"

Rachel blew her nose before holding up the letter in one hand and the policy in the other. She read the letter aloud. "According to the date of this policy, he took it out a little over ten years ago. Since he didn't cash it in, Dave must have meant it when he wrote he didn't hate me."

She burst into tears.

****

When he returned home Jeremy kicked back on his recliner and folded his hands behind his head trying to process the events of the past couple of hours. He was happy for Rachel. Not happy that her about-to-be ex was dead. He would never wish anyone dead. He was happy the guy had at least made an attempt to see she was taken care of in case something happened to him. It was important to a woman like Rachel that, in the end, she may have been discarded, but she wasn't hated.

Since he had been around from the beginning, he was well aware she was confused about the way her marriage had ended. It was a damn shame Dave hadn't tried to actually speak to her, rather than communicated with a note or through their son.

Both boys were going to have some problems adjusting to the present situation, Davy more so than Mike. From his rare meetings with Mike, Jeremy realized the man tried to be fair but was more biased toward his mother. He would have an easier time coming to grips with his father's death.

Davy would probably have periods of remorse that he hadn't done enough to have a better outcome. Jeremy knew this from working with Melody after his divorce. He had to give kudos to Dave. He never would've thought about buying an insurance policy for Patsy. Now, Melody was a whole different story. He had made her the sole beneficiary of his life insurance through the police department. He had also taken out another policy after he retired in which she was also the sole beneficiary.

He picked up the phone and punched in his daughter's number. She answered on the second ring. "Hi, Dad. Are you okay? You don't usually call me at this time of day."

"Caller ID," he said. "What did we do without it?"

Melody's silvery laugh echoed across the miles, making him feel better. "We answered calls from people we didn't want to talk to. Now, to what do I owe the pleasure?"

"I needed to talk to my baby. Had quite an

experience with my neighbor, Rachel, and her family today. I'm sure I mentioned her name."

"Only about a thousand times. What happened?"

He got up and walked to the kitchen, cradling the phone between his neck and shoulder. Opening the refrigerator he took out a can of soda and popped the top. "Her son, Mike, asked me to be there when they told her soon to be ex-husband was dead. It was pretty intense."

"I'm sure it was. But, you've had a lot of experience in that area from your years on the police force. I mean being the bearer of bad news to a family and helping them handle grief. How did she take it?"

"Better than I thought she would. She was shocked, of course. I mean how many people find out their husband was the victim of a shark attack?"

"Ouch! That must've been pretty gruesome. I saw a couple of shark bite attacks when I worked in the emergency room. They're really nasty. Where was he when this happened? California?"

Jeremy walked back into the great room, settled on the couch and gazed at the family pictures on the bookcase. His brother Dan's death had been sudden. He'd been killed in an accident on his way home from work. "No. He was in Pago Pago in American Samoa."

"Are they going to bring his remains back? Have a service here?" Melody asked.

"No. He is going to be cremated over there. They requested his ashes be spread over the ocean. Rachel felt that was the best way to handle it since it appears Dave was very happy there while he was following his dream so to speak."

"She sounds like a lady that has her head on

straight. Then again, you sound a bit...I don't know, distraught is a good word. Do you want me to come?"

"I don't think that will be necessary. I called 'cause you're such a darn good listener, sweet pea."

There was a short pause on the other end of the line. "Dad, I'm always here for you, like you were for me. Just say the word and I'm there. Rob will take care of the girls."

"I know, baby. It's good to know that you're there for me as well, and willing to listen."

"Any time."

He hung up and took a long swig of soda. His experience as a homicide detective taught him that time would heal the family dynamic, but there were all kinds of psychological developments after a traumatic death. He planned to be on hand for Rachel to help her get through it. Davy and Mike as well if they needed him.

Chapter 14

After everyone left Rachel stood at the sink washing the wine glasses and stacking them in the drainer. Kathy and Melinda had wanted to clean up before they left, but she told them she needed to do some ordinary chores. Simple household tasks to help keep her mind off what had happened to Dave.

Try as she might, the picture of him meeting up with a shark kept popping into her mind. Even though she was angry with him, at no time did she ever wish he would die.

Right now she was so keyed up she was ready to scrub the tile grout on the kitchen floor with a toothbrush. She stared out the kitchen window, concentrating on the butterflies flitting around the shrubs in her neighbor's yard. She was still having a difficult time assimilating the events of the past few hours when she caught a movement in the backyard.

God, please don't let it be Betty or Elsie.

She breathed a sigh of relief when she saw it was Anita coming through the lanai screen door. Rachel didn't know if she was up to dealing with her dear friend, but it was too late to stop her now.

She glanced at the digital clock on the microwave. "What are you doing home so early?"

Anita put her arms around Rachel and gave her a big hug. "It's after four. I waited until I saw Davy and

Kathy leave. Oh, my God, I almost fainted when Kathy's sister called to cancel her appointment. Said she was going to watch the kids while Davy and Kathy came here." She glanced in the living room. "Please tell me they didn't leave you alone. If they couldn't stay I thought for sure Jeremy would be with you. You shouldn't be alone at a time like this."

"Settle down, Anita. It's not like I'm a grieving widow. Even though there were times I wanted to kill Dave over the past couple of years, I didn't want him to die." Rachel shuddered and shook her head. "Especially not the way he went out. I simply wanted him to hurt as much as I did when I found his note."

"You know the sad thing about the statement you made is I understand exactly what you're saying." Anita went to the cupboard, took out a mug and poured herself a cup of coffee. "I know there are a lot of times when I say I'd like to kill Lyle, but you know I'd never do it. It's just an expression of frustration."

Rachel nodded in agreement but didn't add anything. She pulled out a chair and sat down at the kitchen table. What would the woman think when she heard about Nafauna and the insurance policy. Anita obviously didn't know about it yet or it would have been part of her initial comments. Actually, the first statement out of her mouth would've been it was the least Dave could do. She would eventually tell her about both of them, but not right now.

Anita went to the fridge and took out some vanilla caramel creamer and poured it into her cup. Stirring it, she came to the table and took a chair across from Rachel. "Still, you and Dave had been married a long time. I'm sure it was still a shock." She shook her head.

"A shark attack of all things. Who woulda thunk it!"

Rachel winced at hearing the incident repeated because it brought a totally ugly, gory image into her head. "All I can say is that was the last thing I expected to hear when I got up this morning."

"I can imagine."

Rachel went to stand. "I think I need some water."

"Sit still, I'll get you a glass." Anita went to the cupboard, took out a tumbler and filled it with ice and water from the dispenser in the fridge door. "So, where did everybody go?"

"They all went home. Davy and Mike are taking care of everything." She explained the arrangements,

"They're not planning to bring Dave's body, I mean ashes, back for a memorial service?"

Without going into specific details Rachel explained, "They were in touch with one of the officials on the island. We decided since Dave apparently was very happy there, it was best to let it all take place there. As for a memorial service, we haven't made a decision about holding one here. You know Dave wasn't raised in any particular church. I think the last time he was in one was when Susan was baptized."

"Right. As I recall he gave you a hard time about attending. He wanted to meet you some place after services. I agree the arrangements y'all have decided on sound reasonable. Dave had a lot of business friends and old classmates, but I don't think he was much for keeping in touch."

"There were, but for the past few years he only ever talked about guys he knew on the job. You know what a couch potato he is...was."

"Don't remind me. Where's Jeremy?"

"He took Daisy and went home, thinking with all the people dropping by, the dog would do better at his place. The family is coming back in a couple of hours for supper."

"Makes sense. You don't need any added stress right now. You know how crazy your dog can get when there are a lot of people here, especially folks she doesn't know. Can I make anything?"

"No, thanks. Jeremy told the boys he was going to call over to the Fork & Spoon and order from their menu. In fact, he called me before you came to say Flora had contacted him and said it was ready for him to pick up anytime he wanted to get it."

Unashamed Anita rubbed her mid-section. "I hope he gets her fried chicken. She makes the best in town."

The thought of biting into food made Rachel's stomach churn. She hoped Flora didn't send any of her fried grouper. It would be a while before she would be able to enjoy fish. "There will be a variety. You remember all the food she sent when Al Kohn's wife passed away."

"Do I ever. He and his wife used to eat three meals a day at the Fork & Spoon. Flora is kind that way. She takes good care of her customers."

"I remember. Connie used to say Al didn't like for her to dirty the kitchen, though Dave said the reason was she was probably a lousy cook. By the way, you might want to call Lyle and tell him to come on down and join us."

"I already did. I'm sure when he hears there's going to be food from the Fork & Spoon he's going to have a miraculous cure of his gastric reflux."

"Is that his malady this week?"

Anita nodded. "It was. It might've changed; I haven't seen him since he read the medical column he found on the computer this morning. I don't think it will be anything to do with his digestion because he was too hungry after his pseudo stomach ulcer. Anyway, he's working down in Ft. Myers today. He said he'd come on down once he got cleaned up. They were working on a condo pool. You know what he looks like after they spray marcite. He's not fit to be seen at a social gathering—not that there is going to be a *social* gathering. I mean you may have a few folks stop by."

"Stop tripping over your tongue. I know what you mean. Why don't we bring our drinks and head for the lanai."

Anita stood to follow Rachel out the door. "I don't know how fresh the air is in the middle of July, but let's go out anyway. We can turn on the overhead fan to help keep the no-see-ums at bay. While we're out there you can fill in some of the details…unless you don't want to talk about it."

She might as well get used to telling the story because she was bound to be repeating it over the next week or so. "The boys didn't give me *all* the details and I really didn't ask." Rachel shuddered. "I imagine they were pretty horrific."

"I don't mean about the shark attack. What was he doing in...where was it now?"

"On the American Samoa island of Tutuila. He was apparently living in Pago Pago."

"Hey, that sounds pretty romantic and totally unlike Dave. Do you think he went native and wore one of those sarong things? You know the kind they wore in the old movies. Maybe he was living on the beach in a grass hut. He might even have had one of those Polynesian beauties as a companion. *Please* tell me he wore one of those sarong things? It will give me a whole different opinion of the man."

Rachel covered her mouth in an attempt to stifle and laugh. "Anita, I doubt Dave would go native. He didn't have the body build for wearing something like that. If you recall he wouldn't even wear shorts, so don't let your imagination run wild. Anyway, what you're referring to, I think I heard Mike call it a lava lava or something similar, rather than a sarong."

"I'm sure he didn't go swimming in long pants," Anita huffed and pursed her lips.

"I didn't ask. Anyway, Pago Pago is pretty modern these days. According to Davy, Dave had an apartment. I understand they even have an international airport."

Anita swung her arm while she snapped her fingers in the air. "Damn, there goes my South Pacific illusion, shattered into a million pieces."

Rachel ran her finger down the side of the cold moist glass. "I can do even better. Davy let it slip that Dave had been emailing him telling him what life was like there. He sent a lot of photos. I haven't seen them. They had the good sense not to bring the laptop with all of the pictures. Davy said he's going to save the emails and print the photos to be put in a scrapbook in case the grandchildren want to read it someday. After all they're all old enough to remember their grandfather. Not that it's important, but Davy also mentioned they have tuna canneries there."

"Did Dave work there? Somehow, I can't picture him working in a cannery."

"I don't know. Davy told me Dave kept bragging about what good drivers the natives were. You know how he spent most of his time here swearing at the other drivers on thc road."

Anita nodded in agreement. "Back in the day, when Dave still socialized, the air would be blue before we got to wherever we were headed."

"While I was a nervous wreck by the time we got to where we were going," Rachel added.

Anita waggled her eyebrows. "Back to where he was living now. Was there anything else he liked about living on the island?"

Rachel took a sip of water, trying to think of something else rather than address her friend's innuendo. She blotted her forehead with the paper napkin. The humidity must be high. There wasn't a leaf moving on the trees, and the fan wasn't keeping her cool. She made a mental note to jack up the thermostat when she went inside. After the sun went down it might be pleasant. At lease she hoped it would be because the smokers would be gathering out here. She had better put out some ash trays. It was very still at the moment, even the birds were quiet. "Oh, yes, they have a McDonalds. That made it absolutely perfect. You know how he loved his quarter pounders and large fries."

"Why do I get the vibe you're deliberately avoiding my question about another woman?"

So much for putting the question of the 'other woman' off until later. Rachel heaved a heavy sigh and bit her lower lip. "Her name was Nafauna. Davy said Dave told him she was named after a legendary princess in island folklore. Mike said she was a real looker. Davy asked if I wanted to look at a picture of her. Once again, I declined."

"Hey, you gotta look at it this way; at least he didn't *leave* you for another woman. He simply found another woman after he left you. I wouldn't mind having a peek at a picture of her. Do you think the boys would show one to me?"

"You can always ask them."

"I think I will, but, relax, I won't do it today."

"Thanks." Rachel got to her feet and lifted her empty glass in the air. "Right now I'm going to go inside and change to iced tea. It's going to take some time to process all this information. Do you want to switch to tea?"

"I'd rather have wine. Do you have any opened?"

"Funny you should ask," Rachel said as she led the way back into the house.

****

An hour later they heard Jeremy's car pull into the driveway. When they came to the door to offer a hand, he turned them down. Instead, he had to make two trips to get everything in the house. Wide eyed, Rachel shook her head as she saw all the food.

"Is Flora expecting half of Calusa to show up?"

"At least. She said you had to be prepared to have people drop by." Jeremy grinned. "She said the buzz started in the restaurant around three o'clock. Now all the folks who come in are talking about it, especially the shark part. Joette and Mandy sent their sympathy. They said they would drop by later when they got off work. Doc McCabe was there having an after school snack with his little boy. He said he and Kelly would stop by this evening after she closed the shop."

"Maybe it is a good thing Flora prepared all this

food." Rachel reached for her purse and took out her wallet. "What do I owe you?"

"Not a penny."

Rachel spread both hands over the bags. "Come on. I can't let you pick up the bill for all this food."

"I'm not. Flora said this one was on her."

With a gasp, Anita laid her hand across her heart. "You *are* talking about Flora Collins at the Fork & Spoon? The same woman who charges her husband for his sandwiches at lunch time?"

"The very same," Jeremy concurred. "And, by the way, I heard all about her charging her husband for his lunch. He never should have given her instructions on how to make fried chicken. You know paybacks can be hell. Anyway, Flora said Dave did all their painting over the years. Always did a good job and charged a fair price. Providing food was the least she could do for his family."

Rachel started to put the containers of cold salads in the fridge. "Dave did have a good reputation as a painter in this area. He always had work. Even during down times in the economy, a lot of people had their homes repainted inside and out rather than buy new."

Anita cocked her head to the side and made a circular motion with her index finger. "Maybe that's what happened to him. He inhaled too many paint fumes over the years, and it mucked up his brain."

Rachel gave her a light back-handed smack on her upper arm. "That's cold, even for you. I remember when you and Lyle were one of those people who made a similar decision during the last slump in the market. I seem to recall you were all set to buy a piece of property out by Roy and Joette Bradley."

Before Anita could answer, Jeremy grimaced and held up his hands as if to halt their repartee before it got out of hand. "Ladies, what do you say we get back to the subject at hand? I don't think I ever spoke to Dave, other than to wave or nod hello as he walked into the house. Also, I'm not a doctor so I can't comment to the effect of paint fumes on the brain. Do you want me to slip this chicken in the oven on low, Rachel?"

"You are a wise man to stay out of this conversation as well as change the subject. We could have been off on a whole other tangent. And, yes, put the chicken in the oven." She headed for the dining room. "Anita, follow me. You can help me set up a buffet table in there."

Anita crooked her finger at Jeremy. "Before you start schlepping stuff out to the garage, how about you give me a hand putting the leaf in the table? Rachel, you can decide what cloth you want to use while he gives me a hand. Depending on who shows this could turn out to be an interesting evening. You could say we'll be mourning the missing."

It wasn't long before cars started pulling up out front and a steady stream of folks came to pay their respects. The first ones in the door were the four neighborhood gossip spreaders: Betty, Al, Elsie and Floyd. Rachel was certain they would stay until she shooed them out the door. They would be sure to mingle in separate areas so they could hear every word that was uttered and compare notes later.

Betty didn't bring any cookies. That was a crying shame because Rachel hoped to pig out on the chocolate chip, which, giving Betty her due, she made the very best. They were always chewy and she didn't skimp on the chips.

The one person who was a total surprise was Chas Martin. The guy was well-known around town as a real player. She was positive he was never a close friend of either her or Dave. What brought him here? Curiosity?

The man in question came up and draped his arm around her shoulders before giving her a big wet kiss on the temple. "Babe, I was stunned to hear about Dave. Man, it must have blown your mind when you heard."

From across the room Rachel caught Betty Bradford's disapproving gaze and tried to extricate herself from Chas' grasp without making a scene. It was an exercise in futility because he had her pinned against his side with one arm. If the guy didn't have such a slime ball reputation she might have thought he was sincere. She was not about to create a spectacle with all these people milling around—especially with all the gruesome elements involved in Dave's passing.

She shot Jeremy a pleading look as he came walking into the living room. Calling him over she reached out and clasped his hand. "Jeremy, I don't know if you've met Chas Martin. He and Dave went to high school together. Chas, this is my next door neighbor, Jeremy Dunn."

While the men shook hands she managed to slip away from Chas' grasp. That didn't stop the man. He snaked out his arm and grabbed her hand. "Rachel, if there is *anything* and I do mean *anything,* I can do for you, please don't hesitate to call. I'll be here for you."

Yeah, sure I'm going to call you. I'd as soon call the devil. It will be a cold day in hell before I want you anywhere near me.

"Thanks Chas, but I'll be fine. I have great family

support. My boys and their wives are taking very good care of me."

He produced a knowing wink and once again put his arm around her shoulder for a one-armed hug. "I'm sure they are, but, ah, sometimes you need someone who remembers the old days. Someone from the same, ah, background. Know what I mean, darlin'?"

Sensing Rachel was getting upset with the way the conversation was going, Jeremy took Rachel's other hand, then pointed toward the dining room table. "Why don't you go get something to eat, Chas. There's plenty of food."

"Thanks, but I'll pass for now. Rachel, I'll check back with you in a couple of days." He slid his fingers down her arm, then put them to his lips before placing them on her mouth and making his way to the door.

"Who is that guy?" Jeremy asked.

Rachel hugged herself. "I understand he's the Casanova of Calusa. He still thinks he's a twenty-year-old stud. He wasn't a stud when he was in his twenties. Even though he was much older, he used to hang out with B.J. Jowett, Kelly McCabe's first husband. They were always on the prowl together. Although I never met the woman, town scuttlebutt had it that whenever Chas got into trouble his mama, Alma Sue, would swoop down and make everything okay, no matter the cost. I don't know why he came by today. He and Dave were never close friends."

"Based on the fact you were in the process of a divorce and now you're a widow, he most likely thinks you're in the market for a new man in your life. Looks like he's going to make sure he's the first in line."

"I don't think so. Must be something else. I mean

my getting divorced is very old news." She took a tissue from her pocket and wiped her lips. "From what I hear he only goes for the younger ones. Dave used to say once the girls were two or three years out of high school they were onto Chas and his inability to have a lasting relationship and so they dumped him. The same scuttlebutt has it that the last couple of times the women were in their thirties or forties, so I assume the young ones are getting wise to him."

"That may be, or he is going for older women because they have some bucks. The cop in me says he already knows about the insurance policy." Jeremy snapped his fingers. "That's it! Bet he's been busy making plans on how to spend your money."

"How could he? I only found out today." Rachel shot him a minimal smile, eyebrows raised in surprise. "If that is the case, Jeremy, my friend, he'll soon learn about the best laid plans of mice and men getting all screwed up."

"I'm well aware of it. My gut still tells me he knows about the insurance policy. All I'm asking is for you to be very careful. You've been through a lot of emotional turmoil these last few months. Trust me, when you're most vulnerable, that's when the Chas Martins of the world start their hunt. Let me know if he does anything, and I mean *anything* to upset you or make you suspicious."

She nodded. "I will. I promise. Now if you'll excuse me, Joette and Roy came in."

Jeremy watched her walk over to greet the couple. He wished he knew more about this Martin character. As he headed for the kitchen, he motioned for Lyle to follow. "How about taking a ride to get some ice."

Lyle had just picked up a piece of chicken. He held it up for Jeremy to see. "Can you hold on a minute? I've only taken one bite out of this."

"Bring it with you, but be sure to grab a napkin; I don't want grease on my seats."

Jeremy was glad Lyle didn't give him any more grief. The man grabbed a napkin and trailed him out the back door. "I don't know what this ice thing is all about. I've got a couple five pound bags in the garage freezer. Always keep some extra on hand during hurricane season."

"Fine. We'll walk down to your place and you can fill me in on this Chas Martin joker."

Lyle took a bite of chicken and talked while he chewed. When they got to his house he wiped his hands on his shorts and entered the code to open the garage door. "Martin has always fancied himself a ladies' man. I don't think you have any worries there, he's harmless. I'm sure most of the women in town think he's a creep. At least that's what I hear from Anita."

"The ladies can think what they like, but I picked up on a whole different vibe," Jeremy said as he followed Lyle into his garage.

Lyle held the chicken gripped between his teeth, while he opened the freezer and tossed Jeremy two bags of ice. "One thing you got to say about Flora, she doesn't get those itty bitty two-bite chicken parts. You can carry the ice. I want to finish eating. Back to Chas. Don't get all worked-up over the asshole. I'm sure Rachel can handle herself."

Jeremy nodded in agreement and handed one bag of ice back to Lyle. "What gives?" Lyle asked.

"It was only an excuse to get out of the house so I

could ask you about Martin."

"Hell man, you could've asked me that while I was filling my plate," Lyle griped as he hit the code to close the garage door.

"There were too many ears in the room. Quit complaining. There's more chicken in the kitchen."

Rachel may be able to take care of herself, but he was going to make damn sure that creepy bastard didn't make any moves on her. It was time to give his buddy, Slick, a call and see what he could find out. Going with his gut feelings had never steered him wrong in the past. He was not going to stop going with them now.

Chapter 15

Rachel leaned against the counter and heaved a sigh. Looking around the kitchen she was well satisfied all was in order. Thank God there was no mess because right now she was bone tired and there was no way she could face cleaning up. After everybody left Anita had herded Kathy and Melinda in here telling them everything had to be spic and span before they even thought about going home. They had done a really fantastic job.

Kathy's sister, Sari, had dropped the boys off, but took Susan back home with her saying she would take her to school in the morning and to ballet after school. The boys' ball game was tomorrow afternoon, and they didn't want to miss it. She couldn't blame them. Under the circumstances there was no reason their world should be put on hold. She was flabbergasted when Davy agreed.

God bless her oldest grandson, Chad. He was the self-appointed head of garbage control and made the rounds of the house, emptying trash cans and picking up cups and paper plates. Joette's son, Ned, the fireman, told him not to empty the ash trays because sometimes there was a smoldering cigarette that could cause a fire. Chad's brother, Matt, who didn't want to help, was more interested in listening in on conversations. It only took one look from his father,

Davy, and the boy pitched in.

Rachel opened the refrigerator door and stared, not knowing exactly what she wanted. Did she want to eat it or drink it? Nothing appealed. She closed the door and checked the dishwasher. It still had a while to go before it finished the drying cycle. She opened the base cupboard door and took out a bottle of spray stone polish to go over the tile splash board behind the stove, the only spot that had been missed. She could do it tomorrow, but she had the bottle in her hand so why not take care of it now?

Jeremy walked in from the lanai. "I'm back from taking Miss Daisy out for the night. I'm still going to keep her over at my place." He took the container out of her hand and put it back under the sink. With a smile on his face and firmness in his voice, he closed the door, took Rachel by the shoulders and pointed her in the direction of the den.

"The kitchen is in tip top shape. You, my dear, are not going to do one more thing tonight. Go in the den and put your feet up. I'm going to bring you a cold glass of wine."

"Twist my arm," she said and held out her arm. He gave it a gentle grasp with his hand. "Ouch! Enough. You've convinced me."

Laughing, she headed for the couch in the den, kicked off her sandals, put her feet up on the coffee table and closed her eyes. Was it horrid of her to think she now had the money to redo this room? Anita would tell her it wasn't. She would put it on her list for later.

As for Jeremy, it was nice to have him take charge. What was nicer was she knew there no strings attached, but she was not averse to any suggestions he might have. Did that make her a slut? Not in her mind at the present moment.

Unlike dealing with Chas the octopus. For the short time he was at the house, the man continuously wrapped an arm around her no matter how many times she tried to slip away. When Chas ran his hand down her arm and did the fingers to the mouth gesture before he left she wanted to go to the bathroom, take a shower and rinse her mouth.

She still felt uncomfortable about that particular encounter. Rachel had heard all the stories circulating around the hospital about Chas, but this was the first time she had experienced him first hand. If Jeremy was right, she would have to watch out whenever she happened to meet him.

Jeremy came in a few minutes later, carrying a glass of wine for her and a long neck for himself. He handed her the glass, sat down on the couch next to her and patted her on the knee. Tilting his head to the side, he asked, "How are you holding up, kid? You look like you did a day's work without a break and then ran a marathon."

Rachel took a sip of wine and rested her head on his shoulder. "I hope I don't look that bad."

"I wasn't referring to your appearance. I'm merely saying energy-wise you seem dog-tired. Dealing with a steady stream of people is no walk in the park."

"You're right on the money there; I am weary. I can't believe Dave knew so many people. I'm sure, due to the circumstances, there were a lot of folks who never met him. I'm also sure the four neighbors, who shall remain nameless, dropped by with food more out of curiosity than to feed the family. Have to admit I was disappointed Betty didn't bring her chocolate chip cookies. I could've used a few."

"Maybe she'll show up with some tomorrow looking for updates. I'm sure Kathy and Melinda were glad you told them to take what they wanted. Do you mind if I ask you a question?"

"Shoot."

He scratched his head. "Why are your curtains laying on the floor still on the rod?"

"So Betty and Elsie can see better when they're peeking in the window. I've caught them on two different occasions so I decided not put them back up. Now I can wave when they snoop."

Jeremy chuckled. "That answers my question. Back to this evening. Your grandsons were busy helping their mother pack up a lot of the extra food. Melinda kept telling her to take more."

"Chad and Matt could eat anyone out of house and home. I don't know where they put it. Of course, my boys were the same when they were that age. I swore Davy and Mike had a hollow legs."

"They're growing boys. I always remember my mom saying she'd rather clothe me and my brother than feed us. My sisters were always watching their weight so she had no problems with them."

"I would have to agree with your mom. As for Chas showing up, along with the unusual circumstances of Dave's death, I'd like to be a fly on the wall over at Anita's shop tomorrow. There'll be a constant buzz and the story will grow more bizarre with each telling. I'm sure it will be more fascinating than what happened."

"I'm *sure* you're right about the story telling. It's like questioning witnesses at a crime scene. Each one tells what happened differently. You certainly had plenty of folks going through here for the past four hours. It will be interesting to hear what they spread around town. On the other hand, I didn't think people showed up with food any more. Even with what you gave away you have enough here so you won't have to cook for a week."

She sat up and grasped Jeremy's hand and tucked it against her side. "Thanks for all you've done for us today. And mega thanks for coming to my rescue when Chas had me monopolized."

"Glad I could be of help." No way was he going to announce his real motives. It was much too soon. Besides, she wasn't ready for any kind of an intimate relationship. She had to have time to get her life in order with her new widow status.

"You know Dave was a local fellow. Lived here in Calusa all his life. I didn't move here until I was in my early teens. Like many of the other people who stopped by tonight, he had his own small business."

"What kind of business?"

"He is...was a painter. You heard Anita's remark about paint fumes."

"Right." With everything going on today he had forgotten Flora's comment about Dave painting the Fork & Spoon. As for Rachel, from past experience on the force he knew people needed to talk after a sudden death, or hearing about a sudden death. It didn't matter if they were close to the victim or not.

"He made a good living," she said. "Had a topnotch reputation. Maybe he felt stuck as he got older. Perhaps that's why he felt the need to see some of the world."

"Could be. He wouldn't be the first guy to take off. It's a damn shame he had to die."

"I think you're sincere."

"From the bottom of my heart. Believe me, Rachel, I've dealt with a lot of violent death over the years. It's a helluva way to go."

"Oh, I agree with you there. I wouldn't wish a shark attack on my worst enemy. I was thinking as a lot of his old friends were telling stories about him today, we think we know someone, but we never truly do. We only know what the other person wants us to."

He pulled her next to him and tucked her head in his shoulder. She didn't try to move away, and he took it as a good sign. "It's true, to a point. What made you think that way about Dave today?"

"Well, for one thing, I always thought he was a skinflint. He kept me on a strict budget. That is one of the reasons I went to work when the boys got older. I wanted to have extra pocket money rather than ask him for cash. For instance this used to be Mike's bedroom but when he got married and moved out I decided to turn it into a den. Where we could kick back and relax. From the day the furniture arrived, which I paid for with my own money, Dave took over."

She pointed across the room at the large flat screen television. Her eyes glistened. "He bought the TV and took over the room, said it was his. I thought for sure he would hate the colors of the room and change things but he never did.

"He kept the books for his business and did our personal taxes. I trusted him and never looked at the returns. When he said sign here, I signed. In retrospect, I shouldn't have been so trusting. He most likely squirreled away some money. He used to tell me about a few guys he knew who did a lot of cash jobs on the side. He must've done some as well."

Jeremy gently rubbed the side of her upper arm. "You could be right, but don't beat yourself up. Believe me you're not the first woman to discover that. Come to think of it men don't have the corner on the market."

"Are you speaking from personal experience?" she asked, making no effort to move away from him.

"I bought Patsy quite a few pieces of expensive jewelry over the years. When I'd ask her why she didn't wear them, she always said it was because we didn't go anywhere fancy enough to show it off or that she was saving it for a special occasion. I learned later she was selling it online. Plus, she wiped out our joint savings account and cashed in the few CD's we had before she took off. See, in my case, I trusted her, let her handle all the money."

"We have a lot to learn from each other."

You have no idea, my dear, but we're not going to rush the learning process. We're going to take it nice and easy and enjoy every lesson. Out loud he said, "That's not a bad idea. Now enough about me. Enough about Dave. Why don't you tell me about Rachel?"

"What do you want to know?"

"We discussed what we like and dislike in movies and books but not much about you personally. You said you moved here like a lot of other folks. Where are you from originally?"

"We moved here from Sikeston, Missouri, when I was a teenager. Started Calusa High School in my sophomore year. That's where I met Dave. We were in the same history class."

226

"Nothing about Dave," he reminded her. "I want to know about your life in Sikeston. Was it a big town?"

"Not when I lived there. Don't know about now because I've never gone back. During my life there it was very small. My dad worked for his father making furniture and took over the business after grandpa died. Dad was only thirty-eight when he passed away, leaving Mom, me and my sister, Trina. There was no way we could take over the business. Mom had a cousin living here in Calusa, and she talked her into relocating."

"Sounds like we both ended up here because we knew someone who lived here."

"I do believe that is how most folks get here. There are very few who were born and raised in Calusa. Oh, there's a few like Lyle and Anita whose families have been here for several generations. The McCabe family—you know, the sons have a chiropractic practice—are locals as well."

"I went to Dr. Jim right after I first moved here. Nice guy. Had me in shipshape in no time. Moving can sure mess with your back. Don't know if your sons told you, but my family has been in Tampa from way back."

"They didn't mention anything. Is that what they found out the day they were giving you the third degree out on the lanai?"

Jeremy laughed and rubbed the side of his nose with his index finger. "Actually, the whole encounter was pretty amusing. It felt like we were playing twenty questions."

She sat up and started to say something but he laid his finger across her lips to stop her. "Don't get upset. Like I said, I found it very humorous to be on the receiving end of the questioning. Now I think it is time you call it a day and try to get some rest. Keep in mind I'm as close as your telephone."

****

After Jeremy left, Rachel took a cup of herbal tea along with a book and went to her bedroom. She didn't know if she would be able to fall asleep. Tonight there were so many memories of the good days in this room. She and Dave bought this house before the children were born. What some of the widows she met at the hospital had told her was true. Once death took your partner the good memories bubbled to the surface. Dave was so good-looking back in high school; all the girls were crazy about him. She giggled when she recalled him asking her to the senior prom. Life only started getting complicated after the children came along.

She wiped the tears from her eyes. He missed out on so much of family life not being a hands on father, except when it came to cars when the boys got older. He taught them how to drive and made sure they had a car when they were eighteen and he felt they were responsible. It was only in the past few years that he truly became withdrawn from her.

She put the tea cup with its warming cozy on her bedside table, sat in the slipper chair, and wiggled her toes. Did she have the energy to get up and change or simply crawl into bed fully clothed? Who cared?

She heaved a sigh. That wasn't true. Mike and Melinda had wanted to spend the night. When she refused and shooed them out the door, Anita volunteered to take their place. Rachel sent her home as well. She needed some alone time after all the excitement of the day.

There were so many thoughts running through her mind, mainly about Dave but also about Jeremy. As for her relationship with Dave, never in her wildest imagination did she anticipate facing his death.

As for Jeremy, was it too soon to be wanting to spend more time with him? Should she be feeling guilty? No. Her marriage had been over for a very long time. She was...was...well, not young anymore, but she was healthy and sure she still had some good years left. Did she want to spend them alone?

No way Jose.

Rachel stared at the queen size bed, inviting her to crawl in. Old habits were hard to change. She got up and went in the bathroom to perform her nightly routine. That was what she needed right now to help her feel some degree of normalcy. She slipped out of her clothes and threw them in the hamper. Grabbing her nightgown from the hook on the bathroom door she slipped it over her head. Yes indeed, wash my face, brush my teeth and drink my tea. Tomorrow will be another day. She could only hope it would be less stressful than this one.

On second thought, having experienced Dave's skulking off in the night, filing for divorce, family discord and now his unexpected death, the road ahead had to be smooth. Compared to these events anything else would be a walk in the park.

****

Jeremy grabbed the leash and whistled for Daisy. The pup came running from the bedroom and sat at his feet waiting for him to fasten the leash. "It's been a wild day, girl, I'm sure you're ready for a nice long walk."

He jogged behind the dog past Rachel's house. The lights were out and most of the houses were dark. Unlike the streets in Tampa, those in Calusa did not have a streetlights on every corner so he had to depend on the bright moonlight to find his way. The same went for sidewalks so he kept to the middle of the road.

He hadn't wanted to leave Rachel alone and almost offered to lie down beside her until she fell asleep but knew that was inappropriate. He made sure she had his number by her bed in case she needed him during the night. The expression on her face told him she would not call. That was okay because he would be on alert just in case.

He was walking by Al Kohn's on his way home when the man called out asking why he was walking in the dark. Jeremy damn near jumped out of his skin. Al was sitting on a chair in his front entry. When Jeremy asked what he was doing sitting outside in the dark, Al said he was keeping an eye on the street.

Jeremy shook his head and went to the backyard to go through the lanai door. When inside he unclipped the dog's leash. "You and I can sleep better tonight, Daisy. The neighborhood watch is on duty."

****

Two days later, loaded down with tote bags in each hand and balancing a box on one forearm, Rachel maneuvered her way into Anita's beauty shop, The Hair Lair. Since it was the heart of lunch time she was surprised the shop was empty. Anita was behind the appointment desk while Harriet leaned on the counter top. Rachel sniffed the air, even the scent of hair spray was missing. Must be no one wanted a trim today.

Anita jumped up and ran to grab a bag and gasped

in mock surprise. "Let me give you a hand. Holy crap, please tell me you don't have two bags of wine. If you do I might be raided by the liquor licensing board, and I certainly don't want them knocking on my door. On the other hand, we're not expecting anybody. If there's any alcohol, I'll have Harriet put the closed sign on the door and drop the blinds so we can celebrate whatever you want."

"Cool your jets, woman. There's no need to close the shop. You should be so lucky that I would bring any left over fruit of the vine, when I can sit in my easy chair and put my feet up at home. The way my life has been going lately there's no way I'll add drinking and driving to my problems."

Anita started laughing. "I don't think drinking and driving entered your head when it came to not sharing wine. You wouldn't do that, drink and drive I mean. I mean I know you would gladly share with me."

"I know what you're trying to say." Rachel set the box on desk ledge. "I think—no, I know—we like kicking back to enjoy a glass or two, though three is more like it these days."

"Are you implying y'all spend all your time together swigging wine?" Harriet asked, amused at Anita trying to clarify her statement and only digging herself in deeper with each word.

"Don't be silly. I'm not strictly talking about us." Anita waggled her eyebrows. "I have two good eyes. I saw how Jeremy hovered over you in that 'I'm here to guard and defend' manner when good old Chas showed up and surgically attached himself to your side. Man, he was as close as white on rice!"

"Sleaze bag Chas Martin?" Harriet squealed. "How

did I miss him?"

"He left before you came by, Harriet," Anita said, "and homed in on our recent widow as soon as he came through the door."

"Speaking of that, Anita, I owe you big time for sending Jeremy to my rescue," Rachel said. "He said you saw what was happening, then went to the kitchen to get him."

"What are girlfriends for? I knew I wouldn't have any sway with Chas. He would've thought we both wanted him."

Rachel shuddered. "God forbid!"

"Amen," Anita said. "Now, what *do* you have in these bags?"

"A lot of food and way too many sweets. There are several zip bags of cheese cubes, raw vegetables and that tasty dill dip Celeste brought over."

Harriet took one of the bags, headed for the small refrigerator in the back break room and called over her shoulder, "I felt my mouth start to water when she walked through the door with the container. I swear I could eat that stuff with a spoon. Oh, there goes the buzzer on the clothes dryer. I'll fold towels while I'm back there. Be sure to talk loud enough for me to hear."

"Go for it," Anita said. "I'll listen for the phone."

Rachel mugged a face at Harriet's statement about the dip. "I like it, too, but don't think I could eat it with a spoon. There's also a couple of cheese balls and three boxes of assorted crackers." She pointed to the box on the appointment counter. "This one is filled with sweets. I'll never use them and I know Friday and Saturday are two of your busiest days. I thought you might want to put out a small spread for the ladies."

"You could've cut up the cakes for the freezer, the cookies as well, but I'm glad you didn't." Anita scanned the box. "I take it there was none of Flora's fried chicken left?"

"There was, but Kathy took the rest home with her. Chad and Matt love it. So does Davy. Mike and Mel didn't get any either."

"It figures." Anita sighed as she patted her hips. "They're young and a lot more active than me. They'll work it off a whole lot quicker than I could. These days I can feel the fat calories sliding right to my hips with each bite."

"I noticed it didn't stopped you from digging into the fried chicken and potato salad."

"No, it didn't. Every time Lyle brings home an order of fried chicken from the Fork & Spoon, I tell myself, with each bite, I'll do extra time on the treadmill."

Rachel grinned. "Ah, yes, the good old treadmill. The piece of equipment you keep in your bedroom to drape clothes rather than hang them in the closet or throw them in the laundry."

"The very same," Anita said, giving her friend a back handed swat on the arm.

Anita directed Rachel to the chair at her station and sat in the one opposite her. "So fill me in on the latest. I haven't seen you in a couple of days. You were so busy after you heard the news and then you were in demand greeting everyone who paraded through your place. I called a couple of times yesterday and got the answering machine. I assumed you weren't home."

"I was out most of day. I really appreciate you helping Kathy and Mel clean the kitchen."

Anita wave the comment aside. "Don't mention it. You looked ready to collapse when I left. The last thing you needed to do was take care of the mess in the kitchen."

"Why didn't you leave a message? I would've called you back."

"I figured you were up to your eyeballs in alligators because somebody drained the swamp. Even though you and Dave were in the process of divorcing there's probably a ton of legal stuff to be handled."

"Amen to that statement. Mr. DeCarlo told me the government can be a pain when it comes to letting someone die."

Anita nodded. "I remember when Harriet's father passed away, it took her about two years to get everything settled and all because the bank put her social security number on his bank account as the primary owner after her mother died. The IRS kept adding it to her income every year. She finally had to hire a lawyer to take care of the problem."

"Now that you mention it, I do recall what happened. It was a nightmare. Then again, I'm a step ahead because I already have an attorney."

"I knew we would catch up with each other sooner or later. I don't want to interfere if Jeremy is busy consoling the widow."

"What makes you think he's *consoling* me?"

"Come on," Anita responded, one brow raised clear to her hairline. "You're talking to the woman with the beauty shop. All the news worth repeating passes through here. Plus, you don't live out in the boondocks like Roy and Joette Bradley. Your comings and goings hit the neighborhood telegraph almost the moment they happen. Then there's the hospital grapevine. So far there's been no report from the Fearsome Foursome that the lights go off and he doesn't leave."

Rachel knew she would have to be very careful in the near future. No one would believe if the house was dark it was because she'd blown a fuse. Thank goodness she had circuit breakers and knew how to manage them.

Where did that thought come from? Not everybody turns the lights off when they're making love.

"Speaking of Jeremy, he came over yesterday. He drove me to Mr. DeCarlo's office, the bank, then took me to lunch." She swiveled from side to side in the chair. "He doesn't want me to be alone in case I need someone neutral to talk to."

"So he's pulling a Julius Caesar?"

"A what?" That statement threw Rachel for a loop. What in the world was the woman talking about?

"You know that Shakespeare thingy—lend me your ear."

Rachel burst out laughing. "It may be apropos, but Julius Caesar didn't say that, it was Mark Antony. It's what he said at Caesar's funeral. *I've come to bury Caesar not to praise him.*"

Anita waved her hand in the air. "Whatever, whoever. English Lit wasn't my strong suit. Lilly Beth Helmick had a tough time teaching me. All I know is I read it somewhere. So fill me in. What's happening in your life these days? I know you haven't been working for the past couple of days."

"I took two weeks off to try to get the legal stuff resolved. It seems every time I turn around I'm signing another piece of paper. Since our divorce wasn't final, it's up to me to handle Dave's estate. I have to get death certificates in order to get the house transferred solely to my name. Then I need one to satisfy the insurance company so I can get the money. Also, I learned because our divorce wasn't final, I am liable for any of his outstanding bills. Considering where he lived when he died, that may take a while."

"Lordy mercy, a person can't die these days."

"I hear you. After my sister's husband died, she even had to get a death certificate for a tire dealer. Seems Patrick had purchased some kind of insurance when he bought tires. She still gets at least one phone call a year for him. After a while she started telling the caller good luck reaching him."

"Let's hope that doesn't happen to you. You need to get Dave out of your life and get a started on a new one of your own."

"Don't be so harsh, Anita. The man's dead. Besides not every year was bad except last two." Rachel rethought that one. "Well—maybe it was more like three or four. Last night when I was going through a closet and packing up the rest of the clothes he left behind, I came across a couple family albums."

"And you sat down and paged through them."

"Yes, I did. We had some good times. Dave was a good provider, but he wasn't as active with the boys as he could have been, especially when they played sports. He would brag to friends when they won an award. Sad part was he didn't tell them."

She scooted down in the chair and glanced around the shop, uncomfortable with the feeling her chin was about to tremble. "Even with everything that has happened I don't want to get rid of those pictures.

There was the one with him and the boys the one time he took them fishing and Mike is holding his catch…it was the size of a sardine. And the one of him holding Davy on his bicycle without training wheels." Her eyes started to water and she took a deep breath. "I'm going to let Davy and Mike pick the ones they want."

"Sounds reasonable, but that was part of the problem with you and Dave. You were always too reasonable."

"It's past history and that's where it will stay."

"I have to admit it was decent of Dave to take out an insurance policy." Anita gave a quick disbelieving head shake. "I always thought you and I were pretty close. I was really hurt that you didn't tell me about the insurance policy."

"I didn't know he took one out. He told me years ago he had, but that was years ago, then said he had cancelled it when the premiums were hiked. Are you sure I didn't tell you about it the day we got the news?"

Anita shook her head.

"If I didn't, how did you hear about it?" Rachel shifted in the chair. She was sure life insurance wasn't mentioned except among the family and Jeremy; she couldn't picture him saying anything to anyone.

"Believe me, my dear; I would've remembered that kind of windfall. As to how I heard about it, there aren't many events in Calusa that aren't discussed in my shop. Fern Martin couldn't wait to reveal that tidbit when she came for her weekly manicure. She said her husband wrote the policy."

Rachel got up and went over to the box on the counter, grabbed a bag of cookies and brought them back and offered some to Anita. "With so much going on, telling you about the insurance policy must've slipped my mind."

She took two. "I'll cut you some slack this time. Anyway, let's concentrate on the present and your options for the future."

"I talked to the boys." Rachel paused to brush some crumbs from her shirt. "I wanted to set up trust funds for them, but they declined. Told me to take the money and enjoy myself."

"Sounds like a sensible plan to me." Anita watched Harriet set up the six foot folding table. "Harriet, I think we'll keep the perishables in the refrigerator until the afternoon rush starts." She glanced at the clock. "Never mind, your next two appointments should be here in about fifteen minutes."

"Okay. In case you're interested, I've been listening to your conversation and so far you don't need any input from me," Harriet chirped as she placed the towel at the shampoo stations.

"I'm sure Rachel is relieved to hear that." Turning back to Rachel, Anita said, "So did you drop by to deliver food, or do you need a trim?"

Rachel looked in the oval mirror and tilted her head right and left. She lifted up her bangs and moved them around before finger brushing the sides behind her ears, then toward her face. "If you have time, I'm getting a bit shaggy around the ears. What do you think?"

Anita viewed her with a critical eye. "It wouldn't hurt and your timing is perfect. My next appointment called to say she was running about a half hour late." Anita stood, glanced at the clock, then grabbed a cape and draped it around Rachel's shoulders and fastened it in the back. She picked up her comb and scissors. "We have plenty of time. Any plans for tonight?"

"Since we've had leftovers the past two nights, Jeremy suggested driving over to Portofino's in Charlotte Harbor. We both like the food there." She also liked the fact that she usually didn't run into anyone she knew.

"You've been there often? I thought his favorite place was the Captain's Net?"

"It is, but tonight we thought we'd go somewhere else for a change. I wouldn't say we go to Portofino's *often* unless you count the two times we went with you and Lyle. Other than that, we've only been there once."

"Don't get me wrong, I think it's great you're getting out. Plus, I'm sure it is nice to go where not everybody knows your name, if you get my drift."

Rachel rolled her eyes. "I get your drift and I'm soooo glad I have your okay."

"Watch your sassy mouth, my dear, or the scissors might slip and you'd end up with more than a trim."

"What do you mean *sassy*? I'd never be sassy with someone holding a pair of scissors next to my ear."

Chapter 16

Rachel hurried into the house. It seemed life had been going at breakneck speed since Dave died. Each day was spent dealing with the lawyer or the bank.

Today was her first back to work since she got the news about Dave and all day had felt like a new employee. The hospital installed a much-needed new computer program during the two weeks she was away and though she'd attended training sessions before she left, it seemed like nothing had gone right.

After a quick glance at the clock, she knew there was no need to rush to get ready but she couldn't dawdle either. Jeremy was picking her up to take her out to dinner. He insisted the first day back to work, after being off for almost two weeks, was not a day to come home and worry about cooking dinner.

She had no complaints. It was good to get out of town for a while, even if it was only for a few hours. No matter where they went in Calusa they ran into someone she knew. Somebody who would try to get an update on her life, especially about the insurance policy. Apparently that bit of news circulated faster than the speed of light. No one actually came out and asked her what she planned to do with the money, but it was easy to pick up that they were definitely trolling for information.

Rachel was out of the shower and half-dressed

when she heard Jeremy's voice coming from the kitchen. "I know I'm a bit early, so don't rush. I'll keep Miss Daisy company for a while."

"Thanks," she called from the bedroom. "It was a wicked day at work, I'll tell you about it later over a cool adult beverage."

"I'm all ears."

"Help yourself to something to drink while you wait."

She went to the closet and took out a slim line white skirt and a new top in lipstick-red. She bought it because the square neckline was flattering and gave her a sense of confidence. The only drawback was the attached spaghetti string undershirt in the same color. Not only were they attached at the neck, but they were sewn into the side seams. Luck was with her. She slipped it on, then donned her favorite half circle gold earrings. She went to the mirror to give herself a last minute check.

Poop on a stick!

Her sensible white bra straps showed beneath the undershirt no matter how she pulled and tugged them into place. Securing them in place with safety pins wouldn't work because the neckline always came out uneven. She rummaged through her lingerie drawer to find the right bra and grabbed a red lace underwire she'd bought last week because it made her feel wicked sexy. She should have put it on to start with rather than be in a hurry. Glancing at the clock she realized it was later than she thought.

She quickly shimmied her arms out of the sleeves and straps of the cotton camisole and changed her bra. *Okay, now all I have to do is slip my arms back in the sleeves.* It only took a few seconds for her to realize she was hopelessly stuck. The strap on one side of the camisole was caught in the hoop earring. On the other side one arm was lodged between the camisole and the blouse. If she tried to pull it over her head, she'd rip the thin strap—or jerk the earring out of her ear. Either way, she was between a rock and a hard place.

What could she do? She couldn't stand here with her arms over her head and the blouse covering her eyes. She recalled a woman who had come through the emergency room a couple of years ago in a similar situation. In that case, the patient got so stuck, she yanked on the top and managed to slice through her ear lobe with the post of the earring. Lots of blood as Rachel recalled—and many tears, mostly of embarrassment. There was only one solution.

Voice muffled by a couple layers of fabric, she called out, "Jeremy, could you come in here for a minute? I'm in a bind."

Jeremy grinned to himself. Now there was an interesting invitation—if one wanted to read an underlying meaning into it. Knowing Rachel, he was sure a roll between the sheets wasn't what she had in mind. He stopped suddenly and laughed out loud when he walked in her bedroom.

"I wish I had a camera," was all he got out as he gasped for breath and continued to laugh.

"I'm glad you don't."

"Honestly, Rachel, this picture is worth more than a thousand words," he hooted. "You look like you're being swallowed by a giant strawberry."

"I'm not up to any light-hearted banter at this point. Please help; I'm literally stuck here."

He stood back, wondering where to start. "Give me a minute here so I can assess the situation."

He would've had to be blind not to notice the sexy red lace bra and hoped he didn't start perspiring. It wouldn't look good if the first thing she saw when she was free was him, tongue hanging out and panting like Miss Daisy. "No problem. Stand still until I get this, whatever you want to call it, unhooked from your earring."

He took his time only to notice that whatever was under the sheer blouse was now twisted sidewise...on the wrong side. "Do you want me to help you slip the whole shirt off so you can start from the beginning?"

He heard her audible sigh as she begged. "Please."

"Okay, as long as you don't think I'm being fresh or taking advantage of the situation, this disrobing is going to go more smoothly if I get my hands under the inside shirt and sort of peel it back."

"Go for it." She didn't give a rat's ass if it sounded suggestive as long as she was free of the damn top. The first things she was going to do was throw it in the trash.

She was acutely conscious of his warm hands as they skimmed up her sides so he could try to slide the shirt up and over her head. When he completed the task he handed it to her. She held it in front of her in an attitude of modesty and hoped her face was not as flushed as the heat she felt there.

Jeremy didn't say a word. He simply kissed the tip of her nose. "I'll wait for you in the kitchen, kid."

She was too old to be embarrassed. After all, she'd been married many years. Jeremy had been married for years. Other than police work, she was sure he had seen women in their underwear before. Bottom line, he'd never seen *her* in her underwear. She had to give him major kudos for not making a move.

As for her feelings, she was not quite ready to address them. When his hands moved up the side of her body her skin tingled. The sensation was so darned good she didn't want him to stop. Damn, it felt so *pleasurable* it made her wonder what it would feel like to have his hands on other places. She would have been okay with a kiss on the lips rather than the nose.

****

Back in the kitchen, Jeremy poured a glass of cold water and took a big gulp. Was this a missed opportunity? A lesser man might have taken advantage of her dilemma, but that was not his style. Rachel was a real lady. A gentleman took care of a lady. But she looked so darn cute when she stood there holding the top in front of her he couldn't resist stealing a kiss, even if it was on her nose.

He couldn't pounce when she was in distress. Guys who did were labeled as slimeballs. No way did he want that title at his age. He would maintain the status quo. Go with the flow. Enjoy the moment. Even if it killed him. He was not the type to hit on new widows. On the other hand, if she had given him any hint she was ready for more, who knows what would've happened?

****

It was a perfect summer night in Southwest Florida to dine outdoors, provided you were in a screened area and the ceiling fans were moving the air and no-see-ums. Some might say she was crazy, but Rachel preferred sitting in the open air rather than in a more formal air conditioned restaurant. On the way to Port Charlotte she asked Jeremy if he would mind going back to Portofino's. He said her wish was his command. She also liked the more casual atmosphere in the bar area with the tiki hut theme. Of course it would be noisy and the TVs would be on but not the sound which was okay with her because it was essentially a sports bar.

Jeremy led her to a table for two, close to an open area with a view of the water. As always, he pulled out a chair to seat her. He signaled to the waitress and gave their drink orders. "I know you like to sit so you can look out over Charlotte Harbor. Who knows? We might be lucky this evening and catch sight of some dolphins or a manatee."

Chalk up another point in his favor. He remembered what she liked and made sure these past few weeks were as stress-free as he could make them. In her mind that was the essence of being a good friend. Her family, co-workers and other friends were supportive, but there always seemed to be a question mark at the end of their sentences, as if they were waiting for her to reveal some deep dark secret. With Jeremy it was different. He let her set her own pace. He was a good listener and he didn't ask intensely personal questions.

"Wouldn't that be lovely," Rachel said as Jeremy took a seat across from her.

"Wouldn't what be lovely, sweetheart?" a male voice said, from behind her.

Before she even heard the voice, Rachel saw the perturbed look on Jeremy's face. The entire ambiance of the place slid down the tubes at the sound of Chas

Martin's pronounced southern accent. Before she could answer or an invitation was offered to join them, the guy dragged a chair from another table and pulled it up next to her.

He was so close, she swore if she turned her head she could count the hairs in his prominent nose. This was too much, but she couldn't move. He had her pinned against the side wall. So much for having a nice dinner and enjoying the view. Jeremy had to see her cringe from Chas' actions. For God's sake the man was an ex-cop. Observation was his forte. He seemed to be waiting for her to take the lead.

The place was packed with the Friday after-work crowd. Under the present circumstances, the last thing she needed was make a scene. As she recalled, Chas was known for his short fuse. Dave used to say back in the day he'd always been quick to start an argument.

She couldn't sit here mute, staring at Jeremy, hoping he would take the lead. Mouth dry as an old wine cork she pasted a weak smile on her face. "It would be lovely to see some creatures out in the harbor. Maybe something dangerous, like an old rogue alligator, but so far I haven't spied any. Maybe they're roaming around on dry land this evening."

She raised an eyebrow and glanced at Jeremy. He grinned, gave a quick wink, and covered it by rubbing his eye. Yes indeed, he got her message.

Chas rocked back on his chair, totally missing the underlying meaning to her comment. "Yeah, I read in the paper about a couple of folks around here finding 'gators in their yard lately. One lady I know almost ran over one a few of days ago. I don't think you're going to find any here, not with a chain link fence along the

246

back by the water. Do y'all come here often?"

The waitress came with their drink order. Rachel was thankful Jeremy didn't ask for a menu. He was obviously picking up on her discomfort.

"Not too often," she said. For sure she would not suggest they come here again. "In fact, we only stopped in for a drink."

"Oh, are y'all going someplace else? Where?" Totally ignoring Jeremy, Chas inched his chair closer. "Maybe I'll tag along."

How am I going to get away from this jerk? She cleared her throat and shot Jeremy a pleading look.

"I don't think so," Jeremy said, glancing at his watch. He stood, gave the waitress the high sign for their check, and walked around the table. He managed to move Chas' chair with his leg so he could help Rachel out of hers. "Sorry, honey, I didn't realize what time it was. If we don't hurry we're going to be late meeting Elmer and Minnie."

Without giving Chas further regard, Rachel took Jeremy's hand. "My heavens, you're right. Time got away on us. Elmer is such a stickler for punctuality. So sorry to cut this short, Chas, but we've got to run."

Once they got to the car she asked, "If you don't mind my asking, who are Elmer and Minnie?"

Opening the car door for her, he grinned. "Elmer Fudd and Minnie Mouse, who else? And I hear Mickey is really ticked off about them seeing each other on the side. Goofy spilled the beans."

Rachel held her hand over her mouth, but a girlish giggle escaped. "I'm sure he would be. Incidentally, it was very generous of you to slip the server a tip on the way out. I'm sure she appreciated it greatly, along with the entertainment."

Jeremy shrugged. "No problem. If she works there she probably knows all about your friend Chas."

Rachel winced. "He's no friend of mine. The few times I've been around him, he always makes me feel like I need a shower."

Jeremy started to go the side. He had to chase the picture of Rachel in the shower, water beading up on her skin, out of his head. Not that it was an image he *didn't* want to dwell on.

He got in the car, started the motor and drove out of the parking lot, checking the rearview mirror to be sure they weren't being followed. "Honestly, Rachel, your face went sheet white when you heard his voice. In fact, I thought for a minute you might faint."

"I'm no shrinking violet, but I did feel like I wanted to upchuck."

"Glad to hear it…that you're no shrinking violet. While we're still on the subject, I loved the 'gator comment. I had to bite my tongue so I wouldn't laugh out loud. Chas is so obtuse, he never caught on."

She gave him a gentle elbow poke in the ribs. "I saw you wink. It was mighty slick the way you covered it by pretending something was in your eye."

"Glad you caught on. Is the guy giving you any problems I don't know about?"

"Not so far. At least none I can't handle."

"What do you mean?"

He had dealt with guys like Chas Martin in the past. The last thing Rachel needed was a stalker. He would have to be more alert about the traffic in the neighborhood. He had a contact in the sheriff's office. He'd meet him for a brew and pick his brain. If Chas was the local Lothario, there was bound to be a buzz.

"Of late he's left quite a few messages on my answering machine, but I've deleted them."

"Be careful " He reached over and took her hand. "Promise me if it gets out of hand, you'll call me and we'll report it to the sheriff."

She squeezed his hand. "I don't think we have to worry about it going that far."

Jeremy pulled out of Bayshore Drive and merged onto US 41 to go over the bridge. "Maybe, maybe not. Be careful and keep me posted if he tries anything kooky."

"I will. Now, where are we meeting our new best friends, Elmer and Minnie?"

"I heard they absolutely love the food at the Oyster Bar at Fisherman's Village over in Punta Gorda."

"Really? Talk about coincidences, I heard the same thing. As for Chas, I think he's probably harmless. You know one of those guys who is all talk."

"Could be, but I want you to be alert. You live alone and you can't be too careful."

This whole scenario gave Jeremy the willies. Two cases from his days on the job at the Tampa PD came to mind. One woman lost every penny to a smooth talking con artist. The other poor soul was not so fortunate. Apparently she didn't cooperate with him and later her neighbors found her dead in the bathtub with rose petals covering the water.

"Not quite alone," she said. "I have Miss Daisy. I'm sure she'd let me know if someone is sneaking around."

Even though he was very fond of Miss Daisy, if the perp had a biscuit or a bone the dog would lick his hand

and beg for more. All the way to Fisherman's Village, Jeremy kept one eye on the rearview mirror.

****

Monday morning Rachel stood stock still, astounded as everybody stopped talking and stared after she walked into The Hair Lair. She felt like one of the spectacular displays over at Kelly McCabe's store, Memories. The kind everyone talked about. There was no way Rachel could believe she was *that* interesting.

No, ma'am, this was certainly not your typical small town beauty salon, Calusa type greeting. Her daughter-in-law sat quietly but couldn't hide the grin on her face. When Melinda didn't look her in the eye or jump up to greet her with a hug, Rachel was sure something was up. One quick glance told her the reason: her daughter-in-law had both feet in the pedicure foot bath.

Obviously this was not going to be a y'all come in, sit down and tell us what's been happening kind of gathering. It was more the come fill us in on the latest happenings in your life and once you do I can't wait to get out of here and spread all the juicy details. Not one person offered to start a conversation, other than the standard hello. They all acted like mimes. At least their mouths weren't gaping open with drool dripping down their chins.

Rachel felt she had to either break the ice or turn around and leave. She squared her shoulders, mentally took a deep breath and remained in the lion's den. "What gives, ladies? It's not like I'm not in here all the time." She glanced at her feet. "Am I wearing two different shoes?" She walked up to the edge of Harriet's empty station, leaned forward to look in the mirror and bared her teeth. "Nope, no food stuck in my teeth."

As she turned back to the room she noted Anita's expression. It was one of curiosity as she wrapped Sophie Jackson's head with a bright pink hair net. She hit the pedal lowering the chair, took Sophie by the arm, and led her to the dryer.

Pointing to the vacant chair, Anita said, "Grab a seat and take the load off your feet, Rachel, I'll be right with you as soon as I finish getting Sophie settled." She quickly got a cup of coffee and some magazines.

Rachel nodded and sat in the chair at Anita's station, wondering if she was in the proverbial *hot seat*. There was no wondering about it, she was. "I only stopped for a visit. Now I'm not so sure I should've."

Anita bent down close to Sophie's ear so she could hear over the noise of the dryer. "Do you want a stool to rest your leg, Sophie? I know you have to keep it elevated since you had a laser vein stripping."

"Thanks, hon," the older woman answered. "I appreciate your thoughtfulness. Could you get me a couple of pillows?"

"No pillows, but I can fold up a few towels." Sophie gave her a thumbs-up gesture.

When Anita finished, Rachel lowered her voice. "Why was everyone staring at me when I came in? Did I make the morning paper or something?"

"Don't be coy." Anita waggled her eyebrows and leaned back on her heels. "From what I hear it seems a lot has happened since you were in here last and that was only this past week. Are you holding out on me?"

"No way. I talked with you yesterday and caught you up on all the news." Rachel furrowed her eyebrow. "I don't have a clue what you're talking about."

"I think you left out an important incident." She leaned close to Rachel's ear. "There's a lot of talk going around town and, trust me, you're the star of those conversations."

Sophie ducked her head from under the dryer. "No whispering over there. It's difficult to hear under this dryer. I have to be on time for another appointment so get right to it. I don't want to miss a word."

"What she said," echoed Harriet.

Melinda sat in the electronic massage chair with a head full of foil wraps while Harriet worked on her pedicure. "Yes, Rachel, we're all ears." She glanced at the clock on the wall. "Hurry up because I only have a half hour before Harriet finishes my color. The word is, socially you're in great demand. Since you are such a fox, it won't be long until men will be fighting over the Widow Benton."

In order to give herself a few seconds to get her thoughts in order, Rachel got up, walked to the coffee pot, poured a mug, and carried it back to Anita's station. Clearing her throat, she took a sip and turned back to her daughter-in-law. "Really? Where is all this great *information* coming from?"

Anita went to the closet, got the broom and started sweeping up the hair around her station. "Colette told us this morning when she was in for a haircut."

"And, pray tell, who is Colette?" Rachel asked. She couldn't ever remember hearing that name before and she'd been coming to The Hair Lair since the day Anita opened the door.

"Colette is a new client. She was the server Jeremy slipped a twenty buck tip when y'all made a fast exit from the sports bar at Portofino's on Friday night.

Seems most of the folks there were disappointed when you boogied out so quickly. They were enjoying the performance."

"What performance? I don't recall seeing any kind TV show there, except for the baseball game and I can't say I was paying attention. Never did find baseball exciting to watch on TV. Going to a game is exciting. Jeremy left the big tip because we had to leave before she, Collette, had time to get our order," Rachel stated. Had she missed something while she was concentrating on trying to send distress signals to Jeremy?

Once again, Sophie ducked her head out from under the dryer bonnet and barked, "Don't be dense. From the account I heard, you did get your drinks and you left them on the table untouched. As for the game, nobody pays attention to the TV because there's no sound. We're talking about the Chas and Jeremy show. It must've been a doozy."

Rachel choked on her coffee. She grabbed a napkin to keep from spewing the rest of the liquid on her white Capris. She couldn't quite deny being there for that one. Instead she tried to diminish the issue. "What was the big deal? Chas was being obnoxious and intrusive, as only he can be. We simply got up and left."

Harriet slipped a pair of flip-flops on Melinda's feet and led her to a shelf of nail polishes to choose a color. "Even after he tried to invite himself along when Jeremy told him you were meeting another couple? The ones with the funny names. Oh, yeah, Elmo and Minnie. I don't ever remember hearing their names before. Are they from Calusa?" Harriet asked. "How did you meet them?"

Correcting Harriet on the names would open up

another can of worms. Enough had been opened already. "Do they have the place wired at the sports bar?" Instead of waiting for an answer she continued, "Have you heard anything from Corinne and Laura about their trip?"

Anita shot her a look that said *nice try*. "We'll discuss their trip later or better yet when they get back. I'm sure they're going to be sorry they missed all this excitement. Right now we want to hear from you. Details, please."

Melinda chuckled and raised her hand. "I second the motion. Aw, come on, Rachel, you know how the folks around here like a bit of gossip."

"Since Dave died I seem to be on center stage," Rachel muttered.

"We all get our turn, but everyone wants to hear the latest episode about Chas Martin and how he fancies himself a ladies' man," Harriet snickered. "I'm sure he considers you fair game. I'm also certain you were glad when Jeremy came to the rescue again."

Were there more stories circulating out there? The kind that aren't actually true, but if someone saw something they thought was interesting they added an attention-grabbing chapter before checking facts and passing it on. That was one of the reasons they had stopped going to the Captain's Net each Friday night. If Jeremy held the chair for her, one of the locals had them getting engaged.

"What do you mean, *again*?" she asked.

"Why, the day you found out Dave was dead. Davy was watching Chas like a hawk, ready to swoop down and carry him out the front door," Melinda chimed in. "He and my Mike were both upset, but they didn't want to make a scene. Mike held Davy back from wading into Chas. They both breathed a sigh of relief when Anita sent Jeremy to the rescue."

Anita raised her eyebrows in surprise. "I don't think you mentioned anything about your sons watching Chas."

"You were the one who sent Jeremy to rescue me, so don't play innocent with me. I even thanked you for doing it."

"Now I remember, yes you did," Anita commented. "My bad, it must've slipped my mind."

"A very convenient slip," Rachel muttered under her breath.

Anita poked her in the shoulder with the end of the hairbrush. "I heard you."

Harriet fitted the sponge separators on Melinda's toes, then rocked the bottle of Hot Mama Pink polish in her hand. "We all know Chas will hit on any female who is still breathing. Last time I ran into him at Harpoon Harry's he was bragging about how all he has to do is sit at the bar and women stuff their phone numbers in his shirt pocket. Claims he's a real *chick magnet.*"

"Come on," Rachel guffawed. "There aren't that many women desperate enough for male company they'd go for him. You did say it was Harpoon Harry's. Maybe, since he went out of Calusa, they didn't know about him. Was it during season? Perhaps they were tourists."

"Don't underestimate him; the guy has quite a line of bullshit," Harriet snickered. "I thought he was boasting until I saw someone do it."

Sophie pushed the dryer hood back. "Talk louder, I

can't hear you. What was he stuffing and where?"

Anita went over to her and repeated what Harriet had said before putting the hood back in place.

"Oh," Sophie hunched her shoulders, pursed her lips and shouted over the hot air. "I thought *he* was doing something naughty."

"No, he was *hoping* he could do something naughty," Melinda quipped after shooting her mother-in-law a sly smile.

Rachel shook her head. "I have to wonder sometimes if the man isn't all talk. Who in their right mind would put up with his kind of nonsense?"

"Obviously none of his five ex-wives," Anita said. "I heard they were so happy to get rid of him they didn't even ask for alimony. They didn't have a chance of getting any. His momma would not allow it. The man lives way beyond his means. He never met a credit card he wouldn't use. Kind of like the way he treats women. He seems to have a built-in radar for lonely women with money."

Rachel's jaw dropped. She had lived in Calusa most of her life and she had never heard that rumor. "How do you know?"

In a sing song voice, Anita and Harriet answered in unison, "Word gets around in a small, small town."

Harriet shook her head. "Since he's an only child, I understand he will come into a boatload of money when his momma passes. Right now she has him on a tight leash as far as cash is concerned, so he has to look elsewhere."

"His momma?" Rachel queried. "That woman has to be older than dirt. Does she still live in town?"

Anita shook her head. "Mrs. Martin lives on Long

Boat Key and I understand she's in her nineties."

"He must've been a change of life baby," Melinda said.

With a snort, Sophie lifted the bonnet again. "She was forty-three when she got pregnant. At the time, she thought she had a tumor. Maybe she would've been better off because I'm not sure he changed Alma Sue Martin's life for the better."

Harriet offered, "Info on the gossip vine is she never answers the phone without checking caller ID to be sure it isn't Chas."

"Holy moly, if his mother can't handle him, who can?" Rachel commented.

Anita brought a fresh stack of towels to her station and stowed them in side cabinet area. "Over the years Harriet has fixed a lot of hair in this town and heard the ladies talk, so she's got the low down on him. In spite of that she told me she even dated him one time. Said once was enough."

"Why would you do that?" Melinda asked.

"Because I was curious. I'm funny that way. He's not exactly ugly to look at." Harriet snickered. "He's no dreamboat, either, but he does have a good head of hair, and it's his own. Come to think of it he has all his own teeth. Yeah, I suppose you could count hair and teeth as a plus in his favor, until he opens his mouth; then it's all downhill."

Melinda sighed. "Back to word getting around town, doesn't it ever, and Calusa isn't small anymore. I mean when I was growing up we didn't have a place to hang out. If you did anything you shouldn't've your parents and all the neighbors knew about it five minutes later. If it was illegal you found yourself in the police beat section of the newspaper the next morning."

"It wasn't all bad, Mel," Rachel interjected. "If you think about it, that was a great way to grow up. There's something to be said for living in a small community and having folks look out for each other."

"I know now, but back then it was a different story. We felt confined. Not one of us had our own car. We walked or rode our bikes most of the time. We would've loved to have had a mall. There were no real restaurants, except the Captain's Net, and you couldn't go there to hang. We only had one traffic light on the Trail, now it seems there's one at every intersection."

Harriet scowled. "Aw come on, you should have been around when we were growing up. You had the Fork & Spoon and the big frozen custard place by the old Wal-Mart. Plus, you had the burger place. Keep in mind the world Chas grew up in had even fewer places to go for entertainment. Makes you wonder what happened to have him turn out the way he has. Of course, his momma saw that he had a car from the time he got his license. He used to call it his *passion pit*." Harriet said. "Come to think of it, I imagine he loves being talked about."

Anita put the dryer hood back in place over Sophie's head and kicked back in one of the dryer chairs. "You wouldn't believe what some of the women he's dated have divulged to me when they're sitting in my chair. Then, of course, some women tell me things they wouldn't tell a priest in confession. Things I don't want to know, but it doesn't seem to stop them. So short of putting my hands over my ears and singing la, la, la, I have to listen."

Sophie ducked her head out from under the dryer.

"Is that how you found out about Chas and the alimony?"

Anita leaned closer and raised her voice. "I had three of his five wives as clients—when they were married to him, and after the divorce. You know he only had two children and they were by his first wife." Anita held up two fingers and moved them is a scissor motion. "Makes me wonder if he had himself clipped."

Rachel raised one brow. "Could be."

"He certainly did," Sophie called out. "Old Doc Paulson did the surgery."

"How do you know?" Harriet asked.

Sophie shot her a mischievous grin. "I have my sources. What was his first wife's name? I have it on the tip of my tongue."

Harriet led Melinda to her station and started to remove the foil. "Vivian Rogers. She and the kids moved to Connecticut about a year after the divorce. She remarried right after she moved there. Her children are grown. The other two wives I know said they never hear from him, and they're not complaining."

"You sure know a lot about them," Melinda said.

Rachel got up and grabbed a cookie from the tray by the coffee urn and took a seat in the waiting area. "I remember Vivian. She was a gorgeous woman, tall, blue eyes, honey blond hair. Didn't Chas work for her father?"

"He sure did," Anita said.

Rachel bobbed her head. "I thought so. Didn't stop him from running around on her. As I recall his father-in-law caught him with another woman right after the first baby was born."

"It was *the* night the baby was born," Harriet said.

Sophie pushed the dryer hood back again. "I think I'm dry, Anita. Now that you've brought it up, I recall Mr. Rogers wanted Vivian to leave Chas then, but she said she wanted to try to work things out."

Anita led Sophie from the dryer to the chair and started removing the rollers. "All his women were real lookers. As for you, Miz Sophie, it's a good thing your hair is short and dries quickly. Otherwise, you'd be late for your next appointment."

"This conversation is too good to miss. I'll call and say I'm running late. As for Chas' women being real lookers, I have to agree. Back to Hal Rogers, he was furious when he found out about Chas."

"How did he find out?" Melinda asked.

"Someone saw Chas at a bar and called Vivian at the hospital. Hal happened to be there. You know how that old man doted on Vivian. In spite of her begging her father not to do it, Hal drove straight to the bar and fired Chas on the spot." Sophie snorted. "Not that it stopped Chas from chasing skirts."

"How do you know all this stuff?" Melinda asked.

"My husband and I were there, watching Chas and a surgically enhanced blond do some major lip sucking while sharing the same stool. Trust me, it was a lot more interesting than what was going on the TV. It got even better when Hal walked in."

Rachel moaned. "You could say Chas still likes to create a scene. As I recall he always had a thing for blondes. In fact all of his wives were blond."

Anita looked at Rachel through the mirror, placed her upturned hands under her breasts, and jiggled them. "And they all had big boobs."

"Yeah, you might say it takes one to know one,"

Harriet quipped, adding, "Now I have to wonder what's made him move on to redheads?"

Rachel breathed a sigh of relief that Harriet hadn't said flat chested redheads. She wasn't flat chested, but she was no Dolly Parton in that department.

Harriet glanced out the front window as she worked on Melinda's hair. "Would you believe a big old black Mercedes pulled up out front?" A second later she said, "Whoever it is they have a driver. He got out and opened the back door. Oh my God in heaven above, it's Alma Sue Martin. And she's coming in here!"

The door opened and in walked the epitome of the word *dowager*. The women stared as Mrs. Martin scanned the room with narrowed dark eyes, just shy of a sneer that could in no way be mistaken for a smile. Her skin was translucent, her make-up artfully applied. A mass of silver hair was styled in a French twist with a deep wave smoothly arranged by her right eye. She looked like she had stepped out of a salon and into clothes off the pages of *Vogue*.

Mrs. Martin was a striking woman—until Rachel glanced at her hands. The veins were thick as clothesline, but the diamonds drew her eye. She had one on every finger as well as in her elongated earlobes. Despite the heat and humidity of the August afternoon, her white slacks were crisp, the tangerine over-blouse wrinkle-free.

"Who is the woman who insulted my son? Made him the laughing stock of the bar when he was trying to be civil to her."

All of the ladies stared at her, knowing very well who she was referring to as it had been the topic of conversation.

Anita stepped forward and, making an effort to sound above suspicion, asked, "What are you talking about, Mrs. Martin?"

"My son said a woman spurned him at a restaurant when he tried to speak to her on Friday night."

Anita had to bite the inside of her cheek not to burst out laughing. The mere thought of Chas having his mother track down Rachel was ludicrous. "What makes you think that person would be here?"

"Because after I spoke to Charles this morning, I called a friend here in town. She knew who it was and was sure she came to your shop. I went to this Rachel person's house first, but she wasn't home."

Rachel stood. "I'm Rachel Benton. I'm afraid you were misinformed by your son."

Mrs. Martin raised a well-arched penciled eyebrow. "Are you intimating my son is a liar?"

This woman was beyond the pale. She would lose ground if she gave in to her temper. No way would she let the woman intimidate her. "No, ma'am, I'm simply saying your son was mistaken. I didn't hear anyone laughing when I was on my way out of the place."

"It happened after you left. Charles said he was so embarrassed he had to leave as well."

Rachel fought to keep her cool. "I'm sorry to hear that. Why are you here? Does Chas still have to run home to his mother and cry on her shoulder? I'd say he's a bit long in the tooth for that type of behavior."

Mrs. Martin sniffed. "He happened to call me about another matter. It merely cropped up during the course of our conversation. And, my son's name is Charles not Chas. We do not have nicknames in our family. The reason I came to see you is, if you think you have any chance of obtaining any of my money by getting your hooks into my son, think again."

Without uttering another word, the woman turned and made for the door, not waiting for a reply, and—as fast as someone her age could—walked out the shop.

Anita came up to Rachel and put her arm around her. "Did any of that conversation make sense?"

Rachel sighed. "Unfortunately, it did. My take is Chas was talking to his mother, for whatever reason, and he skewed what happened to his favor in hopes of attaining his goal."

"You could be right," Sophie said as she walked up to the register. "Haven't seen Alma Sue in years, but she hasn't lost any of her charm, and I use the term loosely. She always did feel she was too good to live in Calusa with us peons."

"Whatever the reason, I still maintain Chas is not telling the truth," Rachel said.

"I agree with Rachel. The man is a well-known liar," Harriet said. "Either he called his mother or someone she knows was at Portofino's and called her. Get my drift?"

Rachel's hands were shaking when she grabbed her purse and made for the door. "I don't give a rat's ass who told her. All I know is, I have no plans to *get my hooks* into her son. Even if his ass came packed with diamonds, I don't care if I ever set eyes on Charles Martin as long as I live."

Anita put her hand over her mouth. "My goodness, girlfriend, I've never heard you using potty language."

Rachel fisted her hands at her sides and clenched her jaw. "There's a first time for everything."

Chapter 17

Between her sons looking out for her, Floyd Patterson waiting by her driveway when she got home, Al Kohn greeting her when she went outside each morning for the newspaper, or Anita killing her with kindness, Rachel didn't know whether to scream, cry or burst into hysterical laughter from all the protection. Kind of like her own personal bodyguard squad.

If she could locate her sister, maybe she and Jeremy could meet Trina at a half-way point—depending on Trina's location at the moment. Bottom line, she did not want to leave town without him. Though he'd become her rock during all this, there were times when a woman needed her sister.

No use wasting time wringing her hands and hoping Trina would call. Rachel knew she would hear from her in her own good time. No matter how much it appealed, she couldn't leave town until all the loose ends were tied up. A knock at the door interrupted her erratic thoughts. *Please God, let it not be Chas Martin or someone else wanting to know the whole story.* If she had one more drop by visit from either Betty or Elsie she'd run screaming into the street.

"Hold on a minute," she called as the knocking persisted. "I'm coming,"

When she opened the door, she found her sister and a gentleman standing on the other side. Rachel didn't take a minute to say hello, come in, or good to see you. She simply fell into Trina's open arms. "I'm so happy to see you," she cried, knuckling tears from her eyes. "You're the answer to my prayers. Come in, come in."

Trina motioned for the man to follow. "Andy, we can get the suitcases later."

"Why didn't you call?" Rachel asked as they followed her into the living room.

"I did. Several times, but there was no answer. I got worried and that's why I'm here."

"I've been in and out a lot lately. Why didn't you leave a message?"

Trina dropped her pocketbook on the floor. "You know how I hate talking to machines. They're so damn impersonal. Andy and I were on the road and we decided to head straight on to Calusa. Andy," she bellowed, "come here a minute, let me introduce you to my sister."

Trina held out her hand to a tall lean gentleman with kind brown eyes and a gray GI buzz haircut. "Rach, this is my husband, Andy. We got married two weeks ago in Maryland."

Rachel clutched her chest and backed up a few steps. "Oh my God, Trina, I don't know if I can take many more surprises."

Trina put an her arm around Rachel's shoulder. "Rather than stand here, let's go to the kitchen and get something to drink so you can catch me up on everything."

As they sat around the table drinking iced tea, Rachel filled them in on how her divorce had been cancelled because of what happened to Dave. "So I was almost to the end of the waiting period for our divorce to be final when I got the word he was dead."

Trina nodded toward her husband. "I filled Andy in on your divorce on the drive down. That's why he suggested we should come visit to see if you were doing okay, and if we could lend a hand with anything. The divorce was a shocker, but hearing about Dave dying just about knocked my socks off. Was it really a great white shark attack?"

Rachel grimaced and scrunched up her shoulders. "I don't know and I don't think it matters. The end result was the same."

Trina nodded. "I have to agree with you. Didn't mean to be insensitive in asking."

"No problem. I appreciate that you drove all this way. I truly do. It seems like my life has been a series of shocks lately. I can't believe you're married. Fill me in me about the two of you. How did you meet? When? Andy, Trina has never said a word about dating anyone."

Andy took Trina's hand and smiled. "We met at Arlington National Cemetery. I was there visiting my wife's grave. It was her birthday. She's buried three plots down from Pat."

Eyes glistening, Trina kissed the top of Andy's hand. "I was there because it was Pat's and my wedding anniversary. Andy and I have smiled and nodded to each other for the past couple of years. I thought it was about time we introduced ourselves."

"I was on the way back to my car when I saw Trina unlocking her car. I back peddled and asked her if she would like to meet for something cold to drink. You know how hot it is in DC in July."

"I thought sure, why not. You could say the rest

was history. Andy's wife had been a nurse in Desert Storm," Trina explained.

"We found out we had a lot in common, including traveling at the drop of a hat, as well as living out west," Andy said. "Several years ago I spent time in Wyoming, fell in love with the place and bought some land around Cheyenne. Trina told me that is one of her favorite spots as well. We're going to start building a home when we get back."

"How wonderful," Rachel said. "I am so happy for both of you."

Before she could say another word, Jeremy strolled in carrying a bottle of wine. "Hey, Rachel I thought we might...Oh, I'm sorry. I didn't realize you had company. I'll come back later."

Trina said, "I'm not company, I'm Rachel's sister and this is my husband, Andy." Turning to her sister, she said, "And who is this handsome hunk?"

Rachel tried not to blush as she made the introductions, but there was no way she could control the heat covering her face. She linked her arm with Jeremy's. "Jeremy has been my mainstay throughout this disaster. I don't know what I would've done without him."

Trina shot Rachel a crafty look, stood and gave Jeremy a hug. "I'm glad you've been here for my sister. Andy and I both know how hard it is to lose a spouse when the marriage is good. The stress must be a million times worse when it's the result of a divorce and you're left to take care of everything."

Jeremy laid his hand over Rachel's. "Your sister is a strong woman. She has handled the circumstances with great dignity."

Rachel cleared her throat. "We've been drinking iced tea. Why don't you open that bottle of wine I saw you carry in while we talk about where we can go grab a bite to eat."

A devilish glint in his eye, Jeremy said, "I take it you don't want to go to Portofino's. It's a quite a drive over there. I'm sure Andy and Trina are a bit tired of riding in a car."

Rachel gave him a nudge in the ribs with her elbow. "I thought we could go to the Captain's Net."

"Are they still in business?" Trina asked. "I thought they might've gone out of business after Hurricane Charley."

"Cliff Gardener rebuilt after the hurricane," Rachel said. "The inside is updated and the food is still great."

"Why don't you give Davy and Mike a call?" Trina asked. "They can join us at the restaurant or come over here for coffee.

"Sure." Rachel felt it was safe because her son had been on very good behavior. "I'll pick up some dessert at the Publix Market on the way home."

****

One look at Davy's face told Rachel she was wrong. He couldn't wait to share his opinion with his aunt. She should have given Trina a heads-up on what had been happening.

Davy kissed his aunt. "Have you met Mom's new boyfriend?"

"I have and I think he's terrific."

Mike rolled his eyes. "Here we go again. When are you going to give up copping a 'tude, bro?"

"When I'm good and ready," he snapped.

Trina linked her arm in Davy's. "Until you walk in

268

your mom's shoes, button your lip, young man."

"But…"

"You know, Davy, you always were a royal pain in the ass. For pity's sake, grow a pair and start actin' like an adult instead of a know-it-all teenager."

Trina looked surprised when Davy's wife, brother and sister-in-law clapped. Davy's kids stood and looked at her with their mouth hanging open.

Susan's mouth formed a big O. "Daddy, auntie said a bad word."

Davy shook his head and chuckled. "Yes she did, pumpkin, but I'm afraid she was right."

"I certainly am," Trina said. "See that your attitude improves by my next visit."

****

Rachel stood at the door and leaned against Jeremy's chest as she watched Andy and Trina drive away. The two weeks they had stayed seemed like one day. She wanted them to extend their visit for another week, but they were anxious to get back to Wyoming and start on their new home. They talked about getting together over the holidays, but made no definite plans.

Jeremy wrapped his arms around Rachel. "Trina and Andy are enjoyable to be around. I especially liked the way she handled Davy the first night. She didn't have any problem giving him an attitude adjustment. I wish I'd had a camera to record the gigantic grin covering Mike's face when Trina told Davy to grow a pair, quit acting like a know-it-all teenager and more like a grown man."

"I don't think Kathy was offended," Rachel said.

"If I had to guess, I'd say she was taking mental notes for future use."

They went back into the house. Once inside Jeremy framed Rachel's face with his hands and stared her straight in the eyes before he leaned down and taking his time, kissed her square on the mouth with a passion he'd been keeping on a tight leash.

When he stepped back she asked, "Why did you do that? I mean...that is..."

Jeremy laid his finger gently across her lips. "Couldn't resist any longer. I think you're one terrific woman and I've wanted to do that for a long time."

She reached up and covered his hands with her own. "Me, too," she said and kissed him back.

Jeremy cocked an eyebrow. "Could I interest you in a little necking on the couch?"

She took his hand. "I'll lead the way."

"It might lead to more. No, it will definitely lead to more. I can't be around you and hold out much longer." He slid his hands down her back and pressed her close. "If I have to take any more cold showers I'm going to be nominated for sainthood."

"Believe me, I'm more than ready," she said, took his hand and by-passed the den on the way to her bedroom.

Once inside she kicked door shut with her foot and started to unbutton his shirt while he danced her to the edge of the bed. He wanted to undress her but she stopped him. "Let me." She had him down to skin in seconds. "Your turn."

"Aren't you scared the neighbors are counting minutes until I leave?" he said as he slipped off her blouse to see her wearing the sexy red lace bra he'd seen before. Only now he didn't hesitate to unhook it and toss it across the room.

She swiveled to push him onto the bed. "I don't give a damn if they're outside selling tickets."

A growl came from deep in his throat as he pulled her down on top of him. "That's my woman."

****

The next morning she woke up to Jeremy planting kisses on the side of her neck. Ah, it had been so many years since she had felt this good.

"Sleep good?" he asked.

"Better than I have in ages," she said, pulling his face toward her and kissing him deeply.

"Do you want to go out for breakfast?"

She ran her hand down his back, stopping at his thigh. "What I want for breakfast isn't on the menu at the Fork & Spoon."

He chuckled and rolled her over on her back. "In that case, I'll give you my AM special."

****

Life with Rachel was fantastic, especially after their relationship came out in the open. Nevertheless, the nagging feeling that came whenever he thought about Chas Martin refused to leave. Rachel said she didn't mention Chas to Trina for fear her sister would worry. She also didn't think there would be any further problems with Chas since her relationship with Jeremy was known.

He just couldn't ride that train of thought. The seasoned cop inside told him something wasn't right about the guy. For weeks the man had worked like hell to insinuate himself into Rachel's life, then, all of a sudden, he was nowhere to be seen. Jeremy didn't think it had anything to do with Mrs. Martin coming to see Rachel at Anita's shop. More likely it was because

Chas heard that Rachel's sister was in town and staying at the house with her husband. Was it the men in the mix that kept Martin at bay? What would it take to convince the guy? The man's hot and cold behavior didn't ring true, and Jeremy was sure sooner or later he'd slither back onto the scene. He had to have a motive, but according to Rachel, he'd never traveled in their social circle. Plus, she hadn't seen him in years, except to say hello when she occasionally ran into him around town.

So what made Martin start his pursuit at this particular time? Why not when Dave first scrammed out of town? News like that traveled fast around all the local watering holes, and Chas had *watering hole Romeo* written all over him.

If he'd been involved with someone else at the time Dave left, that could be why he waited. Making sure the coast was clear. But from what he'd heard, being involved with another woman at that time would not have stopped Chas Martin. Guys like him excelled at keeping several women on a string at one time. Based on hearsay, he should have been on Rachel's doorstep before the ink dried on the initial divorce petition.

Jeremy had been keeping an eye on the traffic on their street since the incident at Portofino's. He thought for sure Chas would be driving a slick sports car, maybe even a snappy convertible. The only vehicle that came by on a regular basis, and slowed when it passed her place, was a customized shiny black, full size van with lots of chrome trim. All that chrome struck Jeremy as a bit odd; at first, he didn't think anything of it.

Then curiosity got the best of him; he had a buddy in Tampa run the plates. Damn if it wasn't registered to

Charles Martin. Why would a spiffy sports car type drive a van?

It was time for a meeting with his buddy, Slick Hansen, a deputy with the Sheriff's Department. When Jeremy pulled up to the Captain's Net, there was Slick's beat up Honda. At least he wouldn't have to wait. Walking into the packed place he spotted Slick talking to a couple of men at the bar and headed their way.

"Hey, man, you're still in time for happy hour," Slick called out as he waved him over, "I want you to meet some of the locals. Greg McAfee and Fred Nelson, this is Jeremy Dunn. We worked together in Tampa."

Handshakes were exchanged and another round of beer ordered. "So what did you want to talk about?" Slick asked and swiped beer foam from his moustache.

Jeremy straddled the bar stool. "I wanted to find out what you know about a dude named Chas Martin."

The other two men burst out laughing. Greg was the first to speak. "You mean Mattress Chas?"

"AKA the Three-A-Day man," Fred added.

Jeremy shook his head to clear images of what Chas might be doing three times a day. The pictures became especially incongruous, particularly after learning of Mrs. Martin's claims about Rachel. "You've got to be shitting me. At his age once a night should be his max, well maybe twice if he has a long rest in between."

Slick patted Jeremy on the back and grinned. "Word around town is he orders Viagra by the case. Right, fellas?"

"The guy fancies himself a sex machine," Fred said, raising his glass and signaling the bartender for another round. "I don't know how women can fall for his line of bullshit, but apparently thcy do."

"It must be a very good line because he managed to nail your prim and proper cousin Lucy Carol," Greg said, waggling his eyebrows at Fred.

Fred shook his head in disgust. "Yeah, I never have been able to figure out how he accomplished that. Lucy Carol's nickname had been the *Ice Maiden* for as long as I'd known her. Don't know how he managed to thaw her, but he did a helluva job."

"We all wondered," Greg said. "Needless to say she didn't share how he did either; I mean get her to go out with him."

"Got your message," Fred said. "I'm sure you didn't expect her to share her relationship with the family. Chas must have a terrific technique because it took her long enough to get over him."

"I bet the family was glad a baby Chas didn't show up on the scene nine months later," Slick snickered.

"You can say that again. I thought my uncle Art was going to gunning for Martin, but Lucy Carol stopped him, saying it was her own fault for falling for Chas' line of bullshit," Fred said. "It was the first time I ever heard her swear, so she must've been pissed."

Greg grabbed a hand full of taco chips from the basket on the bar. "Well, she wasn't the first and I doubt if she'll be the last of his conquests. Maybe she gave him a scare because after they split he only hit on women past the child-bearing age. Then there's his mother. Don't know if you heard about her."

Jeremy nodded. His worst fears were being confirmed. "Indeed I have. Does she always run interference for him?"

Fred laughed. "Scuttlebutt has it she does, most of the time. My wife was telling me about the incident concerning your neighbor over at Anita's shop."

"News sure travels fast," Jeremy said.

Fred took a quick swallow of beer. "She's sort of got an inside track. She found out from her cousin, Harriet, who works there."

Slick stepped into the verbal fray. "Enough about Martin's momma. Let's talk about that big hulking black van he drives. He keeps the chrome on it shining like a diamond. Don't know where he does his parking for satisfying the ladies, but no one's caught him and believe me, we've tried. With so many undeveloped areas in the county, it's hard to patrol all of them."

Jeremy took a sip of his beer, grabbed a chip and dipped it in salsa. "I've seen it cruising along my street several times lately. I still think he's intent on scoping out my neighbor, Rachel Benton, no matter what his momma says. But what's with the van? I mean the way you said it, makes it sound down right sinister. It sure is sending me some mighty weird vibes."

Jeremy noted the way the three men exchanged glances as if each was waiting the other to take the lead. He was well aware Rachel was at a vulnerable stage, well not as vulnerable as she was right after Dave died, and he wanted to be sure she was protected.

"Come on fellas; is there something I *need* to know about this jerk?" He looked from one to the other. "I'm concerned for my neighbor."

"You should be," Greg said. "Chas has had a van since they first came out. It's always black. He has them customized at a place in Ft. Myers, takes out the two back seats. I hear he has a killer stereo system, mini fridge and a blow-up mattress back there and it's a well-known fact he likes to drive out to one of the more remote areas in the Port Charlotte/North Port area. That's where he likes to make his conquests. Ergo the name Mattress Chas."

"Yeah, and the three-a-day handle is one Chas created, not his women. We don't know if he's bragging or if it's on the up and up," Fred said. "No pun intended."

Jeremy whistled out a long breath. "No one has yelled rape or pressed charges?"

"Not to date," Slick said. "Maybe it's because his mother pays them off or he has a good seduction line and strings the ladies along for a while. In years past he managed to marry five of them, but he hasn't made another trip down the aisle for at least ten years. Maybe nowadays they're using him as much as he is using them. Also, you know there are always women who are attracted to the bad boy—or in this case, man, and are sure they can change him."

"Okay, you guys seem to know all about him. My question is why is he hitting on Rachel Benton now? Why not right after her husband booked? What's his motive?"

Slick leaned on the bar with his elbow. "If you ask me, it's money. Chas always could nose out money."

Playing dumb, Jeremy asked, "Money?"

"Yeah, the buzz around town is Dave left the widow well heeled," Slick said. "And his momma's control on the purse strings likely cramps Chas' style.

"How did he find out so fast? I mean he was on scene the day Rachel learned about Dave's death, does the sonofabitch have some kind of radar?"

"Didn't need it," Fred answered, "His cousin is the one who wrote the policy. Arlo Martin is not too bright when it comes to holding his tongue. He's the one who probably told Chas. In strictest confidence, of course."

"Well, I'll be damned," Jeremy said. "I'll have to become better acquainted with life in Calusa."

He also knew he was going to pay closer attention to the movements of the black van. He knew Rachel couldn't be coerced into having any kind of a relationship with Chas. She was a much too savvy a lady. Plus, she was *his* lady.

What bothered him was, up until the run-in with his mother, she hadn't taken the guy's behavior seriously. She still maintained he was a buffoon. In fact, now she seemed to take him less seriously.

That could be a huge mistake.

Chapter 18

Rachel pulled her purse out of her locker and checked her watch. The work day had gone well and even though she'd been busy as a one-armed paperhanger, she was actually leaving on time. When she got home she'd be able grab a quick shower, change and be over at Jeremy's a bit ahead of schedule.

They'd be able to chill and have a glass of wine before leaving for Chad's baseball game. She was so proud her grandson's team had advanced to the play-offs. She and Jeremy had made every game so far; no way would she miss the play-offs. Jeremy's presence at games, cheering Chad on to victory was giving Davy a whole different outlook on their relationship.

After the game the whole family planned on going out to eat at the Captain's Net. She had promised her grandson she would buy him his favorite coconut shrimp dinner if they made it to the play-offs. She had never reneged on a promise to her children or grandchildren and was not about to start now. When she made the promise, Chad asked if she would do the same if they won the championship. Before she could answer, Jeremy said it would be his treat.

Rachel wanted to cry when she thought how Dave had attended so few of the grandkids' sporting events. She was okay with baseball but had not known a lick about soccer in the beginning—and still didn't know much even after attending every game—but that never stopped her. Plus, Matt was big into soccer so she had a few more years of soccer ahead of her.

As for Miss Susan, dancing was her thing. Dave had missed out on so many of the simple pleasures in life in recent years. What a shame he had to leave his family and travel so far away to experience them.

She fished the keys out of her purse and headed for her car. After the family dinner tonight, she and Jeremy had plans centering on horizontal activity and featured a new nighty currently hanging in the closet. She would only wear it for a short time before it ended up on the floor. Then…

Once in the parking lot, she pulled up short. Chas Martin was leaning against the trunk of her car. She hoped the jeans he wore didn't have studs because if there were any scratches on the paint, either he or his momma would pay for the repairs. Damn, damn and double damn. What was Mr. Sleaze Ball doing here?

No getting around it, he was becoming a major problem as well as a royal pain in her rear. So far, trying to be nice wasn't working. She'd have to discuss the situation with Jeremy, get his advice on how to handle Chas because she was at her wits end on how to make sure the man got the message that she wasn't interested in him. Not now, not ever.

He pushed himself away from the car and started swaggering toward her. The man was too damn old to *swagger.* Add to that he was doing a poor job, and he looked downright silly. Merely seeing him attempt it made her blood chill in the summer heat.

"Hey, gorgeous. Not getting off late today, like you usually do."

Warning flags in her brain popped up. "How do you know what time I get off?"

"Sometimes when I'm passing by I see you getting in your car. Hey, it's Friday and I bet you'd like to kick back and rest. Thought I'd take you out for a drink, maybe get a bite to eat. Then we could head back to your place and for a while. Maybe watch a little TV."

Kick back?

The only thing she'd like to kick was his rear-end from here to Naples. The guy was like gum on her shoe. She'd give being polite one more try. "Thanks for the offer, but I can't do it today. I already have plans."

Moving closer, he rubbed one hand down her arm. "Plans can be rearranged, babe."

She wanted to vomit on his shoes. Stepping away from him, she opened her car door and slid into the driver's seat, making sure to close and lock the doors as she wouldn't put it past him to try to get in the passenger side. One good thing about driving a two-door car, he couldn't crawl in the back seat. She opened the window a few inches when he knocked on it.

"Don't be like this, babe. I want to spend some quality time with you."

In a tight voice, she said, "Chas, I don't like being called *babe,* nor do I comprehend why you would want to spend time with me. We barely know each other. Besides, I'm dating someone."

"If we spend more time together we would get more familiar with each other. We have Dave in *common.* You may want talk about him. About the old days or why he left. I'm ready to listen."

She was sure his definition of *familiar* and hers bore two entirely different slants. "Can't today. Have to be over at Davy's ASAP. My grandson's team is in the play-offs and I promised I'd be there to root for him." She was sure the last place Chas would want to be was around kids. She was right on the moncy.

"Okay, maybe some other time." He rested his hands on the roof of her car. "I'd like to get together with you alone sometime. Soon."

"It isn't going to happen."

A look of surprise crossed Chas' face. "Why not, babe?"

She crossed her fingers because her sister always said crossed fingers negated a lie. "Because I'm engaged."

"Engaged! To who?"

"Jeremy Dunn," she said as she put the car in gear and backed out of the slot. If the guy hadn't back pedaled as fast as he did she would've run over his feet. Looking in the rearview mirror she could've sworn he had a smirk on his face. No, it was more, he looked positively menacing.

It was definitely time to have a talk with Jeremy.

****

He answered on the first ring and after hearing the tone of Rachel's voice, came right over. When he walked through the door she was pacing the kitchen floor, biting on a knuckle. "What happened?"

She raced into his arms. He felt her tremble. "I'm starting to get scared."

"Tell me what happened."

She took his hand and led him into the den. She settled herself on the couch and patted the cushion next to her. "Come sit down. Perhaps I'm making more out of this than there is, but I am very uneasy."

Instead of sitting on the couch, Jeremy parked his bottom on the marble top coffee table in front of her and covered her shaking hands with his. "It must be something drastic because you're shaking like a leaf in a hurricane."

"Chas Martin was waiting by my car when I came out of work this afternoon. He wanted me to go for a drink." Before Jeremy could say anything she held up her hand. "That wasn't the part that bothered me. What frightened me was he knew what time I got off. He even mentioned I was on time today."

Jeremy lifted her hands, turned them over and kissed the palms. "The bastard. Sweetheart, I was afraid this was going to happen."

Her voice choked, tears spilling down her face, she asked, "Why is he doing this?"

Jeremy got up and sat next to her. He looped his arm around her shoulders, pulling her closed to his side. "Hate to tell you this honey, but he knows about the insurance policy. Don't get me wrong, it's not that you're not a beautiful, desirable woman. You are, and then some, believe me. Because I want you to feel safe, I've done a little investigating. The word on the street is he somehow finds out when women have money, then slinks in and makes his move."

"But I've tied my funds up in an annuity...and trusts for my grandchildren."

Jeremy kissed her on the temple. "I know; your family knows; Chas doesn't. He assumes he has a chance at comforting the grieving widow."

Rachel snuggled closer. "Not in this lifetime. Besides, I've met his mother."

"I heard."

"Obviously, it's all over town." She ran her hand over his smooth cheek. "Sorry I didn't tell you. I didn't want you to be upset. In retrospect, I thought it was pretty funny that he told his mother on me. I guess it wasn't so funny."

"Based on today's event, it wasn't. When things happen over at Anita's shop it's only matter of time until the story is repeated, but I didn't hear about it from Lyle. I met my buddy, Slick, over at the Captain's Net. He and a couple of his friends filled me in on Mr. Martin."

Rachel gave him a weak grin. "Lyle must have had a new disease he was concentrating on."

Jeremy nodded. "He bent my ear for a half hour yesterday, something to do with his feet." He smiled. "I only listened with one ear. Back to Chas, I'm getting concerned about his behavior. Not to frighten you, but it sounds like he's stalking you. I'd feel a whole helluva lot better if I took you to work and picked you up afterward for a while. What do you say?"

"I may be making more out of the situation than there is." A flush crept across her cheeks as she gave him a sideways glance. "I may have stopped him in his tracks."

"How?"

"I told him we were engaged."

Jeremy shot her a wide grin. "You'll get no objection from me, but don't be too sure it'll stop him."

"I was afraid you'd say that. As for taking me to work, it sounds like a good plan."

Jeremy turned her face and gave her a deep, tongue to tongue kiss, warm with promise for later in the evening. She didn't push him away. Rather she leaned in closer and enjoyed the moment.

When she finally came up for air, she said, "You always know exactly what I need."

"Glad for the vote of confidence. Now what do you say we get ready to go to Chad's game? We may never make it if we sit on this couch any longer. But later be prepared to pick up where we left off. We will discuss our engagement when we get home."

He watched Rachel walk into her bedroom and resisted the urge to follow. If he did they would never make it to the kid's game, they wouldn't even make it to the dinner. Instead, he went to the kitchen to call his friend Slick on his cell phone.

"Your dime," Slick answered.

"Get with the times. It's been a very long time since a phone call cost a dime, pal."

"You know what I mean. Why the call?"

Jeremy opened the slider and walked out to the lanai to give himself some privacy. "I think Chas the Mattress Man is becoming a genuine problem."

"How so?"

"He was waiting for Rachel when she got off work today. From the sound of the conversation he drives by the employee's parking lot at St. Anthony's to check on her. I've also seen his van on our street. He slows down when going by Rachel's house. Frankly, I think he's tailing her."

"Will she get a restraining order against him?"

"I don't think she's ready to admit he's stalking, but she did tell me she's frightened. What do you suggest?"

"Until the guy does something definite, there's not much we can do without her filing a complaint. Right now it hasn't been going on long enough, so there isn't much to justify a stalking complaint. From past experience you also know restraining orders aren't always worth the paper they're written on. He's free to drive on her street as often as he wants, and there's not much we can do about that. My suggestion is to keep a close eye on her and watch out for him."

"I wanted to let you know in case I have to convince Martin he needs to stay away from her."

"If by convince you're talking about a knuckle sandwich, you wouldn't be the first."

****

Since Jeremy had been driving her to work this past week her stress level had diminished greatly. The morning was fairly cool because there was no humidity, so she took advantage of the weather to work on the plants. The new philodendron was going crazy as was the new Christmas cactus. In past years her herbs fizzled after the first month, but this year they were staying healthy. She loved cooking with fresh herbs. The grapefruit tree Jeremy planted for her a couple weeks ago was doing great. It was a perfect day.

Miss Daisy was stretched out in her favorite corner to bask in the sun. Dave never understood how the dog could spend so many hours in the baking sun, while Rachel felt Miss Daisy was recharging her battery so she could drive her crazy with all that pent-up energy. Since Jeremy had come on the scene Daisy had calmed down more than she could've believed, mainly due to the daily workout he gave her.

Before she had the chance to disturb the pet, there was a knock at the front door. She came in the house and glanced at the digital clock on the stove. Who would be knocking on her door at nine in the morning? Jeremy always came through the back door. Her sons were at work and daughters-in-law always called before dropping by. Besides, if they needed to get in for something they all had a key.

It wasn't the UPS man. She hadn't ordered anything, but the way things had been going lately who knew. Anyway, the delivery person always left any packages by the door. The rapping persisted. Whoever was on the other side, it had better be important. She was going to ignore the knock but thought she'd better see who it was because it might be something regarding Dave from Pago Pago.

She opened the door to find Chas Martin, hand raised, about to knock again. The other hand carried a large donut box.

"Good morning, gorgeous." He slipped past her into the living room and made for the kitchen. Calling over his shoulder, "Do I smell a fresh pot of coffee? I sure could go for a cup."

Rachel couldn't believe her eyes as she watched him open cupboard doors until he found the cups. The nerve of this creep. "No, it isn't fresh. It's probably fried to a glue state by now."

Chas grabbed the coffee pot and poured a large mug full and pointed to the box he had placed on the table. "No matter. Once you dunk a few of those goodies it'll taste fine." He took a sip. "Not fried at all. In fact it tastes like you just made it. Whatcha got planned for today, sweetheart?"

Feeling more uncomfortable by the minute, it was clear that telling Chas she was engaged did not deter him. Everyone in town tagged him as harmless, but was he? The bigger question was how to get him out of her space. She had nothing planned, but needed to make up a reason to leave the house as quickly as possible and get to a safe place. There was no use running over to Jeremy's, he wasn't home. He told her last night that he was going out early to get a haircut.

She went to look at her watch then realized she wasn't wearing one. Relying on the stove clock once again she said, "I'm sorry but your timing is bad. I have a full schedule this morning and I need to be on my way." Thank God she was wearing a shirt and slacks rather than her gown and robe.

Chas put the cup down and walked toward her, backing her against the counter. He spread his hands on either side of her and leaned in close, grinding against her pelvis. She could smell the coffee on his breath.

"No problem, sweetheart. I don't have anything to do this morning. I'll be happy to tag along. I can be handy…carrying packages."

"I'm sure you are, but, I have to do these errands alone. And please do not call me sweetheart. You don't know me well enough." She placed her hands on his chest to push him away and resisted using her sister's favorite response that only men who could afford her could call her sweetheart. "I told you I'm engaged."

He took her left hand in his. "I don't see a ring."

"I didn't want one."

Chas raised an eyebrow and gave her a cunning smile of disbelief. "As for your errands, I can always wait for you in the car."

She tried to move away. He wouldn't budge. For being small in stature, the guy had arms of steel. There was no way she could duck under them. She was sure if she tried they would end up on the floor and she didn't want to take that risk. She was about to give him another shove when she looked over his shoulder and saw Daisy at the door, whining and scratching on the glass. *Hurry home, Jeremy,* she prayed.

"Excuse me, I have to let the dog in."

Chas tilted his head to the side and gave her what he probably thought was a sexy crooked smile but came across as more of a sneer. Now she wasn't simply uncomfortable, she was downright frightened.

Leaning in even closer and giving her a big wet kiss on the pulse beating in her neck he ran his tongue up the side of her neck to her ear. "The dog can stay outside. The fresh air is good for her. Right now I have plans for you and me. The mutt would be in the way."

She was about to start screaming when a familiar voice said, "You'll have to change your plans, bubba. The lady's with me. Almost ready, honey?"

Rachel breathed a sigh of relief. Once again Jeremy came to her rescue. Even though she hardly had time to think of herself as being a widow rather than a divorcee, she was beginning to think of him not only as her lover but as her white knight.

With an quaver in her voice, she said, "All I have to do is grab my purse, then we can be on our way."

Defiance in his posture, Chas stepped back. "So you're making moves on the rich widow?"

Rachel watched Jeremy, cool as an arctic blast, both arms folded across his chest, eyes as calm as a pond at dawn. Please, God, no fighting in my house. All I need right now is to have the neighbors calling the cops. Looking at Jeremy's face she breathed a sigh of relief. Everything would be okay.

"I'm not the one doing that, Chas, you are. I'm sure she's mentioned our engagement. Besides, Rachel is not a rich widow, not in what you probably consider *rich*."

"What are you talking about?" Chas snorted. "Word around town is she's loaded. You sure made quick time getting your dibs in."

Jeremy rubbed his finger alongside his nose. "I'm going to ignore that remark. I was referring to the fact that she is a very wise woman. Rachel made arrangements to receive an annuity, so if you're planning to spend her money like you have with other women, forget it."

Chas jutted his chin in the air, but did not look Jeremy in the eye. Instead he seemed intent on the border of grapevine clusters encircling the kitchen walls. "I don't have a clue what you're talking about."

"Sure you do. I did my homework and checked you out. Your mother holds the purse strings and she clutches them damn tight when it comes to you. Therefore, you like to become involved with women who have money and help them spend it. When they catch on they're paying your way they show you the door. There's no way I'd let that happen to Rachel."

Rachel listened to the two men, hoping they wouldn't come to blows. Jeremy was the calmer of the two, but Chas was an unknown. She slipped into the living room and grabbed her purse. Hanging on to it for dear life she prayed Chas would leave without any further argument. Her prayers were answered when she saw Jeremy forcefully escorting Chas to the front door. He had Chas' arm in a firm grip behind his back as he march-stepped the man across the living room floor.

When they got to the door Jeremy opened it, then

gave him a shove. "If I ever see you cruising up and down this street in your black van I *am* going to call the sheriff's office and tell them you're stalking Rachel. Then I'm going to encourage her to get a restraining order against you. Do you understand?"

"Hey, man, I understand," Chas mumbled and rubbed his arm. "You don't have to make a federal case out of it."

When the door was closed and locked, Jeremy leaded against it. "I don't know if you planned to go out. If you did, let's do it later. I'll drive you wherever you have to go. Right now I think we both need some time to calm down."

He walked up to her, took the purse from her hands, pulled her close. He kissed her on the forehead then tucked her head under his chin.

She shuddered with relief. After a few comforting minutes she stood back, reached her arms around his neck and planted a big kiss of thanksgiving on his generous mouth. She tilted her head back and looked into his blue eyes. "You don't know how glad I was to hear your voice. I was starting to panic. First, how did you know he was here? Secondly, how did you know about the other women and the money? Thirdly, does he really drive by at night?"

"Keep in mind women aren't the only ones who talk to each other. Get a couple of guys at a bar and you'd be surprised what they discuss. I found out more than I wanted to know. First of all I found out his cousin, Arlo Martin, wrote the insurance policy for Dave. As to how I knew he was here, I saw his passion pit on wheels parked in your driveway."

She trembled in his arms and burrowed her face in

his chest. "You must have lost a lot of sleep if you were keeping watch."

"No problem. I had a bad feeling about Martin since the first day I met him. As to keeping watch, I'm a light sleeper and our bedrooms face the front of the house. I didn't worry after I began spending the night with you. Before then, I kept my eye out for trouble."

"We all thought of Chas as harmless. Now I *know* he's more of a creep. There hasn't been a repeat of the parking lot experience but I figured it was because you've been driving me and picking me up."

"Telling him we were engaged obviously didn't deter him. Do you want me to keep taking you to work for a while longer?"

She didn't move back, but stayed where she was, wrapped in his embrace. She tilted her head and looked in his eyes. "I don't think that will be necessary because I resigned yesterday. They weren't very happy about it, but that's tough. I've made a decision; the rest of my life is mine. There are things I want to do."

He picked her up, swung her in a circle, and gave her a kiss when he set her on her feet. "Good for you, babe. What do you plan on doing?"

"I've always wanted to travel. Unlike my sister, Trina, I kept putting it off until next year. Now that I have a clear title to the house, I may put it up for sale and get an apartment, some place where I can lock the door and take off."

"What will we do with Daisy?"

"Mike and Mel would dog sit for me." Then his statement hit her. "*We*?"

He cupped her face with his hands. "You know I love you, what do you say we make the engagement real...ring and all? We can travel, take a trip to Charleston so you can meet my daughter and her family. From there we can go wherever we want. We can even take a trip to Wyoming and spend some time with Trina and Andy. If you decide to sell the house you can move in with me. I don't mind taking off, locking the door behind me."

"I've only been single for a few months."

"What do you say we make it legal and get married? I'm game if you are. It's your call."

"I do love you, too, but I don't want to rush into marriage. How about giving me some time?"

"Take all the time you want. I'm not going anywhere and I relish being your significant other."

Epilogue

Two Years Later

Jeremy called from the garage, "Hey, Rach, are you set? I have the car packed and I'm ready to roll."

"Hold your horses. I'm giving the house one more check."

She glanced around the bedroom. The blinds were closed against the summer sun. She knew Jeremy had unplugged the water heater and put the air conditioning on eighty. No need to worry about that anyway because Mike would be taking care of the dog as well as keeping check on the place while they were gone. Since he and Melinda had bought her house, he only had to walk next door. Melinda's biggest complaint about them being neighbors was that she and Jeremy were never home. The only request they'd made of her and Jeremy was that they try to be back by the time the baby was due in October.

Rachel was glad she decided not to wait to marry Jeremy. A month after the Chas incident they had a quiet ceremony with family and a few friends present. As for Davy, he finally admitted to her on her wedding day, that Jeremy was an okay guy. What a wonderful wedding it was. Anita was her matron of honor and Jeremy's friend Slick was his best man.

Rachel grabbed her handbag and headed for the

car. Sliding into the passenger seat she fastened her seatbelt. "Copilot to pilot, it's time to hit the road."

Before putting the car in gear, Jeremy leaned over and gave her a kiss. "Charleston and points west, here we come. Maybe we should celebrate our second anniversary some place special, like Las Vegas or...or do you have a place in mind."

"I do. After watching a lot of shows on the History Channel, I've wanted to go out West. I'd like to go to Deadwood, South Dakota, and visit Mt. Moriah Cemetery where Wild Bill Hickok and Calamity Jane are buried. Then there's the hotel where he was murdered by Jack McCall while playing poker. Did you know Jack McCall was acquitted of the murder?"

"Didn't have a clue. Fill me in."

"It's a really fascinating town. A man by the name of Seth Bullock became sheriff and cleaned up the town. When Wyatt Earp arrived, hoping to take over as sheriff, Bullock pointed the way out of town toward Dodge—you looked shocked at my suggestion to go there."

"I am bit surprised. But it looks to me like you've done some research on the area."

"I've always been fascinated by the history of the area ever since I watched the series, *Deadwood*. The place wasn't at all the way they portrayed it in the old movies. It was a wide open town."

"Consider the trip to Deadwood already added to our itinerary."

She smiled at him and squeezed his thigh. "I'm looking forward to seeing Melody and her family again. We always have a good time when we're there. I'm sure we'll manage to have dinner at Aw Shucks at least once or twice."

Jeremy patted her hand. "Absolutely, because I know it's your favorite place. Please don't ask me to take another trip out to Ft. Sumtcr. I enjoyed it the first two times, but don't think I'm up for a third."

Rachel crossed her heart and raised her right hand. "I promise. We can work on our travel plans one day at a time. I have all the books from AAA in a container in the back seat. I thought we might go see Trina and Andy in Cheyenne for a couple of days."

"We'll give them a call. You know the two of them are like two peas in a pod when it comes to hitting the road at the drop of a hat. We'll have to make sure they're home."

"They'll be home. I checked with Trina the last time I talked to her, two days ago. Have another news flash. Andy made her get a cell phone so we'll be able to contact her when we're on the road."

"You know, hon, that's one of the many things I love about you. You're organized, but not to the point of being a pain in the ass. Plus, we discuss things and come to a mutual agreement without having it turn into an all-out war."

Rachel started rubbing the back of his neck and playing with his hair. "That's because we're mature and wiser. Amazing what life's experiences can teach you about what's important and what isn't when it comes to marriage."

"Yeah, it a shame Chas hasn't learned that lesson yet. I bet he was extremely disappointed when his mother passed away and left him the money, but without access to the entire amount. So it ends up he is still on an allowance."

"I wonder if he reads the obituaries to check out new widows these days."

Jeremy kissed her hand. "He probably does. Guys like Chas never have enough money and toys."

Rachel squeezed her husband's hand. "I can only hope those ladies are lucky enough to have a white knight come to their rescue like I did."

"No worries, my love, I'll always come charging to your rescue."

A word about the author...

Virginia Crane lives in Southwest Florida with her husband and two dogs. Reading has always been one of her passions and eventually it evolved into writing.

Thank you for purchasing
this publication of The Wild Rose Press, Inc.

If you enjoyed the story, we would appreciate your
letting others know by leaving a review.

For other wonderful stories,
please visit our on-line bookstore at
www.thewildrosepress.com.

For questions or more information
contact us at
info@thewildrosepress.com.

The Wild Rose Press, Inc.
www.thewildrosepress.com

To visit with authors of
The Wild Rose Press, Inc.
join our yahoo loop at
http://groups.yahoo.com/group/thewildrosepress/